CURSE OF THE SANDTONGUE

BRAVELANDS

SHADOWS ON THE
MOUNTAIN

BRAVELANDS

CURSE OF THE SANDTONGUE

CURSE OF THE SANDTONGUE

BRAVELANDS

SHADOWS ON THE MOUNTAIN

ERIN HUNTER

HARPER

An Imprint of HarperCollinsPublishers

Library of Congress Cataloging-in-Publication Data
Names: Hunter, Erin, author.
Title: Shadows on the mountain / Erin Hunter.
Description: First edition. | New York, NY : HarperCollins Children's Books, [2021] | Series:
Bravelands: curse of the sandtongue ; 1 | Audience: Ages 8–12. | Audience: Grades 4–6. |
Summary: "For generations, the Silverback troop has lived in peaceful seclusion high above
the plains, but when a new evil descends on their home, one young gorilla must venture
into the unknown to prevent darkness from taking hold of all they hold dear"—Provided by
publisher.
Identifiers: LCCN 2020044136 | ISBN 978-0-06-296684-1 (hardcover) | ISBN 978-0-06-
296685-8 (library binding)
Subjects: CYAC: Gorilla—Fiction. | Savanna animals—Fiction. | Fantasy.
Classification: LCC PZ7.H916625 Sf 2021 | DDC [Fic]—dc23
LC record available at https://lccn.loc.gov/2020044136

Typography by Ellice M. Lee
21 22 23 24 25   PC/LSCH   10 9 8 7 6 5 4 3 2 1
❖
First Edition

CURSE OF THE SANDTONGUE

BRAVELANDS

SHADOWS ON THE
MOUNTAIN

PROLOGUE

Currents of warm air lifted Freewing the martial eagle, raising her so far above the plains of Bravelands she could see it all: the distant mountains in the west, the forests that wound with the silver rivers, the eastern lakes that bordered the sweeping grass plains. The sky was cloudless today, the air crystal-clear, and the golden land below Freewing was clear to her keen dark eyes. The herds thrived; masses of wildebeests, buffalo, and zebras moved below her, following their ancient migration paths. Rivers and lakes glittered in the high noonday sun. Freewing saw the smudged gray line of an elephant family trekking northward and a spattering of yellow dots that were a grazing herd of gazelles.

But she would not find her prey on the plains, not today. She had cared for her chick for long weeks, rarely leaving their nest of sticks high in a solitary fever tree. Now Stormrider's baby down was almost gone, replaced by feathers, and it would not be long till he began to stretch his young wings and grow into his name. It was Freewing's time to hunt again, and she had taken gladly to the skies. Her mate, Strongbeak, would guard both nest and chick until she returned with her promised treat: a monitor lizard.

There was only one place she knew where such a prize was guaranteed: the slopes of the Rock That Touches the Sky. Tilting her feathertips, Freewing gazed toward the great eastern mountain, towering misty blue in the distance over the savannah. As she soared toward it, its color became darker, greener, till she could make out each individual tree in the forests that swathed its peaks and gullies. Ridges of pale rock jutted from its thick shroud of foliage, and sloping boulders. It was on one of them that she saw what she was searching for.

The spotted brown lizard basked on the flat stone in a patch of sun, between a narrow creek and a dark cave in the rocks. Its tongue flicked lazily. Not the largest lizard Freewing had ever caught, but more than big enough to feed hungry eagles, and she would carry this one home easily to her mate and her chick. *Thanks be to the Great Spirit!*

She was very high still; the lizard would never know what killed it. Tightening her wings closer to her body, adjusting her tail feathers, Freewing swooped out of the sun.

How good it felt, this headlong downward dive, the cool wind racing across her feathers. She was close now, and the flat rock was rushing toward her. She extended her talons to grasp her sleepy prey—

—And was engulfed in a cloud of blackness that sent her spiraling out of control. She flapped desperately, trying to regain her balance, as a multitude of tiny creatures whirled around her. There were so many of them, she could no longer see rock or tree or creek, let alone lizard. The air itself seemed to churn, sparking panic in her breast. She gasped, trying to dodge free of the shrill, squeaking horde.

Bats. How she hated them, and that abomination of a language—Skytongue warped by hissing Grasstongue! In the chaos of the air around her, it took Freewing long moments to find her composure. At last, beating her wings strongly, she burst out of the throng and flapped toward the nearest branch.

She perched there, trembling with fury, as the storm of tiny black wings passed. Of course the bats were not attacking her. They were not even interested in her. But what had possessed them to flee their dingy tunnels in the daytime? Freewing caught only snatches of their squeaking hisses, but there was little to be learned anyway; there was only fear and desperation in their voices.

"Fly fly! Quick quick!"

"Be sssswift, Silverfang!"

"Ssswift and far, ssssoar away far!"

Bewildered, Freewing watched as the cloud of bats dwindled in the distance beyond a forested ridge of the mountain. Doubting even her own eyes, she glanced at the sky.

No, the sun was still high. What could drive them into the midday sunlight? What were they so scared of?

She turned her head and gazed with curiosity at the cave mouth by the rocks. But even her powerful eyes could not penetrate that blackness. As she stared, the very stillness of the black maw made a new trepidation stir inside her. Something cold rippled through her body, and for a moment she could not move.

Freewing turned back to the lizard. It had not been frightened away by the bats, nor by Freewing herself—even though it now clearly knew that she was there. Its yellow eyes met hers, and they were filled with . . . what was that look? Was it *mockery*?

Something in the lizard's nonchalant gaze chilled Freewing's blood. It should have fled at first glimpse of her, yet it perched there unafraid, almost daring her to attack. . . . The heavy dread was swamped by fear, and she spread her wings and flapped into the air once again.

Besides, even if that lizard offered itself to her belly up, she would not return for it. Freewing shuddered as she flew higher and faster into the sky.

Something lurked in that black cave. *It must never emerge*: Freewing knew that with the deepest instincts in her body. She would find today's prey on the savannah after all—far from that unseen presence, and the dark, oozing evil it breathed into the air of Bravelands.

CHAPTER ONE

Bramble Greenback, sitting on the branch of an ironwood tree, rubbed his back lazily against the fissured bark behind him. It was an idle sort of day, but then all Bramble's days were idle. That was just how he liked it. It was easy for a young gorilla to pass his time in the forest. There were so many distractions to enjoy, so many pranks to play, beneath the cover of the dense green canopy.

Grinning, he parted the twigs with his fingers and peered down through the glossy green leaves. Yes, Groundnut Blackback was still sitting there at the foot of the ironwood, glancing in perplexity from side to side and looking grumpy. Groundnut wasn't that bright, for a senior gorilla. He should have worked out long ago where the tiny missiles were coming from.

Bramble pulled another fistful of little black fruits from

their stalk. Nibbling his tongue in concentration, he leaned down and dropped them.

Bang! They hit the crown of Groundnut's head perfectly. The old gorilla gave a growl of frustration and rubbed his head, craning back to peer angrily into the tree. But Bramble had already shrunk behind the foliage, barely able to keep from stifling giggles.

The branch beneath Bramble jerked and swayed a little, and he glanced up to see his half sister, Moonflower, had swung over from the neighboring tree. She approached him carefully, a mango clutched in her hand as she negotiated the leafy boughs. "Bramble, what are you up to now?"

"I can't think what you mean," said Bramble, widening his eyes in shocked innocence.

"You know perfectly well. Don't you ever get tired of teasing poor Groundnut?"

"Never." Bramble grinned mischievously. "Don't be mad at me, Moonflower. I'm very good at making my own entertainment." His eyes drifted to the mango in Moonflower's grip, so velvety and red and gold that he couldn't help licking his lips.

"I can't ever be too mad at you." She offered the mango, smiling indulgently. "You want it, little brother?"

"Yes, I do!" Bramble reached out to take it from her, and she dropped it into his waiting palm.

Or she tried to. Bramble, half his focus still on the grumbling Groundnut below, wasn't paying enough attention. The mango slipped from his palm.

"Oh no!" he gasped, snatching wildly for the lost mango.

But it was no use. It bounced down through the foliage, falling jerkily toward the earth. He stared down, feeling his loss grow along with his anxiety as it plummeted farther and farther. *It won't hit Groundnut. . . . It won't. . . .*

With a last wild bounce from a forked branch, the mango dropped straight onto Groundnut's patchy-furred head. It shattered on impact.

"Well, that was a ripe one," remarked Moonflower.

Groundnut surged up from the ground, roaring in anger and thumping his chest. He spun around and reared upright to stare into the tree. Yellow pulp slid and dripped down the big gorilla's face and snout, but Bramble didn't even have time to snigger. There certainly wasn't time to hide. Groundnut's glittering eyes had already locked with his.

"Oh no," groaned Bramble.

"You!" bellowed Groundnut. Reaching up, he seized branches in both fists and shook them violently. The whole tree began to sway as he tore and yanked at its lower boughs.

"Whoa!" exclaimed Moonflower, tottering where she stood.

"We're doomed," blurted Bramble. He grabbed at a branch, missed, and toppled sideways.

The fall down through the branches was a series of painful thuds, but the sheer humiliation was worse. Bramble hit the grass rump-first, with a yelp. Moonflower was just a moment behind him.

She jumped to her feet, unhurt, and grabbed his arm. "Run!"

Twisting, she slammed her hands knuckle-first into the soft forest loam and loped away on all fours. Bramble had to duck before he could run—to dodge Groundnut's wild grab—but as soon as he was free and clear, he bolted after Moonflower. The big gorilla gave chase, but half-heartedly, and he halted after a few bounding paces, panting.

"You insolent little *monkey!*" bellowed Groundnut, slamming his fists into the ground. "I'll tell your father Burbark Silverback about this. Just you see if I don't!"

"Tell him whatever you like!" yelled Bramble cheekily. "I'm not scared!" He kept loping at top speed all the same, following Moonflower as she charged through a group of peacefully grooming Goldbacks. The females glanced up in irritation but made no attempt to stop the two youngsters.

"He's given up!" barked Bramble to his half sister when they were clear of the Goldbacks. "Groundnut gave up ages agooooooh!"

A huge fist clamped around his hind foot, swinging him up into the air. His heart lurched as the forest flipped upside down, but it wasn't Groundnut who held him by the ankle.

"Cassava Brightback! Let me go!" Bramble wriggled and flapped his arms ineffectually. "Put me down, you big lunk!"

"Not till you tell me what you've been up to, you young scoundrel." Cassava's face was fierce and stern, as befitted the heir to the troop's leadership—but his eyes twinkled; they always did.

"Absolutely nothing at all." Still upside down, Bramble folded his arms and pouted at his older brother.

Gently, Cassava set him down, upright, on the forest floor. "Well, behave yourself. You're three years old, young gorilla—you should be learning responsibility!"

"I'm very responsible," Bramble insisted.

"Yes, you're responsible for all the mischief around here," growled Cassava. "Go on then, get along with you. And don't venture far from the nests at this time of the evening!"

"Don't worry about me." Bramble reared up and pounded his chest grandly with his fists. "I'm as strong as any creature on this mountain. Haven't you seen the silver hairs coming through on my back?" He twisted and pointed over his shoulder to show Cassava.

There was silence behind him. Bramble craned his head around to look at his brother, who had leaned close to peer and frown and scratch his head. As Bramble gave an indignant grunt, Cassava leaned even closer, pressing his snout right against Bramble's back.

"Nope," came Cassava's muffled voice. "Can't make 'em out at all."

Moonflower laughed as Bramble slapped his brother away. Cassava was grinning.

"Moonflower, your mother was looking for you," said the older gorilla.

"Was she? I'll go find her." Moonflower smiled. "Bye, you two!" She loped off through the trees.

"Oh, thanks *very* much, Cassava," grumbled Bramble. "Moonflower and I were having great fun. We were livening up everyone's day, that's all!"

"Nobody needs their day livened like that. Just thank the Great Spirit for a quiet life." Cassava swiped affectionately at the top of Bramble's head. "You could have all the excitement of the plains instead—you know, starvation, floods, being chased by crocodiles or eaten by lions. . . ."

"I could handle a lion," sniffed Bramble.

"Ha! Have you ever seen one?"

Bramble glowered at his brother. "Well, no."

"They're terrifying." Cassava's eyes widened and he spread his paws wide, his fingers hooked into pretend claws. "Golden like the sun, and twice the size of gorillas. They have manes of black fur, and tails that sting. And burning red eyes, and long pointed tusks!"

Bramble shuddered. He wasn't so sure anymore that he really wanted a showdown with a lion. "Tusks *and* a stinger?"

"Yup." Cassava nodded. "They're dangerous at both ends." He rubbed Bramble's head affectionately. "If you want something useful to do, young gorilla, you could go see our father at his nest and take him some fruit."

"Isn't he busy?" Bramble wrinkled his snout. "He doesn't like being interrupted when he's busy. . . ."

Cassava shook his head, looking suddenly more serious. "Father hasn't been himself lately. I think he'd appreciate your company." He passed Bramble a bunch of green bananas, then winked knowingly. "But no dropping them on his head, okay?"

Bramble grinned ruefully. "I won't."

He crept through the trees toward his father's nest. Bramble loved his father, of course, but he was in awe of him, too.

When Burbark was in a good mood and feeling tolerant, there was nobody Bramble would rather talk to. But Bramble had had many a snap or a swiped paw when he'd disturbed Burbark at the wrong moment.

As Bramble pushed through the last veil of foliage, he saw that his father had his back turned. Burbark was staring out into the forest, his massive shoulders hunched slightly. Bramble would never stop being impressed by the vastness and strength of that muscular back, with its gleaming silver hair.

Bramble came to a halt, digging his knuckles into the forest litter; he felt pride swell in his chest. He might not be the Brightback and heir, future protector of the troop, as Cassava was, but he was still the son of this magnificent leader.

Burbark seemed very still and focused, and as Bramble crept closer he heard his father muttering to himself under his breath. He wasn't sure Cassava had been right; maybe he should turn around and go back the way he'd come. . . .

No, that was ridiculous. His father was alone, so he clearly wasn't preoccupied with troop business or discussions.

"Father?" Bramble said.

Burbark did not immediately turn, and Bramble frowned in uncertainty. Usually, Burbark would shout in delight and give his younger son a grin—even while scolding him for the disturbance.

After long moments, Burbark's shoulder twitched, and the muttering stopped abruptly. Burbark twisted his head and blinked at Bramble. Then he swung around.

His dark eyes were glazed and distant, and he said nothing.

Suddenly nervous, Bramble crept forward and laid the green bananas at his father's feet. Still Burbark did not move; he just scratched at his wrist, where a small snake had bitten him a few days before.

"How is the troop?" asked Burbark vaguely.

On another day, Bramble might have mentioned the incident with the mango, but his father seemed in no mood for jokes now. He barely seemed there at all.

I guess he has important business on his mind after all.

"They're well," he replied. "I brought you something to eat, Father."

Burbark cast an eye at the bananas, but then looked away, scratching his arm once more.

The flesh looked raw and painful, and Bramble was surprised that it hadn't yet healed. It was a sore that had done in his mother, starting as a nasty gash from a splintered branch, but worsening until she could no longer keep her food down. His father and older brother hadn't let him see her near the end, but he remembered her groans of pain through the trees as the Goldbacks tended to her. He'd tried to talk to the Great Spirit, to beg for his mother's life, but she had died anyway.

"Why don't you ask one of the Goldbacks to look at your arm?" he said.

"Hunh. A Silverback can't go running to the Goldbacks like an infant every time he gets a scratch." Burbark scowled. "I must show myself to be strong, for the sake of the troop. You'll learn that one day."

Feeling a trickle of hot shame in his gut, Bramble nodded.

"Yes, Father. I know. You're right."

Burbark at last cracked half a smile. "I am always right, Bramble."

Yes, he always was, thought Bramble. And despite his boasts to Cassava and Moonflower, Bramble couldn't imagine ever being a powerful and confident Silverback like his father.

Burbark was still watching him in silence; he was clearly not in the mood for a chat, whatever Cassava had said. Bramble dipped his head. "I'll be going, then."

Burbark nodded. He turned again to stare into the forest, but as Bramble began to turn away, he glanced back over his shoulder.

"Thank you for the bananas," he muttered.

A little deflated, Bramble padded back toward the rest of the troop. Life as the Silverback certainly wasn't all fun and bossing other gorillas around. He felt bad for his father, so preoccupied with protecting the troop he could never relax and take things easy. *And I'm actually quite glad I'm not the Brightback*, he admitted to himself. It was Cassava who would take over all those weighty responsibilities, not him. *Poor Cassava.*

It would be nice if he could be of some help to his brother—and to his father, for that matter—but what could he do. *Well, you could start to practice being a troop defender, instead of playing games all the time.* And with no enemies in sight, he could always try out his moves on something smaller. . . . Glancing from side to side as he plodded on, Bramble suddenly spotted the red-and-yellow flash of a lovebird, pecking around for seeds on the forest floor.

Furrowing his brow, he gave a throaty growl. He slammed his fists into the earth, then bared his fangs. "Hey, you! I'm a lion. See my tusks? You'd better run!"

The bird gave him a sidelong glance and, looking not terribly nervous, fluttered away a little distance. Bramble prowled after it. Irritated, the lovebird hopped and flapped away, and he followed, hunching his shoulders and tossing an imaginary mane.

The lovebird gave a whistle of annoyance and fluttered away again, but Bramble was having far too much fun to stop. He raised his head, swung what he imagined were terrifying, bloodstained tusks, and gave a roar.

The bird glared at him across a small clearing.

"I've got you now!" growled Bramble. He leaped across the glade—and collided in midair with a pale, furry shape that sprang from the trees beyond. Shocked, Bramble thudded to the ground with the spotted yellow creature, their limbs tangled together, while the lovebird flew away with a trill of what sounded like laughter.

The yellow creature gave a yowl of shock and kicked away from Bramble, then lowered itself into a menacing crouch. The young gorilla scrambled hurriedly to his feet and faced his attacker. Panting, they both stared at each other.

A real lion! was his first, panicked thought.

It wasn't *quite* as Cassava had described it. It had no mane and no tusks, and when he glanced fearfully at its lashing tail, he could see no stinger. It was a *lot* smaller than he'd expected. But he was quite sure this was the closest thing to a lion he'd ever seen.

Trembling, Bramble raised himself up on his hind feet and bared his teeth. The creature hunched its shoulders and exposed its own long, dangerous fangs.

"What do you think you're doing?" she snarled. "You got in the way of my hunt! Don't you know it's almost nightfall? You should be safe in your nest and scratching your fleas."

"Me? Look at *you!*" Bramble bristled. "No ugly old patchy-furred lion tells me what to do!"

"Lion?" She gave a harsh coughing sound of derision. "I'm a leopard. Lions don't live on the mountain, fool! They're afraid to!" She laughed again.

Oh. A leopard. "I knew that!" he blurted.

She was circling now, slow and menacing. Bramble circled too, his fists slamming into the ground, keeping the leopard's yellow fangs in view. "You did not know that!" she taunted him. "You've never even seen a leopard before, have you?"

"So what? I bet *you've* never seen a gorilla!"

"Ha-ha! I see gorillas all the time." Her muzzle twisted in derision. "They're always snoring. Because their eyes don't work at night. Leopards *live* in the night! The darkness is our home."

"That just means you're too scared to show your faces in the day," grunted Bramble. "Poor sensitive things!"

Her lip curled. "We hunt in the night because our eyes are so much better than yours. A thousand times better than the eyes of a stinky gorilla!"

Bramble sucked in an indignant breath, but he couldn't think of a witty comeback soon enough. "*You're* stinky," he snapped.

"Pfft. I am Chase Born of Prowl, and I hunt tonight to support my family. You're nothing but a cub. A baby!"

"I am Bramble." Provoked, he blurted it before he could help himself: "Bramble Silverback!"

"Silverback?" Her eyes widened, and she tried to peer behind him. "I thought Silverbacks were grown-up leaders?"

"I—" Something cracked in the bushes behind him, and Bramble twisted around in shock as he heard a high snarl. *More leopards? Is it a pack?*

Shadows flickered between the trees, and brown-and-black shapes emerged from the twilit forest, a whole clan of young hyenas. Their yellow eyes glittered in the shady light, and they licked slavering jaws as they prowled forward, ragged ears flickering.

Bramble felt his heart stutter. He backed away as they approached with wide grins, their hackles bristling. Bramble's movement brought him closer to Chase Born of Prowl, and he eyed her nervously, but there were more of the hyenas, and right now they looked a lot scarier than Chase did.

"Aha," said the oldest-looking hyena, tilting its head and licking its jaws. "Two babies! Tender and delicate."

The hyena beside him sniggered. "Far from home. Yum!"

"Gorilla and leopard go well together," guffawed a third.

The leopard snarled, narrowing her eyes. She spun so swiftly, Bramble barely saw the movement; then she sprang up into the nearest tree, clawing her way up the trunk till she reached the first and thickest branch. She glared down at the hyenas, growling, then padded away onto the leaves.

"Oh well," said the leader, hunching its shoulders. "One left, anyway."

All Bramble could do was leap for the same tree as the leopard, but his movements were slower, his frantic scramble clumsier. He could barely hang on to the bark—he didn't have claws like the leopard's. As his heart raced with terror and he clung desperately to the trunk, he felt an abrupt bolt of pain explode in his leg.

With a howl, he jerked at his leg—but it was held fast in the teeth of the biggest hyena. Panic surged inside his chest, and he screeched and yelled in desperation.

The hyenas hollered in excitement; their leader bit more deeply into Bramble's leg. All its paws were off the ground, and its weight was dragging him down; the branch Bramble clung to was creaking and cracking. Soon he would fall, he knew, and they would tear him apart.

It was over. And so soon. Cold fear flowed through his arms, making Bramble's grip weaken even as he struggled to cling on. He wanted to scream for his troop; *Cassava, help me! Father!*

But the words wouldn't come. His throat was too constricted, the pain too dizzying.

Father . . . Cassava . . .

They'll never even know what happened to me!

CHAPTER TWO

Chase slunk along the branch, keeping her body low. The hyenas weren't interested in her now; all she had to do was melt into the forest as she'd been taught. The gorilla had been slower, and that was his bad luck. It wasn't *her* fault.

She halted when she heard the sound behind her: it was a high screech of terror that seemed to rattle her bones. The gorilla youngster was doomed, but he was cursing and screaming at the hyenas anyway. *That could have been me.* Her heart thundered at the sound of his howls. *Could have been me screaming my last.*

She licked her jaws. She should keep going, back to the den. No gorilla was worth it.

But the sounds were blood-chilling. He was no silverback, that tiny gorilla. He was perhaps no older than she.

As long as I stay up high, I'll be fine. I'll just go and look.

She turned and crept back along the branch the way she'd fled.

He was still fighting for his life. Bramble the gorilla gripped a low branch in desperation, a hyena hanging by its teeth from his leg. As Chase watched, the gorilla's grasp failed and he crashed to the ground, the hyena still fastened to him. *That's it, then. Poor thing. Should have climbed faster.*

But the gorilla hadn't given up. He rolled, squirmed upright, and pounded the hyena's head with his fists. As it released him and snarled, with bloody fangs bared, the gorilla reared up onto his hind feet, beating his chest and roaring.

He had guts, thought Chase admiringly. Pointless, but brave. The hyenas, drooling, didn't look as if they'd be giving up in the face of his bravado. They stalked forward, wary but intent. Hyenas were patient and determined. All they needed was an opportunity to strike, and then it would be over.

"Careful, clan-mates. Work together, remember what the adults say?" growled the leader. "Don't get yourselves hurt."

"He's just a furball," sneered a female. "Nobody's getting hurt today."

"Except him," giggled a small male.

"You two, go for a leg each," said the leader, flicking his ears. "The others, grab his arms."

A roar caught in the gorilla's throat, tailing off to a squeak, and he had to cough violently before he could give voice to another defiant bellow. Despite all the chest-beating and hollering, thought Chase, Bramble looked terrified.

Oh well. Such is the will of the Great Spirit. She could hear her mother Prowl's voice as if she was standing right next to her. *Leave the gorilla to his fate and get out of there.*

So why didn't she?

Chase licked her jaws. Her breath was rapid and harsh in her throat, and she realized why she felt so tense: she was still willing Bramble to survive, somehow—to find a last burst of energy, to knock his attackers aside and flee.

Let him learn his lesson but escape with his life.

But step by step the hyenas were closing in. Bramble spun around, flailing his fists, his teeth bared. One of the hyenas feinted, and the gorilla overextended, slipping. It was the opportunity the pack was waiting for, and another dived in, snatching at Bramble's leg with his teeth.

Oh Stars and Shadows, what am I doing...

Chase leaped down from above and landed square on the hyena's back, digging in her claws and raking hard. She tore at its neck with her teeth. A second hyena, shocked, lunged for her, but she lashed out a paw and caught its ear by pure luck. As it pulled away, blood sprayed, and it screeched in pain.

"Look out!" The bellow of warning came from Bramble.

Chase spun around, flicking her tail to balance herself, and snapped at a young female, but she felt fangs bite into her haunches. Though it wasn't a deep wound, the sharp pain focused her on the dangers.

"Get out of here!" she cried to the gorilla.

Slapping away a yelping hyena, Bramble bounded across the forest floor, springing up to land on the back of the hyena attacking Chase. Using it to propel himself, he jumped up to the nearest branch and hauled himself into the safety of the tree. Chase gave a last savage claw swipe to the nearest hyena, then sprang lithely up the tree to sit at Bramble's side.

The young gorilla was trembling, she could feel it—but then her own heart was racing. Despite the snapping and frustrated yelping of the hyenas below, Chase clearly heard her mother's voice in her head again: *What in the name of the Great Spirit were you thinking, Chase?*

"Thank you," gasped Bramble, panting. He was staring at her in bewilderment; he must have been as confused by her decision as she was. The young gorilla gulped a lungful of air, as the hyenas snarled and barked below. "I mean, thanks for coming back to help."

She gazed at Bramble in silence, letting her heartbeat slow and steady. "Don't mention it," she said at last, crisply. "Nothing personal, you understand. I just hate hyenas."

"Hey, you two!" barked the hyena leader below them. "Come on down here! We're only playing!"

"If one of you's too nervous," panted another, her tongue lolling in a grin, "the other one could come down first. Then you can see we're quite friendly."

"Ha-ha," growled Chase dryly. "Hyenas are stupid. *We're* not."

The hyena clan yelped and whooped in anger and stalked around the base of the tree, but when it became clear that Chase and Bramble weren't going anywhere, they padded off with disappointed growls.

"We're lucky those were only small ones," remarked Chase,

licking hyena blood from her paw.

"They were?" Bramble looked startled.

Chase made a disdainful face.

He grinned at her, which she found endearing and annoying in equal measure. "Well, thank you for your help, anyway."

"I told you, it was nothing." Sitting up, she scratched uncomfortably at her ear. "It'll be completely dark soon, Bramble *Silverback*. You'd better get back to your troop." She gave him a sly look. "I'm sure they need their leader."

He looked embarrassed again; that was better, thought Chase with satisfaction. *Silverback indeed!*

"Bye, Chase Born of Prowl!" He grinned ruefully.

"Farewell to you too," she grunted.

She watched him climb down from the tree, then pause to peer nervously into the shadows. He must be checking for any sign of the hyenas. After a moment, Bramble shambled off into the forest.

Chase shook herself. The buzz of the fight still rippled through her veins, and there was a spring in her pawsteps as she trotted back toward her den. It was always good fun to get the better of hyenas.

She hadn't been telling *quite* the truth when she told Bramble she saw gorillas all the time. In truth she had glimpsed the huge creatures only briefly, through the trees in the starlight. Bramble So-Called-Silverback was the first gorilla she'd ever actually spoken to, and she had to admit she was a little surprised he could hold a conversation. She'd always thought gorillas were as dense as hyenas.

She slowed to a walk as she approached the den and sniffed carefully at the base of the trees. Other leopards had marked their passing, but not recently; she could smell Shadow's mark, but it was old and faded. He hadn't been around for a long time, and Chase's mother would be happy about that. Prowl did not like the arrogant young male who ventured too brazenly into their territory.

Flattening her body to the ground, Chase slunk between the white hollow roots of a dead tree and squeezed into the space beneath. Prowl was in the den, but she barely glanced at Chase; she was focused on the tiny leopard between her paws. The little cub grunted in his sleep, and his whiskers shivered: perhaps he was already dreaming of hunting, thought Chase.

"How is Seek?" she asked, licking her mother's ear.

"As well as can be expected without his mother's milk," said Prowl, peering at the snoozing infant. In a mutter she added, "Slink should have fed him for much longer."

The break in her mother's voice was barely noticeable, but Chase heard it. "Slink would have wanted to," she said softly. "She didn't mean to leave him."

"Indeed." Prowl had composed herself, and her growl was clear and strong once again. "But my sister's death was the will of the Great Spirit. It's up to us now to look after Seek."

Chase nuzzled her mother's head comfortingly, and Prowl raised her head to rub her chin against her daughter's cheek.

Prowl drew back abruptly, her lips flaring. "Do I smell hyena? Is that why you haven't brought back any prey?"

"What?" Chase widened her eyes. Immediately she knew

she was wasting her time; her mother would not fall for an innocent face. She should just have said they hyenas had stolen her prey . . . except that Prowl wouldn't have fallen for that, either. And Chase knew she could never tell her mother such an outright lie.

Prowl didn't repeat herself; she didn't need to. She remained silent, staring levelly at her daughter, until Chase had to avert her gaze.

"I'm sorry, Mother." Chase dipped her head, ashamed. "I did have a"—she didn't want to say *fight*—"an encounter with a pack. They were attacking a young gorilla, and it annoyed me. They didn't give me much trouble, don't worry—"

Prowl grunted in anger. "Chase, how could you be so irresponsible? We both have to stay safe, now that we're taking care of Seek. The life or death of a gorilla isn't any of your business!"

"I'm sorry. They made me furious, that's all. You know I despise hyenas." She had better not tell Prowl, Chase thought guiltily, that it was actually the gorilla who had deprived her of her quarry.

"How many times have I told you, Chase? *Trust only yourself.*" Prowl's voice lowered as Seek stirred. "This forest won't look after you—you have to be on guard *all the time.*"

Guilt churned inside Chase. "You're right." Little Seek was opening his mouth in a huge yawn that showed his baby teeth, and she nuzzled him gently.

"Hi, Chase!" He blinked and batted her chin with his paws. "Can we play now?"

Prowl shook her head. "Chase has to go out hunting again, Seek. She hasn't brought any prey back yet."

"Mother," said Chase, her head drooping, "I need to rest first."

"No, Chase. *We* need to eat." There was an edge of ferocity in her mother's voice. As if to soften her sternness, she licked Chase's cheek. "I will not be here forever, my daughter, and it is my job to make sure you are ready."

Seek placed his little paws against Prowl's chest. "Mother-Sister, I don't want you to leave! You won't ever leave us, will you?"

Prowl nuzzled him gently. "I'm not going anywhere for a long time, my daughter and my sister-cub. But I must know that you are both safe and capable on that day . . . in the *far* future, little one." She licked Seek's face firmly.

Chase pressed her head to Prowl's cheek. "Of course I'll go hunting again. And this time I won't return empty-jawed."

She crawled up out of the den again into the cool night, fired by determination. But as she set off at a trot, she couldn't help her faith quavering. Prowl made hunting sound so easy, but even *finding* prey was hard enough.

The forest was not silent; it was filled with the cries of night birds, the chirping of crickets, and the piping of tree frogs. But she needed to find something bigger than any of them, though a large bird *might* do for now. . . .

Chase padded on through the darkness, her ears quivering at every rustle in the dead leaves, her gaze finding the glow of other eyes as tiny creatures scuttled away in the night. At last she felt the trees thin out, and she sprang up onto a vast fallen pine. She knew it jutted out over an escarpment above a small glade, and she trod silently along its trunk until she could survey the ground below.

There was a gap in the forest's dense canopy here, and starlight bathed the glade in a silvery glow. Chase sat down to wait, suddenly more confident in the embrace of the night. There were grass-eaters down there; she could hear their stamp and shuffle. As she focused on the shadows that moved, she made out pale striped hides, blending into the bands of starlight on the grass.

Half a dozen female bongos had gathered to browse on shrubs on the far side of the glade below her. They seemed alert, raising their horned heads frequently to let their huge glowing eyes scan the forest around them. But none were looking up.

Chase resisted the urge to leap straight from the rock to the glade below. Slowness and patience were needed now; one wrong paw and they'd slip away faster than she could pursue. She paced silently around the edge of the escarpment and down its rock flank. Halfway down she paused on a sloping ledge, one paw raised.

Chase made herself stay absolutely still as one of the bongos stamped its hoof, agitated. That must be the leader, she thought, narrowing her eyes. It broke into a run, guiding the others at a panicked dash across the glade and into the trees, and for a sickening moment, Chase thought she'd lost her chance.

But the group didn't gallop far; the alarm had been too vague. The bongo hadn't really seen Chase, only sensed a disturbing presence. And those disturbances were multiple in the forest night; the bongos couldn't flee from everything. Indeed, she noticed with delight, their flight had brought them closer to her. Perhaps it wasn't Chase who had scared them at all; perhaps it had been only an imagined predator, because one by one the bongos stepped out of the bushes and back into the open glade, shaking their spiraled horns in relief. A tree had died and fallen not far from the escarpment, and the antelopes began to nibble nervously at its rotten bark.

Prowl's eyes would shine with pride, thought Chase, and Seek would yowl happily. A whole bongo brought back to the den would feed them for several days.

She stiffened again as the leader edged right beneath her, then a second. Chase counted one, two heartbeats; then she sprang.

The bongos bolted and she landed between the third and fourth, just missing the shoulder of one as two more skipped and dodged past her. But she twisted, took a flying leap, and felt her claws catch in flesh of the smaller straggler.

The last bongo stumbled, taken by surprise. Chase did not hesitate; she bounded onto its shoulders, bearing it down until it collapsed forward on its forelegs and went head over hocks. She felt the beat and warmth of its blood beneath her paws, and even in the chaos and darkness she knew where that heartbeat pulsed strongest. Her jaws found its neck, and she crushed her fangs together. The bongo went limp beneath her, one leg still jerking as she felt its lifeblood soak into her mouth.

Shaking it one last time, she released her hold. "May its spirit run among the stars," she muttered hurriedly, as was the custom. "Its flesh is mine, but let its bones belong to Bravelands."

Chase glanced to right and left in the darkness. The five remaining bongos had vanished into the shadows of the forest, though she could still hear their bleats of distress. As she craned to listen, they grew silent again. That was wise; even though they grieved the loss of this young female—perhaps the calf of one of the others, going by its size—there would be other predators lurking. There always were, and something that wasn't Chase had spooked them already. If that hyena clan was still around, Chase did not want to lose her kill to their thieving jaws.

Your kill is only truly yours when you put it beyond the reach of the scavengers. Her mother's wisdom echoed in Chase's ears yet again.

She ripped off a few bites of flesh from the shoulder and gulped them down to restore her energy. Licking her jaws, she glanced around in search of a suitable tree.

There. A strong and tall acacia with a forked trunk was perfect; she could cache the bongo there until Prowl and Seek could be brought to it. Gripping the creature's neck in her jaws, Chase took a deep breath and began to scramble up the acacia's trunk.

A youngster it might be, but it was still a sizable creature. The drag on Chase's claws was painful, and her neck already ached from its weight. As she loosened one paw to reach for the next hold, Chase lost her grip altogether. She tumbled back to the ground in an undignified heap of leopard and prey.

"Need any help?" The low, mocking voice came from far too close by.

Chase froze, her fangs still buried in the bongo's neck. She shook it loose.

"Shadow Born of Stealth," she growled.

He padded into the open starlight, his eyes a burning glow in his dark face. "You seem to be struggling."

"I don't need *your* help," Chase snapped. She moved to stand over the young bongo, hunching her shoulders in warning.

Shadow padded closer, smirking. *So full of himself!* He'd always known he was special, that was the trouble: that rare dappled black of his coat, and his eyes, as green as sunlight through the forest canopy.

"I'm only offering assistance," he murmured.

"And I told you, I'm fine! I lost my balance. I'll get my kill up there, but it would be easier if you weren't watching."

Seeming chastened, he stepped back. But his eyes still glowed with mischief as he watched her second attempt at climbing the acacia.

The second attempt went as well as the first, and she fell back, panting. With a rumbling snarl of humiliation, Chase picked herself up off the ground again and licked angrily at her shoulder fur.

In the silence, she could almost *hear* Shadow's tail flicking.

"I can help if you like," he said at last. "It is my tree, after all."

"Oh, is that so?"

"That's so." He shrugged. "Look at the claw marks on the trunk and use your nose. I'm not making it up."

Fuming silently, Chase stared at the territory marks. His scent was there too, but faded.

"So really," he went on, bending down to lick his fore-paw casually, "anything stashed in those branches rightfully belongs to me."

Chase glared at him, her chest swelling with fury. He was right. "You wouldn't dare talk to me like that if my mother were here."

Idly, Shadow glanced about him. "But Prowl isn't here. Is she?"

There was nothing more she could say. Besides, he was bigger and stronger than she was; Shadow could take her precious bongo any time he liked.

"I'll cache it somewhere else, then." With a last snarl, Chase turned and dragged the antelope away. She was never going to find another tree as perfect as that one, but she would *not* stay and argue with that insolent idiot!

When Shadow was far enough away that even her vision could not find him in the night, Chase halted to rest, dropped the bongo, and glared her resentment toward where she'd last seen him.

Even now, she could still feel the mocking glow of his cool stare.

CHAPTER THREE

The last rays of the sun made the plains' grass glow pink and gold beneath streaks of brilliant white cloud. It struck sparks from the yellow coats of the gazelles who clustered in the sunset, settling for another night of uneasy sleep beneath the star-light. Already the gazelles on the outer rim of the herd were watching the savannah, limbs trembling with tension, heads alert and eyes huge.

But all the nights were like this, and they had been since the dawn of Bravelands. Prance knew that. Some might be lost, and never wake from slumber to crop the plains grass; some might find their spirits bounding skyward, released by the fangs of predators. It was always so. Nevertheless, the Us was at peace. The skies were clear, the grass plentiful, and many recent fawns hid in the grass or tottered among the grown gazelles. The herd was as restful as it was possible for it to be, thought Prance, with a warm glow of love and belonging. The beat of her heart, the beat of every heart in the herd, was gentle and easy.

Her friend Skip, grazing closer, nudged Prance with her nose. "Have you heard any more from the zebras about the Great Father's health?"

Prance sighed sadly. "It's said he can no longer see or hear. He lives, but he is failing by the day. So Sunfriend told me."

"Poor Great Father." Skip dipped her head in respect, then shook it from side to side. "How can he govern Bravelands in that condition?"

"Bravelands seems to be doing just fine under his leadership," Prance reminded Skip. "The Great Spirit has not sought a new host, and it's not wise to question its ways."

"Still, if there is a sudden danger—how can a failing Great Father defend us?" insisted Skip.

"When the time comes that the Great Parent cannot do their duty, the Spirit will find a new host," said Prance firmly. "You know this, Skip. That's how it's always been."

Reassured, Skip lowered her head to crop at the grass. Prance joined her, tearing at the short sweet grass that had been trampled and ignored by the zebras. She was glad she'd been able to reassure her friend; after all, things had been good in Bravelands for as long as most creatures could remember. Only the oldest survivors and the elephants remembered a time of chaos or peril—the age of Titan, when the Three Heroes had saved Bravelands. Skip said the stories were exaggeration, but Prance wasn't so sure. After all, Great Father Thorn had been one of those Three Heroes! And Prance was sure that the Lion Fearless hunted among the stars, just as her mother had told her.

Not that I'd want to meet him face-to-face, she thought with a shiver. Great Lions of stories were all very fine, but real ones were no friends to grass-eaters!

Just as she thought of lions, Prance felt a tremor in the Us. Every head jerked up; the fear that rippled through the herd was in Prance's spine and limbs too. She sprang at the same moment the others did, and in the same direction. There was no need to think or plan; the Us took over now, as it always did. Lithe bodies ran alongside her, Skip among them; she knew them all by name, they were her friends. But at this moment she and they were only the Us. The Us had protected them since Time itself had brought seasons to Bravelands; Prance knew that too, from her mother's stories.

As quickly as it had begun, the surge of panic was over. Her herd-mates around her trotted to a halt. A mutter spread through the herd, passed from gazelle to gazelle: it was a false alarm. *This time.* But no gazelle must ever assume the peril wasn't real. *Trust in the Us.*

"Thanks be to the Great Spirit," said Prance dutifully.

"Look," said Skip, jerking her head. "There was no predator this time—but something has changed."

She was gazing toward an elderly gazelle, Leap, who now stood alone at the edge of the herd. Leap looked very quiet and still, thought Prance. Her head hung a little lower than usual, but she seemed calm as the herd gathered close to her, their eyes wide and curious.

And then Prance realized: she saw it, as she had seen it many times before. Leap was searching quietly for her own shadow, yet she had none.

Already Prance could hear the murmuring begin, and she knew the words as well as any in the herd. She spoke them too, as the gazelles quietly bowed their heads to honor Leap.

"The stars summon you; don't look back."

"You are marked, and you are honored. Fly as the savannah birds do."

"Do not fear; run fast to the stars."

As the murmuring died away, Leap raised her elegant head. She gazed around at her herd-mates.

"I do not fear." Her gentle voice carried across the silent assembly. "My life was good, and my fawns were many and healthy. The Us has left me now, but I do not fear Death. I do not fear the flesh-eater that will take my earthbound life. Freed from my shadow, I will fly to join my ancestors on the sparkling plain."

A rumble of warm approval went through the herd. Leap's words were fine, thought Prance, and the herd had received them well; the Us would remember her. *I hope I do as well when my time comes.*

Feeling a swell of emotion in her throat, Prance nodded respectfully to the old gazelle. As she lifted her head, Leap's gaze met hers.

"Ahhh." Leap's voice was soft, yet wondering. "Another herd-mate shares my honor! The Great Spirit's blessing be upon you too, sister."

Leap was talking of another Shadowless—one who stood right behind Prance. A thrill of awe rippled through Prance's blood. *Two of us are to be taken, then.* She swiveled her head to look over her shoulder. *Oh, I hope it isn't Skip!*

No. Skip stood behind her, all right, but Prance saw with relief that her friend's shadow was in place. Skip had drawn back from Prance, though. She was gaping at her, even as her jaws moved around a mouthful of grass.

All the herd were staring at Prance.

The warm emotion and her sense of the Us faded, very slowly, to numbness. This made no sense. Prance surveyed the herd, her head turning from one side to the other, uncomprehending.

The Us watched her from a distance.

With a surge of panic in her gut, Prance turned to Skip and took a few quick steps toward her old friend. But Skip drew away again, slowly, merging into the herd. Prance stood isolated, her throat tightening, her legs trembling.

Skip's eyes were huge with grief. "The stars summon you, Prance," she murmured. "Don't look back."

"What?"

"Do not fear," added Spring, beside Leap. "Run fast to the stars."

Prance thought she heard a muttered *Fly as the savannah birds do*, but in truth she could no longer hear her herd-mates. Her head filled with a panicked buzzing. She did not want to look down. She did not want to see. But she must. *Oh Great Spirit*—

Prance lowered her eyes.

Her delicate hooves touched the soft grass's sunset glow. The dying light was intense now, more beautiful than she had ever seen it, and it cast the herd's shadows in a great dark mass back toward the mountains in the distance.

But it cast none for her.

Prance spun around. The light of the sunset was dazzling. The sun itself was still a blazing sphere that rested on the horizon.

She twisted again, back toward the herd. Every nerve in her body fired into life, searching, searching desperately for the Us. She could hardly breathe.

"There's some kind of mistake!" she blurted.

"Prance," said Skip, shocked. "Accept the Great Spirit's choice."

Spring nodded, her face disapproving. "The stars summon you. Don't. Look. Back."

Prance suddenly hated the words. She'd said them so many times to other gazelles; how could she have spoken them so lightly?

"The Us has left you, as it has left Leap," insisted Skip. "You will die tomorrow. You are marked and you are honored; fly as the sav—"

"No!" brayed Prance in horror. "It's a mistake! It really is! I felt the Us just now, when Leap—it was with me then—I was—"

The words dried in her throat. Yes, she had felt the Us when Leap spoke. But as she stared in disbelief at her herd, she knew the truth: it had left her now. The Us was no longer a part of her.

So this is how it feels. Certainty, fellowship, love, and strength in numbers: all had deserted her. She stood alone beneath a twilight sky, facing the last night she would ever know. Perhaps she would not even witness another sunrise.

As she turned from her herd, the great orb of the sun sank at last beyond the hills, with a dying flash. Prance knew, with a darkness that swelled inside her as swiftly as it encroached on the land, that she would not see it again.

"Accept it," came Skip's voice from behind her.

"But I don't want to die!" cried Prance, in desolation.

Skip trod delicately to her side. "It's a shock, I know. It must be. But look at Leap. Take your example from her."

"Leap is *old*!" exclaimed Prance. It still seemed so unreal, as if the world around her had left along with the Us, and she was alone in a void. "Leap has lived a good life, she has borne fawns! I have lived only three seasons. It's too soon!"

"Now, you must be calm and hold your tongue," said Skip sternly. "The Spirit has chosen, and that's that. It's over. It is an *honor*, remember."

It did not feel like an honor. Terror clutched at Prance's heart and wouldn't let go. It was so easy for Skip to say those words; it had been easy for *her* to say them, every time.

Skip turned very suddenly, cantering with the whole herd a little way from Prance. Prance knew, with a surge of grief, that it had not been Skip's decision; her friend was responding to the Us, as she always had. So this was how the Us had always looked to those outside it: *And I am that creature now.* The Us was lost to Prance; she would never feel it again. A hollow, aching void seemed to open inside her.

"Prance, young one." The soft voice at her ear was Leap's.

Prance turned. The old gazelle's eyes were a little cloudy, but still kind. "Leap," she greeted her, numbly.

"Let us find comfort in each other," suggested Leap. "Come along. We will drink together for the last time."

Prance followed her, her legs trembling. More than anything she wanted to run with the herd, to canter at Skip's side, to sense the Us, but that was no longer possible. Leap's company would have to be enough, until—until *it* happened.

Cold fear surged through her again. Leap nudged her gently.

"Here's a pool," she told her. "Drink, Prance."

As they dipped their muzzles into the cool, clear water, Prance almost forgot for a moment that it was the end. The water felt so good against her hot throat, and the last colors of the sunset and the purple twilight were so beautiful. Raising her head, she stared toward the dark, mist-swirled slopes of the mountain beyond the plain.

"The mountain!" Leap was watching her. "Lovely, isn't it? So grand and commanding. But do you know how it came to be?"

Prance shook her head, wordless.

"My grandmother told me the story, not long before she

lost her own shadow. There was once a very greedy hippo, who ate everything he came across. He ate the river grass till it was gone, and drank the rivers dry to find the last of that grass. He stripped the trees of every leaf and gulped down their trunks. Bush and forest, grass and flower: the insatiable hippo consumed them all, and the whole world was in danger from his hunger.

"So the Great Parent of the time—an elephant—he came to the hippo and told him he must eat stones; only those could quench his tormenting appetite. The hippo obeyed the Great Parent, as all creatures should. He ate the stones and the rocks; he ate boulders and kopjes and whole escarpments, and at last he ate so much, he could not move again. And as he sat there, he slowly became the rocks that he had eaten, and he turned into that mountain, right there. And the land lived and bloomed and grew again, and vast forests flourished, even on the hippo's own stony flanks."

Prance swallowed hard. Staring at the mountain, she could almost see the bump of a gigantic hippo's head, the rounded swell of its back. As its shadow fell across them and the air cooled, she shivered.

"Don't worry," whispered Leap. "Soon you and I will join the greater herd among the stars, Prance. A moment's pain—and then you will run forever with your parents and all your ancestors. There is nothing to be afraid of."

"I know," mumbled Prance. "I'm not scared of that part. It's—I worry that—oh, *Leap*, how do you think it will happen?"

"Does it matter? A lion, a cheetah, a crocodile? All kill

swiftly, as the Code demands; the pain ends, and there is free-dom and wild beauty forever."

Together, the two doomed gazelles walked back toward the herd. Prance could not help her gaze drifting constantly to the noble old herd-mate at her side. Leap seemed so completely at peace; she was even looking forward to the liberty of the stars. For her, the struggle to survive would be over, and she would rest.

But I can't find peace, thought Prance, her mind an agony of turmoil. *Great Spirit, what is wrong with me?*

Life is a struggle, I know it. I know we fight each day to live!

But please, Great Spirit. Please. I haven't finished fighting.

CHAPTER FOUR

"And then one of them tried to sneak up on me. Like this!" Bramble narrowed his eyes and made himself drool as he mimed a creeping hyena. "But I was ready for him. I turned as he pounced, and I *whacked* him, right on the nose."

"And the hyenas were really big?" Moonflower's eyes were wide and horrified; Cassava sat a little farther back, listening intently to Bramble. Beyond the three siblings, other members of the troop had drawn closer to listen. They were enthralled by his tale, Bramble realized. The narrow escape from the hyenas had been worth it, just to see the awe on his troop's faces. And he wasn't exaggerating all *that* much.

"*Huge,*" Bramble emphasized, raising his voice to reach all of them. "Tall as Cassava's shoulder when he's standing up." He patted his brother's shoulder to demonstrate to the watching gorillas.

"That's a very big hyena," drawled Cassava, picking at a tick in his fur.

"Bramble, do *sit still*!" Apple Goldback scolded, shoving him down onto the soft grass beneath the kigelia tree. "I need to check this leg wound of yours, and I can't do it while you're dancing around!"

"And how many were in the pack?" gasped Moonflower.

"At least twenty," said Bramble. "And I fought them off alone! Two attacked at once—and I just stood up, like this—and punched them both, one to each side!"

"Bramble, *stop it*!" exploded Apple, grabbing his arm and yanking him down again.

"Both at once, huh?" said Moonflower. "And what were the others doing?"

"They were all waiting to bite me!" said Bramble. "But they thought better of it when they realized what they were dealing with!"

"Twenty, though?" said another of the other Goldbacks. "Are you sure you're not . . . misremembering?"

"Now, now." Cassava grinned. "Even if there weren't twenty, Bramble's obviously shown a lot of courage, and that's good." He winked at his little brother. "I'll bet the hyenas got a few bites and scratches in, after all. There's no way he could have got away from such a mob with one leg bite."

Bramble took in a breath to spin more details of his strength and bravery. Then he hesitated. Cassava was right; the hyenas would have been bound to take a few more lumps out of him. "Indeed!" he blurted at last. "They were angry, but clumsy. Lucky they only got their teeth into my fur *mostly*. I don't remember much of it, to be honest. It's a blur. Because, you know, I was *so furious* that they'd attacked me!"

"Wow." Cassava nodded. "It's hardly surprising that your memory's hazy after a fierce fight like that. Well done, Bramble."

Bramble nodded and folded his arms, sticking out his lower lip. Apple rolled her eyes and returned her attention to his leg wound.

"It's just a scratch, Apple, honestly," he told the old gorilla.

"I'll decide that," she muttered.

"It was the hyena hanging on my leg that did it." Bramble glanced at Cassava. "But I paid it back. Honestly, I gave it a kick that sent it flying through the air!"

"I bet you did, little brother," said Cassava. "Good for you!"

"Uh-oh," said Moonflower.

"No, I *did*," said Bramble indignantly. "You don't believe me but I'm telling you, they were—"

"Not you," interrupted Moonflower, pointing over his shoulder. "Uh-oh to *him*."

Bramble twisted around, trying not to let on to Apple about the bolt of pain that shot into his leg. His eyes widened, and he almost forgot the bite. Groundnut Blackback was stomping through the trees toward him, his expression thunderous.

"I want to talk to young Bramble," he rumbled. "Never mind flying hyenas, I want to know about a flying mango. My fur is *still* sticky!"

"Groundnut!" Bramble glanced to left and right, looking

for an escape, but Apple was still holding firmly onto his leg as she peered at the wound. "I, uh . . . I didn't do it on purpose. . . . I, um, dropped it, and I didn't know you were there, and—"

"A likely story!" roared Groundnut. "What about the iron-wood fruits, eh? Can you explain—"

A terrible sound split the air, drowning out Groundnut's next words: it was as if thunder had come down from the sky to the earth, and was trying to split the mountain. Apple fell back as the ground shuddered; Groundnut stopped yelling and covered his sticky head with his paws. Cassava sprang to his feet, and instantly stumbled back as the ground shifted, and Bramble grabbed Moonflower and held tight to her in panic. The gorillas who had been watching yammered in alarm, and there were hoots and cries from their unseen troop-mates in the nighttime forest.

As quickly as it had begun, the mountain quieted, and the ground stilled. The gorillas, frozen in place, stared at one another in a new and ominous silence.

Cassava was first to recover. He scrambled back to his feet. "The mountain spoke," he said quietly.

"I always wish it would speak a bit less dramatically," said Moonflower, extricating herself from Bramble's grip.

"All right, everyone." Cassava shook himself. "We must all head to the Spirit Mouth. Moonflower's right; that was no small rumble; the mountain wants us to know something. I'll rouse the friends who have already gone to their nests."

Groundnut nodded, dropped to his forepaws, and began to

guide the Goldbacks up the forest slope. Cassava turned and bounded into the blackness of the forest, already grunting his summons. Just a few moments later, small groups of gorillas began to emerge from the trees, rubbing their eyes and shaking nest twigs from their fur, muttering to one another as they headed after Groundnut and the Goldbacks.

"Wow!" Moonflower whispered to Bramble in excitement. "There hasn't been a Spirit Mouth ceremony since we were little. I wonder what it wants to tell us?"

"Dayflower Mistback will know," pointed out Bramble.

"Of course she will," said Moonflower proudly. "Come on, Bramble!"

They bounded after the others, climbing up through the dense forest toward the black stone ridge that jutted from the mountain's eastern slope. Already most of the troop had made their way there; gathering according to their ranks, gorillas sat patiently at the border of the trees and on the edges of the escarpment as the last stragglers arrived. As they waited for their Mistback's verdict, the gorillas groomed one another and murmured quietly. Cassava had roused all the troop's members from their nests; now he sat in a prominent position by a large jagged boulder, his brow furrowed in thought. Occasionally he glanced up and around, searching the nearest trees with his gaze. Bramble loped up with Moonflower to sit at Cassava's side, in the place reserved for Burbark's offspring, just a little to the Silverback's right flank. Not that the leader had yet taken his place on the black slab of jutting stone.

"Where's Father?" asked Bramble.

"That's what I was wondering," muttered Cassava. "He'll be here, don't worry."

Bramble glanced up toward the top of the outcrop, where loose boulders were piled around a small ledge. A grizzled, lightly built gorilla sat up there alone, her pale brown eyes distant; she paid no attention to the other gorillas as the last few members of the troop took their places.

"Your mother looks very thoughtful," whispered Bramble to Moonflower.

"She always does," said Moonflower. "And I guess this was quite a big declaration from the mountain."

Groundnut shifted impatiently nearby. "Where *is* Burbark Silverback?"

Cassava's brow cleared, and he pointed to the trees just downhill. "Here he comes," he called with relief.

Leaves shuddered and twigs snapped as Burbark's huge shape loomed out of the forest. Rising onto his hind feet, he paused for a moment to scratch at his wrist, then dropped to all fours and shambled forward. He blinked and surveyed the troop with a look of mild irritation; it was as if he'd just been woken from a pleasant nap. Bramble bit his lip. His father looked so distracted.

Then Burbark met Cassava's eyes. He shook himself and padded up the rocky slope with what seemed like renewed determination. He halted on that flat slab of black rock, just beneath the Mistback's perch.

Turning to face the troop, Burbark clenched and unclenched his fists. Bramble waited for his booming declaration.

But when his father at last blinked and gruffly cleared his throat, his words were little more than a rapid grunt.

"Behold the Mouth of the Mountain."

Burbark seized the edge of a vast slab. His shoulder muscles bulging and flexing with the effort, he dragged it aside. Coils and tendrils of pale smoke poured from the cavern beyond, rising and swirling around the Mistback before dissipating in the clear air.

Bramble watched in silence with the rest. The smoke continued to seep from the cavern, wreathing the hunched figure of the Mistback. It was as if the Great Spirit, a nebulous and benevolent presence that he took for granted, was suddenly close to him. Bramble could almost feel its warm breath on his hide.

He knew the history of this place; he had been told it by his mother while she was still alive, just as all young gorillas learned it from their parents and grandparents. Many generations ago, when Kigelia Silverback had led the gorillas away from the perilous plains to live in the mountain forests, the troops had feared that the Great Spirit might abandon them. But Kigelia's daughter, Pepper Goldback, had heard the Spirit's voice through the mountain. She had become the first Mistback. And since then, at this place and at other vents that opened in the mountainside, the Great Spirit had spoken many times to all the mountain troops.

A silence settled over the gorillas; Bramble could hear the rustle of small creatures in the leaf litter, the flutter of birds in the high branches, and even the distant bark of a jackal.

Dayflower Mistback rose from her perch, then padded with dignified steps down the short slope to the mouth of the vent. Swathed in smoke, she paused, glanced at the sky, then dropped to all fours and vanished into the cavern.

Bramble held his breath. He felt the fur rise and tingle along his spine.

"Has your mother ever told you what it's like in there?" he whispered to Moonflower.

She shook her head. "Not much. Only that it's a little confusing but very special. She hears voices, sees shapes in the smoke. But it isn't always clear what they mean."

"I'd love to go in and see," murmured Bramble.

"You know you can't," said Moonflower sternly. "No one can, except the Mistback. Not even Burbark Silverback."

Bramble turned to peer at his father. Surprisingly, the big Silverback looked rather bored. He scratched at something on his shoulder, stared into the forest, and heaved a sigh. Bramble blinked, confused. How could his father look bored on such a special night? And wasn't it disrespectful to the Mistback and the Great Spirit itself?

A shadow moved at the entrance to the vent, and Bramble turned back to the Mistback. Dayflower was emerging slowly, her eyes vague and her fur glistening with moisture. As she gazed around at the troop, her features creased into a frown.

She rose up onto her hind paws and made a ringing declaration. "Hear me. The Spirit spoke tonight with a warning."

There were gasps and murmurs around the troop, but

silence quickly fell again. Bramble sensed the quivering tension in his bones.

"Evil will spread from this mountain to all of Bravelands," Dayflower intoned.

The gorillas cried out in alarmed grunts. Bramble felt his fur on his neck spring erect, and his stomach went cold. How was that possible? The mountain was a peaceful place; it was why the gorillas had come there so many moons ago! "Evil?" he whispered hoarsely to his half sister.

Moonflower gripped Bramble's arm, and he could feel she was trembling with shock. "*From* the mountain?" she gasped.

"Evil will spread from *this* place," Dayflower emphasized, with a glance at her daughter, "infecting the plains below—unless wisdom stands in its path."

"This is not possible," grunted Groundnut, rising to his hind feet.

"I agree," called Lantana Goldback. "There's been a mistake."

"They're right. It makes no sense," said Bramble, bewildered. "This is the safe place!"

"It doesn't *seem* to make sense," Moonflower corrected him. "The Spirit's voice does not lie to my mother."

Cassava was eyeing Burbark, but the great Silverback showed no sign of reacting. After a moment, Cassava cleared his throat, stood up tall, and thumped a fist against his chest.

"We must send a delegation to the Great Parent on the plains," he declared. "This warning is meant for all of

Bravelands, and it should be passed on!"

"Not if it's wrong," muttered Groundnut, shaking his head.

"It's like I say," put in Lantana, "the Mistback *could* have misunderstood."

Moonflower shot her an indignant glare. Bramble glanced at his father to gauge his reaction, but Burbark was quite still, his features impassive.

"Going to the *plains* . . . I mean, is that really necessary?" Bindweed Blackback stood up. "The Great Spirit will surely deliver the message to the Great Parent—directly."

Moonflower jumped up, looking a little embarrassed but determined. "I agree with Cassava," she said in a shaking voice, as the older gorillas watched her. "The warning's too stark to ignore—and the mountain *chose* to warn us directly. That can only mean that the Great Spirit wants the message to come from us. It's relying on the gorillas to take its warning to the plains!"

A grinding sound came from higher up the slope, harsh and echoing. The gorillas turned, and Moonflower put her paws over her ears, wincing. Burbark Silverback had risen at last and was shoving the flat boulder back across the vent.

No one could speak as the grinding noise continued. By the time the rock was in its place, every gorilla was watching Burbark in silence.

"We are not going *anywhere*!" he bellowed. Burbark glared directly at Cassava.

Bramble too looked at his brother, nervous. Cassava,

though, simply seemed taken aback. He opened his mouth to reply, but closed it again without saying a word. His eyes were wide with shock and hurt.

Burbark nodded to himself as he surveyed his troop. "Have you all forgotten why the gorillas came here in the first place? This mountain is our refuge. The Great Spirit wishes us to protect our *own* home; the rest of Bravelands can look after itself."

"But Father." Cassava surged to his hind feet, his fists clenched in frustration. "The mountain spoke, and the Mistback interpreted. She has never let us down—"

"NEVER forget!" boomed Burbark, silencing his son with a glare before turning back to the startled troop. "*Blood pools on the plains.* That is why we will not go there. And I will not send the best of my troop to die on a whim!"

Bramble glanced at Dayflower Mistback. She was crouched back on her ledge, and she looked both troubled and a little perplexed as her gaze drifted to Burbark.

"How about we speak to some of the other troops?" suggested Cassava, after a long, awkward moment. "We can ask if they received the same message and how they interpreted it?"

"What would be the point?" demanded Burbark, thumping his chest with both paws. His eyes flashed. "The message sounds clear to me; the only confusion is yours and Dayflower's."

Cassava looked shocked. "But Father—"

"I said enough!" shouted Burbark. Bounding down from

the ridge, he shoved roughly past Cassava, who staggered in surprise.

When the great Silverback had crashed back into the trees, and the sound of his thumping steps had faded downhill, the gorillas turned to one another, shocked.

"That's not like Burbark," said Bindweed.

Groundnut patted Cassava's shoulder. "Are you all right?"

Cassava shook him off gently. "I'm fine. And so is my father. I'll try talking to him again in the morning."

"I still say it's unusual," put in Lantana with a scowl. "Burbark's behaving very oddly in the last few days, and this—"

"I never saw him treat the Mistback like that before." Bindweed shook his head in dismay.

Bramble chewed his lip, silent. He didn't like to hear the troop questioning his father, but he had to admit they were right.

Moonflower had wandered off to speak to her mother, who was shaking herself out of her smoke-induced daze. Bramble sat down, his gaze switching between Cassava and the trees where his father had disappeared.

Of course we must do what the Great Spirit wants. It's just that we're not sure what that is. . . .

He frowned, tugging at his lower lip. The plains were a terrifying place; he had heard the stories. Even if Cassava had exaggerated the lions, Bramble didn't much want to meet one after all. And lions were far from the only notorious villains of the great grasslands. *Cheetahs. Crocodiles. Rhinoceroses, with spikes on their heads as big as trees . . .*

He found himself far from disappointed by Burbark's decision. *Blood pools on the plains.* Gorillas did not belong there, and Burbark Silverback's word was final.

No one from the troop was going anywhere. *Thank the Great Spirit.*

CHAPTER FIVE

Oh, the bliss of a full belly! Chase lay sprawled on her flank in the den, barely able to imagine moving again, let alone hunting. She puffed out a sigh of contentment through her nostrils, feeling her whiskers shiver.

The bongo had fed all three of them, and well. Seek was fast asleep on his back beside her, his paws twitching in the air; perhaps he was dreaming of chasing down his own prey. But even better than the food had been the look in Prowl's eyes as they had feasted on the carcass. She had glanced up frequently at her daughter, yellow eyes burning with gratitude and pride. It had warmed Chase's innards even more than bongo-flesh.

Chase had not told her mother about that run-in with Shadow. She had certainly not confessed her failed attempt to cache her prey in the tree. Instead, she had dragged the bongo all the way back to the den, fighting off exhaustion and a few cheeky jackals, and had managed to feign some remaining energy when she arrived.

It was no problem, Mother. I didn't want Seek to have to trudge all the way to the prey; I decided to bring it here instead.

The struggle and the weariness had all been worth it. Prowl was delighted with her; Chase had reveled in her triumph and in Seek's adulation.

Her ears twitched; her mother was stirring. Chase rolled over to catch the shape of Prowl, slinking out of the den mouth.

"Where are you going, Mother?"

Prowl turned her head, her whiskers twitching. "It's nothing important, Chase, so don't worry. I want to patrol the territory, that's all. Stay with Seek and go back to sleep."

Chase rose to her forepaws. Prowl was gazing at her very directly; worse, she was using the voice Chase had heard before. That had been the voice Prowl had used when she told Seek, over and over again, that his mother was coming back soon.

But Slink didn't come back. Slink was dead all along.

Prowl's eyes were still fixed on hers. *She's not telling the truth,* thought Chase with a shiver of certainty.

"Chase, you mustn't worry," Prowl told her gently. "I've patrolled this land more times than I can count. I'll be all right."

Chase took a breath to argue. But her mother's eyes were warm, so she simply nodded. Prowl turned again and squeezed out through the den mouth into the night.

Chase glanced down at Seek. His rounded little belly rose and fell steadily, his eyes were tightly closed, and he wore an unconscious smirk of pure contentment. Chase waited a few moments longer. Despite her mother's reassuring tone, she had been hiding something. The cub was not going to wake up any time soon. Waiting a few moments to give her mother a safe head start, Chase crouched and slunk out of the den after her.

Beyond the cave mouth, starlight outlined the ridges and the forests in an eerie silver glow. Chase paused for a moment to inhale the cool night air through flared nostrils. She closed her eyes briefly. She loved the nighttime; it was impossible to imagine hunting in the heat and glare of the day, with flies buzzing around her sticky fur. How did lions and cheetahs tolerate it? In the darkness of the night, the air felt purer, lighter, and every scent was enhanced—grass, flower, river, or prey. The birds were quiet, but for an occasional night screech; insects buzzed and whirred and chirped in a constant chorus that she loved. Her ears caught every rustle in the grass, every creak of a branch, every tiny susurration of dry leaves.

She flicked one ear back as the grass stirred close by. Tilting her head, she measured the sound, estimated the speed of what was there, and slapped her paw down hard.

There was a squeak of terror; she felt soft fur and fragile bones beneath her paw pad. Very slightly lifting her foot, she peered down at her catch. The huge eyes of a pygmy dormouse stared up at her, glazed with terror.

Chase lowered her head to sniff at its long bushy tail. There wasn't much meat on it, and she was hardly desperate. She could feel the creature's violent trembling through her forepaw.

She stepped back. "Go on. You're lucky I've already eaten."

It gazed up at her for an instant in petrified disbelief. Then it squirmed upright and fled into the night.

She watched the grass close behind it, feeling rather pleased with herself. She'd obeyed the Code as a proud leopard should: *Only kill to survive.* She certainly hadn't needed that poor tiny creature to sustain her existence.

Swishing her tail, Chase padded on after her mother, following the clear trail of her scent. She was so preoccupied with her achievements of the day—an excellent hunt *and* respect for the Code!—that it took longer than it should have for a new presence to penetrate her awareness. When her instinct grew too strong to ignore, Chase paused, one paw raised, and frowned. She glanced slightly to the side, twitching her whiskers and flaring her upper lip.

There was something downwind of her: not some insignificant small prey, but a large creature with blood on its breath. It was impossible to catch the precise scent, but her hide tingled with the awareness that she was being followed. She glared into the darkness behind her.

Nothing moved. Chase widened her nostrils, but she couldn't trace the scent. If it was the hyenas, back for revenge . . . *I must get out of their reach.*

There was a thorn tree a few paces away; she could make

out the glimmer of its bark in the starlight. With six loping bounds she was beneath it, and without a gazelle to weigh her down, it was easy to scramble silently into its branches. Chase stretched herself along a lower bough, breathing as calmly as she could and gazing down at the grass below her.

Not far away, the long grass was stirring. It waved and swayed, and suddenly a shape that seemed darker than the night itself emerged from the pale blades.

Shadow . . .

He paced slowly toward the thorn tree where Chase hid, then hesitated. His whiskers jerked, and his nostrils flared. He narrowed his glowing eyes.

How dare he! thought Chase angrily. She stood up on her branch, her tail lashing. "Why are you following me?"

Shadow looked up, startled, but his face swiftly took on that rather smug expression of his. "Chase. You should be careful at night, out alone like this. I saw another leopard in this territory today. A big one. He's looking for a mate and for land."

Chase wrinkled her muzzle. "I've smelled no other leopard. And Prowl hasn't mentioned any strangers lurking."

Shadow hunched his dappled black shoulders. "Believe what you like, Chase. I've seen him with my own eyes. Be careful, that's all I'm saying."

Chase narrowed her eyes and peeled back the corner of her lip to show her fangs in derision. "You sound scared, Shadow."

"So what if I am? It means I'm smart. You shouldn't joke about such things, Chase. If a new male homes in on your mother, and then finds Seek, there'll be trouble."

A chill rippled along Chase's spine. There would be more than trouble; there would be death. *Seek's death.* No male would tolerate another's cub in his territory.

"Don't let me interrupt your precious nightly hunt," said Shadow, turning with a flick of his tail as he stalked away. "I thought you'd appreciate the warning, that's all."

He merged with the darkness of the forest night, and Chase waited only a moment after he'd gone before bounding down from her perch. She looked toward her mother's trail, then turned back toward the den.

If Shadow's right—if a new male is in the area—I have to get back home. Now.

Chase started out at a brisk trot, but quickly broke into a run, streaking through the trees toward the den. Her heart swelled and raced, faster with every step, and she laid her ears back, desperate.

The thick-rooted tree was in sight; she sprinted for its shadowy base and squirmed into the cavern. Relief melted into horror as she felt its emptiness; there was no cub here. She could hear no light, quick breathing, no squeaky dream noises. Chase's blood throbbed in her ears, in time with her thrashing heartbeat.

"Seek!" she cried out loud. "Seek!"

He was nowhere to be seen. There was a flattened patch of earth where he had lain, and a couple of tiny broken roots; all that remained was his cub-scent.

Chase dragged herself back out of the den onto the open plain. *"Seek!"* she wailed, as loudly as she dared.

A hyena could have taken him; they could burrow into the den quite easily. Or, if he'd wandered, a night bird of prey would find him easy meat. He was still so small! The forest night was home to Chase—but not to Seek, not yet. A thousand dangers could find him here. . . . *How will I tell Prowl that I lost him?*

"Seek! Seek, call to me! I'll come for you!" Her plaintive roar resounded through the trees.

She could barely hear it for the thudding of her heart, but at last she did: a mewling squeak, muffled by distance, at once remorseful and frightened.

"Seek!" Chase bounded toward the noise. There was a shallow gully between the tree and a neighboring copse, and it was there that she found him, cowering beneath a patch of thorny scrub.

Seek crept out from beneath the thorns, quivering. His glowing eyes were huge in the darkness.

"I'm sorry, Chase," he whimpered. "I woke up and you weren't there, so I went to look for you, but I got lost."

Chase fell on him, licking his head and pressing his small body down with her forepaws. She licked harder at his jaw.

"Ow, Chase . . . that hurts . . ."

She drew back, torn between relief and anger. Then she drew a few sharp breaths and closed her eyes as guilt washed over her.

"It's my fault, Seek. Prowl told me not to leave you, and I shouldn't have. I'll stay now till morning, I promise."

Far more gently, she picked up the little cub by his scruff

and trotted as fast as she could back to the den. He dangled limply, not resisting at all; he seemed simply glad to be found and rescued. Chase's hide felt cold with terror and relief. *What if I'd lost him?*

Back in the musty dimness beneath the tree roots, Seek fell asleep again almost instantly, in his usual flattened-earth spot. Chase curled her body around him, tucking her tail carefully over his face; she was determined not to let him wander away again without waking her.

The important thing was that Seek was safe. There had been no strange male leopard, no intruder to pursue Chase and Prowl and dispose of his predecessor's cub. *Shadow was wrong.*

Or we were just lucky. . . .

Perhaps the stranger was lurking close by, and simply hadn't yet stumbled across their den. Perhaps he'd never existed at all.

After all, thought Chase darkly, Shadow might have his own motivation. He might just want to frighten the family off so that he could take this fine territory for himself.

The stranger might be a pure invention of Shadow's. Chase closed her eyes, but she coiled her body even tighter around Seek and pressed her muzzle close to his.

All the same. I'm not taking any chances.

CHAPTER SIX

It happened at dawn, as the first pale rays of the rising sun pierced the violet cloudbank.

One moment there was easy peace: the murmur of waking gazelles, the rip-and-crunch of their morning grazing, the soft braying calls of the gazelles on the outer rim of the herd; and huge eyes blinking wide all around Prance.

Then panic.

It was not the terror of a single gazelle; it was a charge that bolted like lightning through the Us. Every head snapped up and reared back, every tail stiffened, and a thousand slender legs raced into motion. The herd fled, galloping headlong for every life within it.

It had happened so many times. Prance knew how it should be, and she raced with the rest, matching her speed to theirs—or trying. She knew, even as fear surged through her veins, that it was different this time. The Us did not carry her; it was as if she was striving with every instant, every hoof-fall, to remain with them. There was no instinct carrying her on, only her own singular desperation. The herd surged and thrummed like a vast heartbeat; all she could do was pound along with them, her whole body tightening and trembling with panic. She didn't know where they were going, when and how they would turn. She was separate, an individual.

I am alone.

Her hooves struck the ground, her muscles worked to carry her along, but it was all such an *effort*. It was as if the air she ran through was thicker than the air that surrounded the herd. When the gazelles, as one, veered sharply to the west, they collided with her clumsy body; Prance stumbled and almost fell as she made a frantic, conscious effort to turn with them. Almost at once the herd swerved again, and this time she could barely keep up. The effort was more than she could bear. Her legs were heavy, her lungs bursting, and they were leaving her behind; all she could see in her blurred vision were the white flashes of their rumps as the throng outpaced her.

"Wait! Friends! Wait!" It was a strangled gasp, and of course they did not hear her. The Us moved them like water flowing over stone; they could not have turned back even if they'd heard her, even if they'd *wanted* to turn.

Prance knew how it felt. But only now did she understand it fully.

Her body ached, and her lungs were seized by a searing

agony. She should not look back, she knew; she should not
strain to see what it was that pursued them. It would slow her
down. Running with the Us, there was never the time or the
need for such distractions.

Prance had no choice. She twisted and galloped as fast as
she could in the other direction. There was no point following the herd now; the Us was lost to her. She was on her own.

Don't look back. Don't look back. It was taught to them from
the moment a gazelle was born, because the alternative was
unbearable: *Don't look back. Don't watch for your own death. Run.*

Don't look back. . . .

Yet Prance couldn't help herself; it was as if another instinct
had taken over, one that had been dormant during her whole
life of oneness with the Us. She twisted her head and saw
the predator at once: the pale, fast body of a lioness, streaking through the grass toward her. It ran strangely, lurching
on three legs while the fourth barely touched down; but the
speed of it was not affected at all. How could a lame, wounded
lion catch her? *I am a gazelle! I am the wind!*

More lions ahead. The blurred streaks of their tawny bodies coming in to intercept her.

Putting on a burst of extraordinary speed she hadn't known
was in her, Prance hurtled toward a nearby copse.

Don't stay on the open plain. Not now. That is for the Us.

Her head and shoulders burst into dry rattling foliage, and
Prance felt a brief spurt of triumph. But then, far sharper and
stronger, she felt the hot lethal pain of claws in her rump. She
stumbled forward into the bushes, but the big cat was dragging

her back, pulling her toward the grassland with a remorseless strength.

It was strange how time had slowed. Prance almost felt as if she could catch her breath. The safety of the scrubland receded, and she knew a cold certainty: this was the end. All she had to do now was wait: for the bite of fangs in her neck, for the heavy strangulation that would bring merciful darkness. Perhaps it wouldn't hurt so very much. Perhaps the lioness would snap her neck, unintentional but quick; Prance had seen it happen. It was kind.

It was final.

It was now—

I AM NOT MEANT TO DIE!

The knowledge burned through her, firing her heart into renewed, angry life. Prance lashed out with her hind legs and felt her hooves hit a warm body. Her hooves were hard and sharp, and the yielding body fell backward. Prance thought she heard a yowl of agony, but it was so distant it seemed to come from another world.

Her kick was not enough, of course. Those claws still clung to her rump, and Prance found herself rolling and falling, tangled with the hot, reeking body of the predator. As they crashed into a fallen branch, the lioness grunted with pain, and all but one of her claws lost their grip. Prance took her chance and tore herself free of the last dragging claw. She felt the warm trickle of blood where her hide had ripped, but the lioness was dislodged at last.

Prance staggered to her hooves, backing away. The lioness

crouched opposite her, panting and growling; blood streamed from the flesh-eater's left eye. Her tawny flanks heaved with exhaustion and her good eye burned with frustrated rage, but Prance did not wait for the lioness to catch her breath. Spinning, she sprang away through the trees.

This was not her land; she was used to running on the open plain. She was terrified that one of her thin legs would catch on a bush or a branch, sending her tumbling head over hocks and leaving her easy meat for the pursuing predator. But Prance fled at full tilt anyway, praying to the Great Spirit to keep her feet sure.

The run seemed to last forever, but when her lungs at last burned unbearably and her legs could carry her no longer, Prance faltered and trotted to a shivering halt. Panting, she stared wide-eyed into the trees behind her.

There was no sign of the lioness.

Prance could no longer stand. Her legs gave way beneath her, and she collapsed onto the soft bush litter beneath a thorn tree. She stretched out her neck, gasping, her flanks heaving.

It was some time before her legs felt strong enough to carry her once more. Tottering, Prance rose painfully to her hooves. She took an experimental step, and though her legs shook, she didn't fall. Drawing in huge breaths through her flared nostrils, she began to walk unsteadily back through the trees.

It was even eerier now that she was not fleeing for her life. Yet at the moment, Prance didn't dare leave the cover of the trees. She wound back through them, retracing her steps as best she could, and when she reached the border of the woodland, she stood for a long time gazing out fearfully at the plains beyond.

I cannot stay here. I don't belong.

Taking a deep, shuddering breath, Prance stepped out beyond the tree shadows onto the grassland. Her herd was nowhere to be seen.

The full impact of her solitariness struck her. She had never in her young life been alone before. *But at least I'm alive.*

If she could just find the herd again, they would take her back. The Spirit had made a mistake; that was clear now. Even Skip would accept that! Indeed, Skip would probably be ashamed of herself for giving up on Prance so easily. But Prance would forgive her old friend. She would forgive *all* of them. Once more she would be one with the Us, and all would be as it was before. Why, she probably had her shadow back already—

She glanced down, heartbeat pulsing in her dry throat. The sun was bright above her, undimmed by any clouds.

She still had no shadow.

The disappointment was like a kick in the belly. But then, it had not been so long since she had thwarted death. The Great Spirit could not be expected to put everything right immediately. Her shadow would return before the end of the day, Prance was sure of it. *And I did* cheat death!

Feeling a new energy course through her, Prance picked up her hooves and trotted out farther onto the plain. There was a big churned area of scuffed hoofmarks in the dusty grass, and she recognized many of them. Her herd was close after all! Head bobbing, ears pricked, and short black tail switching from side to side, she headed eagerly after them.

There was something ahead of her, on a pale patch of sandy earth: a humped shape with vultures flapping and squabbling around it. Prance's steps slowed. It was impossible to tell what the thing was at this distance, but her instincts had buzzed into nervous alertness. Her legs trembling, Prance approached the slumped creature. As she edged closer and closer, the wobbling heat haze cleared, and the shape resolved into something recognizable.

She halted, shivering. Leap had been caught here, out on the open plain, and the lions had already finished with her. Tattered and ripped and dusty as her hide was, its markings were familiar. Her rib cage was exposed, her limbs torn, and as Prance stared in dread, two vultures began to fight over a strip of throat-flesh.

She wouldn't want my pity, Prance told herself, as she swallowed hard. *Leap was a good gazelle, and she loved the Spirit. She's free now.*

All the same, this could have been her. *Should* have been, perhaps. Prance too might have lain here on the plain, torn and battered and lifeless, food for the vultures and a host for fly grubs. A horrible shudder rippled through Prance's gut.

A vulture craned its scrawny neck to stare at her and took a couple of flapping steps in her direction. Prance backed away hurriedly.

"Run well among the stars, Leap," she murmured quickly. "You were kind to me."

With that she twisted and fled from the awful scene,

galloping in a wide swerve around Leap's remains and racing eagerly toward the herd in the distance. She could see them now, shimmering in the haze between earth and sky, and suddenly she could not wait to be with them all again. They would be amazed at her tale of escape; she would tell it for seasons and seasons! A Marked gazelle who escaped death—it was unheard of, yet here she was, returned to the herd, blessed by the Great Spirit and joined once more with the Us! Prance could almost feel the Us reaching out to her, flowing into her limbs once more. She would be part of the herd again, and she would soon forget that her friends had abandoned her. It was the way of the gazelles, after all!

All is forgiven. All will be well!

Why, she was witnessing the Us at work even as she ran toward her herd. Heads came up simultaneously, hundreds of eyes widening. As soon as the first gazelle turned to face her, they all did, their ears coming forward as one. There was Skip! Grazing was forgotten as they stared in wonder and . . .

"Prance?" Skip took a hesitant step toward her, her ears twitching and drawing back.

"Yes, it's me! I escaped my death!" Even to Prance, her own voice sounded too bright and strained.

Skip's voice grew wary. "What's the meaning of this?"

"I . . ." Prance looked from gazelle to gazelle. "The Great Spirit spared me. I have returned as one of you! We will be the Us once more, together!"

Some of the gazelles tossed their horns. Others stamped their hooves, restless and frightened. Fawns edged closer to their mothers, trembling, and older gazelles backed away, nostrils tightening in disgust.

Skip made a sudden darting motion toward Prance, striking the ground with her small hoof. "Get away with you!"

Prance's heart plummeted. For a moment, she couldn't breathe.

"Skip, my friend—I survived! Nothing happened to me, I'm Prance Runningherd once more!"

"No!" bellowed an old doe. She lowered her head angrily, jerking her horns at Prance. "You are cursed. Leave the herd, Marked One!"

"Yes!" brayed another, younger doe. She edged in front of her fawn as if Prance might attack it. "You're not welcome. Go and find the fate that missed you!"

"Yes!" exclaimed Skip. "You know that is the right thing to do, Prance Herdless."

"What?" Something cold washed through Prance's blood. She could hardly breathe, and her heart slammed against her delicate rib cage. "What did you call me?"

"You heard us," commanded Skip, as the others nodded and stamped their hooves. "You are not Prance Runningherd, not anymore."

"Please," begged Prance, although she was already backing away. Somewhere inside her, she knew it was hopeless. *I am Marked. And it's forever.*

"Go, Prance Herdless. *Go!*"

CHAPTER SEVEN

His father had been right; the plains were no place for a gorilla. There was
no emerald-green canopy to shade him, no cooling mountain breeze; the
unforgiving sun was a white blaze of heat above his aching head. Bramble
was horribly exposed here; there were no trees, no hillsides, not so much as a
boulder or a bush. In every direction, for as far as he could see, lay nothing
but dry yellow grass and flat cracked earth. He would at least see predators
approaching, though.

Wouldn't he?

I'm so thirsty! *thought Bramble. His throat was raw, his mouth*
dry. He was so weak, he could barely lurch on his aching knuckles toward
the shimmer of water ahead. Was it true water, or some horrible, taunt-
ing mirage? Everything shimmered and wobbled on these dreadful plains!
Everything—

No, it was water. Gray and murky and unappetizing, but he collapsed
onto its gritty bank in gratitude. It was a perfectly round, stagnant pool, with

a single log floating in its center. Bramble didn't care. I have to drink!

He reached down, cupping the water in his fingers. Just as he was about to bring it to his lips, he looked again at the log.

It had eyes. Slitted, yellow eyes, cruel and devoid of mercy. The log lurched up out of the water, parting its scaled jaws to reveal rows of jagged yellow teeth.

Bramble was too shocked to move. There wasn't time. The jaws parted above his head, plunging his life into blackness, and snapped closed—

Bramble jerked awake with a gasp, his heart pounding. He clutched his chest. It had been a dream, only a dream; still, his mouth felt horribly dry. Why would he have such a nightmare? It must have been because of all that had happened yesterday: the hyenas, the shaking of the earth, the quarrel at the Spirit Mouth.

He was three years old, and it was a long time since he'd scuttled to find his mother in the middle of the night, but he very much wanted to do it now. His mother had always comforted him after a bad dream, had taken him in her warm, strong arms and rocked him back to sleep. A bolt of grief surged through him, and he swayed where he stood, feeling more alone than ever.

Any company would help. With trembling paws, Bramble clambered out of his nest, picking leaves from his fur, and peered around in search of the troop. Someone had to be awake. . . .

The closest nest was empty. He furrowed his brow. Loping to the next, he found that it, too, had been abandoned. So had its neighbor—and the next, and the next. As he scrambled up through the branches, searching every cluster of bedding, panic rose in his chest. *It's another dream. I only dreamed that I woke up, and I'm still asleep, and I just need to shake myself awake again properly. . . .*

His toe found a thorn on the branch, and he yelped in pain. Sitting down, Bramble tugged the spine out of his foot. No, he was awake all right. He blinked in fear. So where was everyone?

Bramble stopped to catch his breath. There was a reason for this. It didn't make sense right now, but it would. After all, his father wouldn't leave him alone. Nor would Cassava.

Of course! He felt a rush of relief. Even if the others wandered off or were playing some kind of mean trick, Cassava wouldn't abandon him. Feeling instantly better, Bramble shinned along a fallen trunk and hopped down to the ground on the other side. A gray and misty light was peeking between the trees and through the canopy above his head; not long until morning. Here he could make out the crushed leaves and the broken twigs where many gorillas had passed.

"Cassava! Groundnut!" he called out. "Bindweed! Hey! Where are you?"

The sound of his own voice reassured him, and he set off along the track of the troop through the smashed foliage.

They weren't far away at all. With relief, Bramble made out the shapes of gorillas beyond a small dip of clearing. He speeded up, loping toward them. They were all staring at the same thing, something on the ground, and they hadn't noticed him yet.

"Hey!" he called cheerfully. "What's going on?"

Groundnut turned, startled, with the others. The big Blackback's eyes were wide with shock, but he didn't scold Bramble for appearing so unexpectedly. Instead he shambled toward him, rising up to block his path with his massive body.

"Stay back," he said, but his voice was gentle. "Don't look, Bramble."

Bramble's gut clenched. "What? What happened? What is it?"

Groundnut reached out an arm, stretching it across Bramble's chest. Bramble tried to push forward, but the big gorilla was implacable, and far stronger. Very quietly, Groundnut murmured, "Don't."

Something in that single word made Bramble's blood turn as cold as a mountain stream. He backed away a step, then one more, his pulse beating hard in his throat. *What won't he let me see?*

Groundnut might have been stronger, but he wasn't agile. Bramble ducked beneath the arm of the Blackback and bounded forward, too fast for the older gorilla to stop him. He expected Groundnut to yell with rage and come after him, but when he glanced over his shoulder the old gorilla was simply watching him, his shoulders stooped and his eyes full of regret.

Bramble's heart raced with confusion and fear. As he shoved his way through the cluster of gorillas, he realized who was missing. Then, at his feet, he saw a mass of black fur.

"Cassava?"

It came out as a throaty rasp. The gorillas around the body fell silent. Bramble was shaking, yet his limbs felt completely numb. He stared across his brother's unmoving form. His father stood opposite, staring down at it. There was no expression on his face, none at all, but his burly chest rose and fell rapidly. Burbark slowly raised his eyes to Bramble's.

"Father, what happened?"

For a long, horrible moment, Burbark said nothing. Bramble noticed Moonflower in the crowd, crouched next to Bindweed Blackback. His half sister's eyes were moist, and she had her hand over her mouth as if she couldn't bear to speak.

He felt someone take his arm gently. It was Groundnut. "Your brother is dead," he murmured in his ear. "I'm sorry, Bramble."

The Blackback's gaze was level and sorrowful, and no other gorilla spoke, not even Burbark.

"No!" Bramble gave a screeching howl of anger. *How dare he say such a thing!* "No, he isn't!"

He yanked his arm out of Groundnut's grip. Bounding forward, he crouched to take hold of Cassava's wrist; his fur and skin felt oddly cold, as if his brother had sat exposed in the mountain wind too long. That was bad for him, thought Bramble crossly; bad for any gorilla. Instead of setting up this silly prank, Cassava should have been in his nest last night, curled up safely with the rest of them.

Scowling, Bramble shook his brother's arm. It felt limp and heavy, so he shook it a little harder. "Cassava, get up! Stop it! Stop fooling around, *please*. Please . . ."

His voice faded, caught on the dryness in his throat. Cassava's flesh was much too cold; it was the kind of rigid, lifeless chill that had nothing to do with mountain breezes. There was no movement in his burly chest, no whisper of suppressed breath from his lips. There was blood there, too, on Cassava's flank and throat; how hadn't he noticed it before? Bramble didn't want to look at it, so he jerked his head away.

He had never given his heart much thought; now, from the searing pain, he knew it was breaking. He heard a wail of awful grief, and realized it was coming from his own throat.

"How? How? *How?*"

"No one knows," rumbled Groundnut, shambling to his side. He seemed almost relieved that the tension had broken, that Bramble had finally seen the truth.

"We thought it was hyenas, Bramble," growled Lantana. "They were around him when we found your brother, and they fled pretty quickly. But no hyena did this."

"For certain," murmured Bindweed. "Everyone agrees the hyenas weren't responsible."

Moonflower suddenly seemed able to move again, and she rushed to Bramble's side. She put her arms around his shoulders and rubbed his cheek with her lips. "Oh, Bramble. I'm so sorry."

"But this doesn't make sense," cried Bramble. "Cassava doesn't get into fights! Who's done this? *Who?*" Pleadingly, he stared at his father.

Burbark gave a weary shrug. His eyes were just as dull as they had been for days. "Cassava was foolish to wander off in the night," he muttered. "It's clear to me what happened. He went against my orders; he was determined to venture onto the plains and find the Great Parent. He was trying to do the Great Spirit's job, and his arrogance was punished by that same Spirit. Let that be a lesson to all of us."

Lantana stifled a gasp of shock; even Groundnut cocked his head in puzzlement. The other gorillas exchanged startled looks. Some gave Burbark surreptitious glances of pity.

"Father, no!" Bramble stared at Burbark, aghast. He clenched his fists, shaking off Moonflower's embrace. "You can't say that. The Great Spirit would not punish Cassava that way."

"Bramble's right, you know," Groundnut told Burbark, hesitantly and very gently. He chewed on his lip. "The Great Spirit wouldn't punish a gorilla; it knows we are the most peace-loving of Bravelands' creatures."

"And the Spirit itself gave us the warning," murmured Dayflower Mistback. Her eyes glistened with tears. "Burbark, you mustn't blame the Spirit. After all, if Cassava only tried to do its bidding—"

"He didn't!" blurted Bramble, interrupting. His eyes burned. "Cassava wasn't disobeying you, Father. He wouldn't. He wouldn't have left without saying goodbye, either!"

Burbark's expression did not change. He surveyed the others, then turned his cold stare on Bramble. "What other explanation is there? Your brother was impetuous and disobedient, and it was the death of him. Whether Dayflower accepts it or not—such is the will of the Great Spirit."

It was as if Bramble's innards had tied themselves in knots. His chest ached, and he could barely breathe. But before he could form a retort that was more than a scream of rage, Dayflower Mistback shambled closer. Gently she touched the motionless corpse of Cassava.

"I do not agree with your interpretation, Burbark," she said quietly. "I bow to your leadership, of course. But I can say with certainty that the prophecy from the Spirit Mouth is already coming true." She raised her head and gazed levelly at her leader. "Cassava's was an unnatural death. An *evil* death."

"It's a disaster for us, for the whole troop," said Lantana bleakly. "What are we going to do? Cassava was the Brightback. Burbark, say something to comfort us. Your own heir is dead!"

Not even that provoked a reaction from the Silverback. He gazed down frowning at his son, as if he was a curious plant.

Moonflower was scratching at the ground with her fingers. "There's a blood trail," she said, glancing around sadly at the others. "Cassava may have died here, but it's not where he was wounded."

"Then let's follow it," said Bindweed with a heavy sigh.

Bramble felt detached from his own body. He did not much want to see the place where Cassava had been attacked; it seemed so unimportant against the stark fact of his brother's death. But Burbark remained rooted to the spot, expressionless eyes still locked on Cassava's body, and Bramble found he didn't want to linger alone with his father. He traipsed after Moonflower and the others.

They did not have far to go. After only a few trees, Moon-flower and Bindweed stopped and crouched down.

Groundnut shambled forward. "Looks like we've found the culprit," he grunted.

Despite his misgivings, Bramble pushed forward through the other gorillas. He breathed hard as he stared down. A fully grown female leopard lay there, sprawled awkwardly, her neck twisted, her open eyes glazed, and her muzzle frozen in a death snarl.

"She's big," muttered Groundnut. "They must have fought to the death. Ah, Bramble, be comforted." He patted Bramble's shoulder. "It was no punishment from the Great Spirit, and no evil creature broke the Code. Now we know what happened: your brother died bravely, fighting for the troop."

Bramble's throat tightened with grief and anger. "So why would he leave the troop? What was he doing, wandering off at night into the path of a leopard?" He thumped his fists hard against the ground. "If he wanted to protect the troop, he should have stayed with us!"

It was as if his furious words had sparked something in the whole troop. The Blackbacks began to whoop and holler with rage, slamming their fists into the ground, jumping up and down until the ground shook beneath them. Bindweed darted forward and punched the leopard's head hard. At that signal, all the Blackbacks fell on her, hitting and tearing and kicking the limp corpse.

Bramble stayed back. He felt no rage toward the leopard, only a cold numbness that spread remorselessly through his

body. What was the point, anyway? The leopard was already
dead, and Cassava was too. The troop's rage could not change
that. All the bared fangs and flashing eyes and thudding fists
in the world would not bring back his brother.

His heart weighted like a stone with grief, Bramble turned
and shambled back to where Cassava's body lay.

Burbark had withdrawn and was sitting with his back to
both his sons, rubbing at his wrist. Bramble touched Cassava's
shoulder.

A slight breeze stirred the black fur. Taking a deep, painful
breath, Bramble moved around to look at his brother's face.
Cassava's eyes were slitted open, but as dull as the leopard's.

There was a tick buried in Cassava's armpit; at least that
wouldn't bother him again. Bramble reached down and
twisted it, tugging it out.

With a huge effort, Bramble worked his hands beneath
his brother's shoulder and tried to heave him over. It took his
three fumbling attempts, but Burbark made no move to help;
he didn't even turn. At last, with a final clenching of his jaws
and a violent thrust, Bramble tumbled his brother over, to lie
sprawled on his back. He stood for a moment, panting, his
chest heaving.

Cassava's chest did not stir; of course it didn't. Why had he
dared to believe it would?

Sighing, gritting his teeth, Bramble began to pick leaves and
bits of twig from his brother's fur. He tidied and smoothed,
removing more ticks, untangling the matted fur around his
brother's wounds. He stroked Cassava's fur back from his face,

caressing his creased brow and gently closing his eyes.

"If Father won't perform the Last Grooming, I will," he whispered, touching Cassava's scarred cheek with his knuckle. He bowed his head.

"My brother. I will miss you, more than I can say. But I'll make sure of this: you will look your best when your spirit reaches the stars."

CHAPTER EIGHT

When dawn seeped into the den between the old tree's roots, Chase wasn't sure she'd slept at all. That was not unusual, but on any other night she would have been hunting till sunrise, eager for the kill, reveling in the stillness of the forest's dark hours. Lying beside the sleeping Seek, she had been able to think of nothing but Prowl.

Where was her mother? Why hadn't she returned with the daylight? Wasn't Prowl eager to make sure that Seek was safe, to lick Chase's ears and tell her how well she had protected the cub?

There were bushpigs out there, quick-tempered and surly. In her mind's eye, Chase saw one of them charge, its wild tusk-thrust goring her mother's ribs and tossing her aside. Chase shook her head to dispel the image, growling, but more terrible visions leaped into her mind, unbidden and unwelcome:

Prowl as she paced along one of the many ridges of these jagged foothills, missing her usually sure footing and slipping to her death. A rotten branch breaking beneath her weight, sending Prowl plummeting into a ravine.

Chase sat up, curling her tail around her. She licked her jaws, washed her whiskers. Seek mewled happily in his sleep. Chase trod an impatient circle around him, then lay down again, staring at the patch of light where dawn showed at the den entrance. Twitching her ears, she craned them for any sound of paws in the leaf litter, for the crack of a twig that would signal her mother's return. *But she's always so silent*, Chase reassured herself. *I won't know Prowl is back until she slinks into the den with prey.*

Perhaps her mother had simply gotten lost? It was possible. Not *likely*. But even a leopard as stealthy and confident as Prowl might be led astray if she wandered too far. She might have run into that strange leopard Shadow had mentioned. She might have driven him off so far, so fiercely, that now she was having trouble retracing her steps.

Prowl getting lost would be unexpected. A little shocking, even. But Chase would far rather that than any of the other visions that troubled her.

The morning seemed *unnaturally* quiet; Chase could barely hear any birdsong. She grunted a cough, partly to clear her throat, partly just to break the silence. Seek stirred, stretching out a foreleg and licking his jaws, before falling back into a doze.

Then, quite suddenly, there was a sound. Not far off,

something was hollering and screeching. No, many some-things. A flock of birds, perhaps, disturbed by a predator?

Mother! Perhaps that was Prowl out there now, too tired to worry about scaring a bunch of starlings from their roosts. *Maybe I should venture out to meet her?*

But she didn't want to move out of the den. That noise didn't sound like birds. It sounded as if it came from bigger, more dangerous creatures, screaming with fury. It sounded, she thought with a quiver in her belly, like enraged gorillas.

Her hackles sprang erect and she bared her fangs at the den entrance. Something warm nudged her forepaw, and she realized the racket had woken Seek. He stood at her side, tail quivering, as his ears swiveled and flicked to the sounds. His eyes were huge.

"Chase, what's that sound?"

"I don't know, little one," she growled. "I think it's gorillas fighting." They couldn't be far away, she thought, flattening her ears and narrowing her eyes. And she'd never heard goril-las fighting—not like this.

Seek padded closer and put one small paw on hers. There was real terror in his eyes now. "Chase, where is my Mother-Sister?"

Bending closer, she licked his head. "Nearly home. Don't worry."

It was a silly thing to say to him, she told herself—even as a thrum of fear tightened her own gut. Leopards would always worry. The dangers were too many. But she couldn't bear to watch Seek's anguished little face any longer without doing something. She gave him a last, warning growl—"Stay here"—and scrambled up out of the den.

In the open, warm air of the forest, the furious screeching seemed to rebound from the tree trunks, louder than ever. It wasn't hard to follow the screams; Chase's sensitive ears ached. All the same, she ran swiftly toward the commotion.

The racket became overwhelming, and she slowed to a walk, pacing cautiously through the dappled shadows. When she saw a massive, black-furred back, she stopped and flared her nostrils.

Chase couldn't see beyond the gorilla, but he was too intent on what was in front of him to notice her. She stayed absolutely still, one paw raised; after only a moment he gave a roar and bounded forward to hammer with his fists at the ground. There must have been ten or more of the troop in the glade, old and young, male and female; they took turns loping to something in the center of their group, stomping and kicking and punching it. Chase furrowed her muzzle in perplexity. There was another smell, one she recognized. She stepped forward, heart suddenly a hot weight under her rib cage.

And now Chase could see what they were hitting: a tattered, misshapen, bloodied body that would be unrecognizable but for the ragged, spotted pelt.

"Mother!"

Rage swept through her; Chase threw all her natural caution to the winds and sprang forward into the midst of the gorillas, snapping and snarling.

"GET AWAY FROM HER!"

Taken utterly by surprise, the huge apes staggered back a few steps, leaving Prowl's corpse clear for a moment. Chase took her chance. She straddled her mother's body, hunching her shoulders, and turned, slowly, eyeing each gorilla.

One of the biggest gorillas lumbered toward her, his lips curling back in a vicious sneer. "Stand aside, you stupid cat."

"It's none of your business," growled another.

"She's—*she was my mother*!" The growl burned deep in her throat.

The bigger gorilla shrugged. "And now her corpse is ours, to treat as we wish." He gave a deep growl of anger. "To treat as she *deserves*!"

Chase's tail lashed. "Do not touch her again!" She kept twisting, her fangs bared, so that none of the gorillas would have a chance to dart forward and attack her.

There was no question Prowl was dead. The gorillas had all but destroyed her corpse. But Chase would not leave her. Before she could mourn Prowl, she must protect her body.

The gorillas circled her slowly, shambling on their knuckles. Two of them rose up on their hind legs, intimidating; others bared their fangs; and yet others thudded their huge fists against the ground, hard enough to make it tremble. It was all Chase could do to keep her eyes on more than two at a time, and she had to keep twisting constantly. She knew if she had to that she would claw and bite to the end. The great apes were wary, but they didn't look afraid. That was hardly surprising. They were so much bigger than she was—far larger even than Prowl, who had been a good-sized leopard, strong and wily. . . .

No. She couldn't think about how much she was going to miss her mother—not yet. Chase spun again as a gorilla shifted behind her, but it had already backed off.

Chase panted, her jaws parted. The rush of energy was wearing off, and she was beginning to be viscerally aware of everything about the gorillas: their bunched muscles, the tension in their limbs, the blazing anger in their black eyes. She had startled them, but they were too furious to retreat back into the forest.

"Why have you done this?" she yowled. "She never harmed you!"

But they were silent, their stares sullen. And Chase became aware of something else: the circle of gorillas was closing. They were shuffling toward her, barely perceptibly, but one knuckled fist was planted firmly after another, and their eyes glittered with menace. They were almost on her. If they all charged at once, Chase knew she was as dead as Prowl. Her heart thundered in her rib cage. *If they kill me just for defending my mother's body . . . they shatter the Code!*

Chase hunched her shoulders and lashed a paw forward, extending her claws to score deep gashes in the ground. Baring her teeth, she snarled her challenge at the nearest gorillas.

For a moment, she thought her bravado had worked. The gorillas exchanged hesitant glances before drawing back a little. One of them grunted in anger.

But the snarl that answered him did not come from another gorilla. Chase twisted in surprise.

Behind her, the gorillas had fallen away a little, breaking

their threatening circle. Through the gap stalked the biggest leopard Chase had ever seen. His muscles rippled under his sleek pelt, his ears were laid tight back against his skull, and his jaws were wide to display glistening, long fangs. He swung his head as he paced on, eyeing each gorilla directly as if daring them to attack him.

And those eyes of his were the most extraordinary thing about him. Chase had never seen anything like them. They were ice-blue, like shadows in the snow on the high slopes of the mountain. When he turned them on her, Chase's heartbeat seemed to falter.

"Flee while you have the chance," the strange leopard's snarl rang through the clearing.

She almost did. Taking a panicked step back, she turned. But that movement made her glance down once more at her mother's torn body. Her lips curling back from her fangs, Chase felt her rage surge again.

"No," she roared. And as the gorillas hesitated, held back by the eerie blue gaze of the newcomer, Chase sprang at the nearest one, swiping her unsheathed claws at his chest.

Startled, the huge gorilla flinched back and staggered. But he recovered his composure almost instantly. He beat his chest and thundered forward, baring his own yellow teeth.

All the gorillas roared, throwing their heads back; some thumped their fists against the ground. Chase felt the earth tremble beneath her paw pads, but she did not regret her aggressive strike. *They deserved it!* she told herself. *I'll still die with honor!*

A huge female gorilla charged forward, swinging a powerful fist that Chase only just managed to duck. Behind her, another attacked, and she had to roll onto her back, then leap to her paws.

"Leave my mother alone!" she snarled at them.

"Your mother was a Codebreaking killer," spat the big female.

Crouching, Chase sprang for her, claws reaching for the gorilla's black eyes. "Never! She never would, *liar!*"

The huge apes were surprisingly quick movers; the female dodged, and Chase felt the blow of a fist against her flank that knocked the breath from her. She tumbled head over paws and leaped up again, panting. She could still do them some damage! There were so many of them. . . .

No matter. I'll leave a few lifelong scars!

"I said *flee!*" roared an exasperated voice behind her.

Chase felt something grab tight hold of her neck, and for an instant she was sure a gorilla was about to snap her spine. *It's the end.* She kicked and squirmed, but something dragged her backward, away from the enraged gorillas. As Chase twisted, baring her teeth, she saw that her captor was no gorilla; that massive leopard had her scruff between his jaws and was dragging her away.

"Your mother is dead," he mumbled through her fur, and released her. "You are alive, so run!"

Something in his voice penetrated the mist of rage in Chase's head. As the gorillas bounded toward them both, muzzles peeled back to show their fangs as they roared, Chase came suddenly to her senses. *I've done all I could for Prowl. I tried!*

She spun and bounded after the big male leopard. Behind her, she heard the crack of branches and the gruff bellows of the angry gorilla troop, but they were dwindling now that she was racing through the forest; she and this new leopard were far faster than those slow-bodied, slow-witted apes. Chase felt her muzzle curling in anger even as she ran.

"Run, you cowards! Run, murderous cats!" It was the last taunt she heard, and for a moment it almost made her twist and fly back at them. But the strange leopard beckoned her on with a warning growl, and the voices of the jeering gorillas were soon lost in the forest behind them.

Chase could no longer take out her grief and rage on the gorillas, but resentment swelled inside her at the leopard who had interfered. As his racing steps slowed, she skidded to a halt on a fallen log and snarled at him.

"What did you think you're doing? I needed to avenge my mother!"

He halted and trotted back toward her, looking not in the least remorseful. "By getting yourself killed? I'm sure your mother would have loved *that*."

She glared at him. Those blue eyes were so disconcerting. "I could have taken those apes!" she snapped.

"No, you couldn't." He blinked slowly and sat down to wash a paw. "I just saved you from certain death. *That's* what I thought I was doing, to answer your question."

"I didn't ask for your help!"

"Yet I gave it anyway." He placed his paw back on the ground and tilted his head to stare at her. "You saw what they did to your mother. However brave you were, they'd have done the same to you."

What they did to my mother . . . Chase felt a surge of grief overwhelm her anger. The big leopard was right; those gorillas would have torn her limb from limb.

I'm sorry, Mother. I'm so sorry. I'll have to honor you by living on. By looking after Seek in your place . . . Chase had a sudden vision of the vulnerable cub, back in the den, still unaware of what had happened to his Mother-Sister. Poor little Seek . . . he'd been bereaved twice in such a short time. Chase's heart ached for him. *Yes. I have to take care of him; he'll need me more than ever now.*

And that meant the arrogant blue-eyed leopard was right. Chase averted her eyes and glared at the ground. "I suppose I should thank you, uh . . ."

"Range," he told her, twitching his whiskers. "Range Born of Sprint. And you are?"

"Chase," she said bleakly, "Born of . . . of P—Prowl."

"And that was Prowl back there." He nodded sympathetically. "So where is your territory, Chase Born of Prowl? How far did you come, just to find gorillas to fight?"

The gleam of his gaze was disarming, and Chase opened her mouth to answer him truthfully. Then she stiffened, remembering Shadow's warning about a strange leopard in the area. She heard her mother's voice clearly in her head.

Trust only yourself, Chase.

"Thank you for your help," she growled, "but we keep our . . . I mean, I keep my territory to myself."

"Wise, but bear in mind I did just save your life," Range murmured. "It's not as if—"

He broke off abruptly, his head snapping round, his ears quivering. Distantly, but drawing closer, there were sounds of crashing branches and angry grunts.

"The gorillas." His blue eyes widened. "They're coming this way."

As Range poised there, judging the direction, every muscle tense with the weight of his decision, Chase took her chance. Twisting, she bolted away from him, plunging into the undergrowth and running fast as she could for the deep forest.

He had taken her by surprise before, but she had been taught by Prowl. She knew this side of the mountain as well as she knew her own den, and she knew how to travel silently, how to leave no tracks. Yes, he would know all the same tricks she did; he was a leopard after all. But with her head start and a fast run, that stranger cat should not be able to follow her home.

Sure enough, the sounds of the gorillas faded quickly. Pausing, Chase twisted her head, nostrils flaring and whiskers trembling. No. There was neither noise nor scent behind her of a leopard in pursuit. Maybe the gorilla troop had gone after Range instead, thought Chase a little guiltily.

But no doubt he'd be able to outrun them again. What was important to Chase now was getting home to Seek.

Just to make sure Range could not pursue her, Chase

followed one of Prowl's more cunning diversions, taking a broad sweep around the mountain's flank and through a narrow gully before turning toward home once again. By the time she came in sight of the old twisted tree, she was weary and footsore. Her flank ached where the massive gorilla had struck her, but she did not think any bones were broken. And for the first time since she had evaded Range, the grief returned in a wave to buffet her.

Her throat went dry as she saw Seek wriggle out of the den. His eyes lit up as he trotted to meet her. Her own paws dragged, heavy as stones. *How do I tell him?*

"You've been gone for so long!" Seek reared up on his hind paws, batting at her cheek. "What happened? Where's Prowl? I'm hungry!"

"Seek." Her voice was hoarse. "Seek, I—"

He dropped back onto all four paws. Laying his ears back, he stared at her. "What? What is it, Chase?"

There was so much fear in his eyes. *He's heard this kind of news before*, Chase thought, her gut wrenching. *He knows what's coming. He knows from my face what I'm about to tell him.*

But that didn't make it any easier.

"Oh, little one," she sighed, crouching down to press her face close to his. "It's us now. Just the two of us. Alone."

CHAPTER NINE

Prance could not help herself. She might not be part of the Us any-more, but every bone and nerve in her body *wanted* it. It was a longing she couldn't resist, drawing her remorselessly in the wake of the moving herd. She followed them at a distance as the white sun rose higher and higher in the sky, as the heat made their forms shimmer, as they grew ever more unclear on the horizon. Forcing her weary legs to move, she trudged after them, head hanging low. Every so often, she would close her eyes for the briefest of moments, willing her shadow to return. Hoping for a miracle.

It never came.

The day's heat was intense now, but she could barely eat; no ripped mouthful of sweet grass could fill the gaping emptiness inside her. Her throat grew dry and hot. She must try to graze, just for the moisture.

Lowering her head, she tore listlessly at a patch of crushed grass. Even as she chewed, she recognized some of the hoof-prints that had trodden it down, and her heart ached.

She raised her head. She blinked. In the blaze of the sun and the wobbling horizon, she had lost the herd. She was alone.

Her gut lurched. Breaking into a gallop, she bolted across the grassland, her breath rasping. There was a darker line, a visible mass in the dazzle of the glare . . . and there they were. Relief rushed over her as she made out the hazy shapes of her erstwhile friends.

I must not fall so far back again! Prance trotted closer, as fast as she could without breaking into a run. The forms became clearer; she could make out individual gazelles once more.

A few of the herd outriders raised their heads and turned to stare at her. Prance knew what would be happening now, though she could not feel it: a buzzing ripple of recognition, a knowledge that came without having to watch.

More gazelles glanced up from their grazing. The closest outriders began to walk toward her. Their heads were lowered in aggression, and Prance stopped suddenly, immobilized by sharp dread. She could neither flee nor move forward; *How can I run from the Us?*

But I can't feel it! I've lost it! I—

"Get out of here!"

She knew she should have expected it, but the throaty bray from old Hop was shocking.

"I . . . I can't."

Then they broke into a gallop, charging at her. As panic and distress flooded through her body, Prance twisted and fled in despair.

"Stop following us!"

"Leave us be, Herdless One!"

"Go find your death! It searches for you!"

When Prance slowed and looked back, the three gazelles were already trotting back toward the herd, their heads tilted high and satisfied. Before long, their forms became indistinct, then blended back into the distant shimmer of the Us.

Prance halted altogether.

It's no use. I have to stop trying. I'm an exile forever.

Perhaps they were right. Perhaps she should seek out her death. . . .

No. Lifting her head abruptly, Prance glared at the horizon, where the herd was already moving on. *No.* She took a step, then another, and began to walk. *I'll go somewhere. Anywhere. On my own!* A mistake had been made, by her herd and by the Great Spirit itself. *I'll show them!*

Except . . . she wouldn't. A constant nagging dread pulsed in her body as she trudged aimlessly across the plain. Hop and the others were quite right; her death had missed her, but even now it was hunting her down, and it *would* find her. She was defenseless and utterly vulnerable without the shelter of the Us.

Every whisper in the grass, every stir of leaves made Prance's heart jolt. Her head twitched anxiously from left to right, and she spun around at every touch of the breeze on her rump. She was sure she could feel the burning eyes of predators on her hide, more and more of them with each step she took. It was as if all the flesh-eaters in Bravelands had homed in on her at the Great Spirit's behest; they were coming closer all the time, coming to *make it right*.

It could only be a matter of time.

Still, Prance couldn't help this dragging knowledge: something *wasn't* right about what had happened to her. So many gazelles had gone before her; her own mother had lost her shadow and had fallen to a hyena clan within a morning. And all those doomed antelopes had grown calm in their final hours. Her mother's eyes had gazed on her in that dawn light, still loving, but distant and strangely peaceful. Prance remembered the grief, but also the acceptance. Her mother had died well, and rightly. They all had.

So why not me? Why hadn't the Great Spirit touched her with that calm sense of fate at the end? Why had it abandoned her . . . and why had it left her alive to question and suffer?

Her legs ached, and her throat burned, but Prance didn't dare dip her head again to snatch a mouthful of grass; each time she thought of grazing, she imagined sharp claws digging into her flank and rump. She could only plod on, placing one hoof in front of the other.

The ground became a little softer beneath her hooves. Prance raised her head. Only a leap away, a trickle of water cut a tiny gully through the sandy soil.

She turned to follow it, the ground growing damper and more yielding with every step. It felt so cool and soothing against her tender hooves. The rich, earthy smell of water filled her nostrils, and she halted, gratefully, before the silver gleam of a watering hole.

No Code-following flesh-eater could attack her here. The customary truce would always hold. Swamped with relief, Prance trotted toward the bank.

Something stirred a little way ahead of her, something reptilian and huge but lithe. With a cascading gush of water, a crocodile lifted its long snout and grinned at her, all its long teeth showing. Others, too, woke from their basking doze and swiveled their heads in her direction.

Prance groaned inwardly with despair. Crocodiles did not respect the sacred truce, any more than they followed the Code. These ones seemed sluggish and well-fed, but they would move quickly if such an easy meal came closer. She would not get near the bank before meeting her delayed fate.

Perhaps this was the end the Great Spirit planned for her: simply to wander, lost, until she dropped from thirst and exhaustion. Perhaps she had done something so wrong—and had forgotten it so easily—that her body would not even be allowed to nourish the predators of Bravelands. She would shrivel to a skeletal husk, food only for the scavengers.

What did I do that was so wrong, Great Spirit?

"If you don't know, there's no point asking it," rumbled a deep voice some way behind her.

Prance's weary head jerked up. She must have rasped her despairing words out loud, she realized. A line of elephants was approaching—five females and a big bull. They had a couple of older calves at foot, but no babies; it must be mating season for them. And the big bull's broad, splayed ears had caught her unthinking cry of misery.

The elephants kept moving steadily toward the watering hole; twigs snapped and foliage crackled as they reached out their trunks to tear lazily at branches. A yearling calf flapped its ears at Prance.

"She shouldn't question the Great Spirit anyway, should she, Aunt?"

"No indeed," confirmed the huge old female at her side, giving Prance a disapproving look as she walked past.

Their scolding didn't sting; Prance was too exhausted to care. Besides, she had noticed something else, with a surge of hope—some of the crocodiles had spotted the elephants and were already slithering grumpily into the lake. The big bull elephant shook his tusks and flapped his ears at the remaining crocs. He made a few short and aggressive charges, and within moments, all the crocodiles were gone.

Prance did not have the energy to be afraid of the elephants; anyway, despite their haughty rebukes, she knew they wouldn't bother her. Sidling in among them for protection, she followed their lumbering legs to the bank of the watering hole. A tingle of happiness ran through her own limbs; for a fleeting instant, she felt part of a moving herd again.

But it was not the Us. She was not truly a part of this elephant group.

Prance was so relieved to plunge her snout into the murky water, she didn't even notice that the massive, intimidating bull was right beside her. By the time she raised her dripping muzzle, she was too blissfully relieved to be scared.

He blew a spray of water droplets from his trunk and turned his head to gaze curiously down at her. "You're alone?"

"I am herdless." Prance spoke the words quietly, for the first time, and at last she accepted it was true. It came with a wave of shame. *Herdless.*

The bull watched her, his eyes sympathetic. "Well, be careful around water."

"Gazelles are careful everywhere," she said ruefully.

He chuckled. "True. But the crocodiles have grown unusually aggressive lately. They seem a little bored with their usual prey, and they're attacking big flesh-eaters—lions, leopards." He cast a dismissive glance at the lake. "They won't challenge an elephant, though."

"Then I'm glad you came along," said Prance softly.

He lifted his trunk to sniff at her. "Why *are* you herdless? Are you lost?"

She shook her head. Shame silenced her again for a moment, but she cleared her throat. "I . . . it's a long story."

"Elephants have nothing if not time," he reminded her gently. "Tell me."

And so she did. Once she began to speak of her exile and

humiliation, Prance found she couldn't stop. The shocking loss of her shadow; the mortal dread of that morning; the horror of the chase and the incredible fact of her escape: it all came tumbling out in a heartfelt rush. Her voice truly faltered only when she came to her herd's rejection.

"I tried to explain," she whispered. "I knew there must have been a mistake. But they . . . they wouldn't listen. They fear me now. They *hate* me."

"I don't think so," murmured the bull. "Afraid maybe, and that can look like hate. But perhaps you can find another herd and run with them?"

"I don't think so," she muttered. "Not while I'm shadowless. No gazelle herd would take in such a cursed creature."

The big elephant was silent for a long moment, looking thoughtful. He stared at the ground beneath her hooves, still unmarked by a shadow. Then he blew out another breath through his trunk and nodded.

"Perhaps," he murmured, "it needn't be a gazelle herd."

Prance gave a sad chuckle. "You think wildebeests would have me? Or a warthog family? Or *elephants*?"

"You'd be surprised what can happen," the bull told her gently. He was gazing very directly into her eyes now. "My own sister once led a vast herd of animals, and few of them were her own kind. If an elephant can do it, why not a gazelle? We are all capable of more, so much more, than we think, young . . . I'm sorry, I don't know your name?"

"I'm Prance Runni—I mean, Prance Herdless." It didn't

hurt as much, now that she said it to this great elephant. Something in his eyes and his words wakened a faint hope inside her.

"I am Boulder," he said, dipping his head slightly. "And take my word for it, Prance Herdless. Bravelands is mother and father to all of us, in many ways." His eyes twinkled. "And it can bring us together with some *very* unexpected friends."

CHAPTER TEN

Even the scents of the forest seemed dulled now. To Bramble, the shadows no longer held dancing beams of sunlight or the flash of bright flowers. He didn't even glance up when blue starlings erupted with a clamor from the treetops. Everything around him seemed infinitely dark, and dank, and miserable.

Moonflower gently groomed Bramble's back as he crouched in a corner of a glade, but he wasn't even enjoying that soothing ritual. He sat still and tense, watching the rest of the troop. They were still downcast, but life for them went on; they chatted, ate, and even laughed sometimes. Bramble felt as though he had forgotten how to laugh, and his pranks and tricks seemed like something in his distant past, or games played by some other young gorilla.

"Oh, Bramble," sighed Moonflower softly behind him. "I know we had happy times with our brother, and we'll never forget them. But he's gone. He wouldn't want you to mourn him forever."

"I can hardly recall the happy times," mumbled Bramble, his head drooping. "I've tried. But every time I remember a joke Cassava made, or the way he used to rub my head with his knuckles . . . I can't see him clearly. All I can see is his body. All I can imagine is the fear he must have felt when the leopard attacked." He shut his eyes tight. "I miss him, Moon-flower."

"Of course you do. We all do. You and I especially. But we *must* remember him as he was!" Moonflower hesitated, as if she was thinking. "That time he was giving a terribly solemn speech, and he fell through a rotten branch! That was hilarious, and we teased him for days. Oh, and when Father called him to council—do you remember, Bramble?—he was late and in a terrible hurry, and he sat on a porcupine. How he squealed!"

"I remember," said Bramble softly. "I do, Moonflower. But I can't stop thinking about his . . . his death. How could it have happened? It doesn't make sense!"

"Death doesn't always make sense." He felt her shrug.

"No, but Cassava wasn't the type to take on a leopard, especially a big one like that. Not alone, and not unless it was a last resort." He shook his head. "My brother didn't pick fights."

"No," said Moonflower, "but maybe the leopard did? Perhaps it was mad, or starving, and it attacked him first. Leopards are so fierce—so defensive, too. It might have seen Cassava as a threat."

Groundnut shambled out of the shadows on the opposite side of the glade and sat down closer to the two siblings. "I still say that no single leopard could have killed Cassava," he growled, picking the skin from a banana. "There was more than that one cat involved, I'd stake my own life on it. It must have formed a pack with others."

Apple Goldback raised her head and turned to him. "Leopards don't hunt in packs," she said firmly. "Not ever."

"That's a very sweeping statement," complained Groundnut. "How are we sure of this, huh? Do you know everything there is to know about leopards, Apple?"

"Do *you*?" she retorted. "I've been around leopards all my life, and I've never heard of them teaming up."

"Well, maybe you haven't seen *everything*," began Groundnut indignantly, as Apple rolled her eyes. "I doubt you've got proof of that, Apple, and—"

A deep, commanding grunt reverberated through the forest, interrupting the squabble. "Gather and listen, friends." Burbark lurched out of the trees and rested on his knuckles as his black eyes surveyed his troop. "Gather, and speak if you will."

Bramble glanced over his shoulder at Moonflower as he scrambled to his feet. However sad he was, his father's formal summons was not one to ignore. The council members were rising, padding toward Burbark.

"All of you," added Burbark, meeting the eyes of the gorillas who still looked questioning. "The whole troop. Join me in the Flame Glade." He turned and stalked away.

Moonflower shambled at Bramble's side toward the Flame Glade. "I've been wondering when Father would summon the whole troop to council," she remarked. "It's been days since Cassava's—"

"Yes," interrupted Bramble. He did not want to hear that awful word spoken again.

As they made their way with the other gorillas to the largest glade in the territory, Moonflower seemed to understand Bramble's wishes; she didn't speak any more. They sat down together beneath the spreading branches of the huge flamboyant tree that dominated the clearing, and Moonflower touched Bramble's arm in a gesture of gentle reassurance. Close by, their father Burbark crouched at the very foot of the tree, watching with an unreadable expression as his troop assembled.

They had been quietly settled for long moments before he spoke.

"Every troop must have a strong leader," he grunted. "This is the wisdom of all creatures through all ages. But the gorillas are wiser than others; we have always been more foresighted. Every troop has a powerful Brightback, second to the Silverback, who is ready to take command the moment it is necessary." Burbark paused, gazing at the gorillas. "Our troop has lost our Brightback. Therefore, another must be chosen."

Bramble could not help himself. Under his breath he muttered, "Already?"

Moonflower gave him a stern nudge, and Dayflower

glanced in his direction with some sympathy; the old Mistback must have heard him. She cleared her throat.

"I agree with Burbark," she declared apologetically, watching Bramble. "A strong successor must always be in place, because no troop can afford the leaderless chaos that would otherwise follow."

Groundnut edged a little forward, raising his chin. Other Blackbacks shifted uncomfortably where they sat, eyeing one another appraisingly. A few of the Goldbacks shot hopeful glances at their favored males.

"It'll be Groundnut," whispered Bramble to Moonflower. "He has so many silver hairs already."

"I think you're right," murmured his half sister.

"I have taken time to make my decision," growled Burbark. His eyes turned to his surviving son. "And I command Bramble Brightback to step forward."

There were gasps from the assembled troop.

For a moment that felt as if the whole forest had stopped moving, Bramble did not understand. He wanted to ask *Who? Who's that?* But he was dumbstruck.

Groundnut's eyes had opened wide, and some of the Goldbacks began to whisper frantically.

"Bramble? *Him?*"

"Burbark isn't serious."

"He *looks* serious?"

"Yes, but *Bramble?*"

Bramble had to clear his throat before he could speak, and

the sound of it grated. He coughed again. *"Me?"* he echoed the Goldbacks.

"You are my new heir," said Burbark, with what looked like a shrug.

"That isn't possible!" Groundnut rose and punched his fists into the ground.

"He's years from being a Silverback!" added Bindweed.

"There are many Blackbacks who are far more suitable," agreed Apple, with a disbelieving glance at Bramble. "Stars above, *Moonflower* would be a better choice!"

"Don't listen to them," hissed Moonflower angrily in Bramble's ear. "Go to our father."

The troop had fallen silent again, though their expressions ranged from confusion to annoyance. Bramble swallowed hard. It was difficult enough to approach his father in this formal setting, but the gaze of the other gorillas made it far worse. Burbark seemed huger than ever, sitting there alone beneath the bright red canopy of the flamboyant tree; his face was stern and noble.

I'm not at all like my father, he thought miserably. Burbark was powerful, solemn, magnificent. *I'm just a joker.*

Burbark extended a hand toward him and gave a slight nod. "Come, my son."

Bramble's heart raced as he walked forward. At last he stood before his father, gazing up. His throat was dry. He was entirely in Burbark's massive shadow.

"You are young, Bramble," growled his father, "but I know you will rise to this responsibility. It was Cassava himself who persuaded me of this: he always spoke very highly of you and your potential."

Bramble's heart lurched. *Oh, Cassava, you did have faith in me.*

"May you lead this troop well and wisely," Burbark went on. "When the time comes."

Bramble opened his mouth, but no words would come. He was still terrified, yet he didn't think he had ever loved his father more.

"And now, there is important business I must deal with." Burbark rose, turned, and shambled away into the trees without a backward glance. The whole troop stared after him, slack-jawed and stunned.

Their obvious shock brought Bramble back to himself, and he blinked hard. He wished he hadn't come forward. He wished he had stayed at Moonflower's side, however much he shamed his father. He wished he had not agreed to this at all. Standing in Burbark's place, in full view of all these older, larger, wiser gorillas, he felt like a fool and a fraud.

But I didn't actually agree to it. I just didn't have a choice.

Groundnut took a few lurching paces forward, gazing at him quizzically. All Bramble could give him was a helpless shrug.

With an almost imperceptible shake of his head, Groundnut turned to the troop. "We must get to work," he announced. "All of you can help build a more suitable nest for Bramble tonight, one that's more fitting for his *new* status."

"I'm a baboon if I will," grunted Branch Blackback, and a few others nodded in surly agreement.

"And I'll feed you to the wretched baboons if you *don't*!" snapped Groundnut. "Show some respect for your Bright-back."

Bramble was torn between embarrassment and gratitude. As the muttering Blackbacks set to work, he shot the old gorilla a grateful nod. *I don't deserve his loyalty after all the pranks I've pulled, but oh my, I'm glad of it.*

It was the oddest feeling, watching the big Blackbacks go to work in his honor. He stared, having to clench and unclench his fists to stop himself joining in. He should really be help-ing build a nest for some other, more fitting heir. Instead of which . . .

Moonflower nudged him. "Don't get cocky about this."

Bramble was mortified that she might think he would. "Of course not!" he exclaimed.

The other gorillas were shambling back and forth between Bramble and the forest, gathering up dead leaves and branches. He felt a sudden sharp pinch in his ribs and spun around in shock.

It was one of the Blackbacks, Woodnettle, and he wore an insincere grin. "Saw a tick on your side," he said, holding up his fingers to display something completely invisible.

Bramble scowled, but he didn't dare argue back. This felt so wrong! Sure, he used to fantasize about leading the troop, and hunt awkwardly for silver hairs on his back, and joke with Moonflower and Cassava—but this was too soon, *far* too soon. What if something happened to Burbark tomorrow? This afternoon, even! Any one of these Blackbacks would be a far better leader than he would. If Burbark died, one of them would probably challenge him on the spot, and Bramble could never win such a fight. He might even be killed!

"You'll be fine." Moonflower, reading his thoughts as usual, squeezed his arm.

"I don't see how," he said. "I'm not the right choice, Moonflower."

She didn't reply, and his heart sank even further.

Even my half sister thinks this was a crazy decision. Bramble stood up a little straighter and clenched his jaws. "Moonflower, I'm going to talk to Father. He's got to change his mind about this. For the troop's sake!"

He set off into the trees, his determination swelling inside him. With every pace he took, he was more convinced that his father would listen. This wasn't a rejection of responsibility, Bramble told himself—he was being wise! Burbark would see that. It would even stand him in good stead to be Brightback later, when he'd grown and matured more. When he was *ready*.

Burbark, despite his *important business*, was not hard to find. He was sitting on a mossy rock behind a veil of creepers, one of his favorite spots for thinking. As Bramble approached, he heard his father muttering to himself. It seemed to be becoming a habit. *Well, if it helps him think.*

"Father?" He didn't bother with a formal greeting. *I'm the Brightback now*, he thought ruefully. *Almost my father's equal. Even if it's just for a day!*

Burbark snapped his head around to give his son a glare. "What?"

"I just . . . want to talk to you . . ."

"I'm sorry, Bramble." Burbark shook himself and seemed to make a conscious effort to smile. He rubbed at his wrist. "What did you want to tell me?"

Bramble had almost forgotten, in his sudden concern. He stared at the snakebite, anxiety churning inside him. It was still raw, with black flecks and patches of ugly yellow. "Father, I really think you should let the Goldbacks look at that. Remember what happened to Mother!"

"Nonsense!" Burbark waved a dismissive arm; it was the wounded one, and Bramble caught the waft of an unpleasant smell from the bite. "Your mother's case was entirely different. Now, what did you want to say?"

Bramble licked his lips and picked nervously at his armpit. "It's about this Brightback business, Father. I don't think I—"

"Thanked me? You don't have to, son! Listen, I have a mission for you already." Burbark smiled. "It will be good experience, and a chance to ground you more firmly in the troop's minds as their Brightback."

"I—but, Father . . ."

"Don't worry, Bramble. It's a straightforward enough task." Burbark relaxed back against a tree trunk, rubbing at his wrist again. "A simple survey of the mountain. Find out more about the other troops here; bring me news of their numbers, their strength, and recent important happenings."

Bramble's heart sank. How could he reject the position of

Brightback when his father had already started to assign him duties? "I don't understand, Father. Why do you need me to do that?"

Burbark tilted his head to give him a sharp look. "I know you haven't been Brightback for long," he grunted, "but that's not the kind of question you get to ask. Do as I tell you, please. It's a simple enough request."

Bramble sighed inwardly. It was clear that his father didn't want to hear his protests, he thought, but at least a journey like this would take him away from the troop for a while. In that time, they might even get used to the idea of him as Brightback. *And it'll take my mind off things, too.*

"All right," he agreed slowly. "Yes, Father. Of course."

"Good." The older gorilla gazed at him levelly. Clearly it was a dismissal.

But Bramble couldn't help noticing how red his father's eyes were, how raw and bloodshot. His heart turned over with pity. Burbark had to look strong at all times—of course he did—but his feelings ran deeper than he showed. Perhaps, now that Bramble was the Brightback, the two of them could at last share their grief?

"Father," said Bramble quietly, "I'm so sorry about Cassava."

Burbark blinked. He shook himself, looking almost perplexed, as if the name meant little to him.

"We cannot dwell on the past, Bramble!"

Bramble flinched. "I only . . ."

"No. It is the future of the troop that should concern you

now, as it concerns me." Burbark turned away with an air of finality. "You are the Brightback, after all."

It should have been the proudest moment of his life. *I am the Brightback.*

But it was the wrong choice. Bramble knew it with certainty.

I'm in way over my head. And this won't end well—for me, or for the troop.

CHAPTER ELEVEN

She'd always wanted to become her own leopard. To be as independent and strong as her mother.

But it had happened too soon, thought Chase as she slunk through the dark forest. However proud she was of her hunting skills and her self-reliance, however confident she felt when she was at one with the night—she was not ready.

But the truth was, she had no choice. Prowl had not meant to leave them; she had promised not to. But she'd been taken anyway. *Such is the will of the Great Spirit.* That was what Prowl would have said.

But Chase had a hard time believing the Spirit would be so cruel to Seek.

He'd been deprived of his mother, and now of his mother-sister too; Chase would have to look after him now as if he were her own cub. She was too afraid of jackals and hyenas to leave him alone in the den, so she had brought him out with her into the blackness of the night. It must be terrifying for the cub, but it was safer for him to be with her.

The moist and leafy scents of the forest became tinged with something fouler and darker: old blood and rotting flesh. Flaring her nostrils, Chase clambered onto a log and sniffed the air. There was pale movement beneath her as Seek tried to follow, but he was too small to jump up beside her. Clawing the log in frustration, he whispered, "What is that smell, Chase? Is it something we can eat?"

Her whiskers twitched. "I don't think so, little one." Leaping down, she led him through dense undergrowth as the smell grew stronger. She halted as she was overwhelmed by its stench and stared down at the source.

"A monkey. It's been dead too long, Seek, and only the flies have touched it. I reckon it died of some sickness."

"So we shouldn't eat it?" he said. He sounded half-disappointed, half-relieved.

"No. I know you're hungry, but we'll find something better, I promise. This might make us ill ourselves."

It was hard to catch any new scents until they had made their way far from the dead monkey; the reek of it lingered in Chase's nostrils as she crept between trunks and through mossy gullies. Her stomach growled with hunger, and she could only imagine how ravenous Seek must be—but he padded valiantly along behind her and did well to make as little noise as he could.

I'm already proud of him, thought Chase with a pang in her heart.

Her whiskers bristled almost before she registered the new smell of prey. Halting, she flared her nostrils, turning her head until she homed in on the creature in the undergrowth. Behind her, Seek stopped; she could barely hear his nervous breath.

"A bushpig, or maybe a warthog," she murmured to him. "A young one. Follow me."

She flicked her ears as she stalked forward, placing each paw with care. She could hear the pig rustling and rooting in the dry foliage, not far ahead; it hadn't noticed her approach. Slowing her paws even more, she crept patiently toward the sounds of snuffling.

There was an explosive sound behind her, high and sudden, and she froze. Seek had sneezed, spooking the pig. Battling her frustration, Chase sprang after it as it scuttled away through the dense brush.

It was fast, but it was little. Surely she could catch it. It knew its surroundings, and it was smart enough to flee through the thickest vegetation, but Chase was agile too. She raced after it, hearing its desperate panting squeals grow louder—

Chase skidded to a halt, sending up a shower of dry leaves, as a vast shape loomed out of the darkness. Glowing eyes fixed on her, and her ears were buffeted by an enraged squeal that definitely didn't come from the youngster.

Her prey's mother was definitely a bushpig, not a warthog,

and the huge creature looked more than ready to gore a leopard. She plunged forward, raking her savage tusks at Chase.

Don't mess with bushpigs, Chase. Her own mother's warning ringing in her ears, Chase dodged and twisted, fleeing back the way she'd come. Even then, she heard the crash and rattle of the bushpig mother as she came in pursuit through the undergrowth, and it was all Chase could do to outrun her.

Panting, she slowed at last, and Seek came trotting to meet her, his eyes huge and remorseful.

"I'm sorry, Chase. A bug got in my nose!"

Repressing her urge to scold him, she nuzzled his flank instead. It really wasn't his fault; it had just been bad luck. "Don't worry, Seek. You couldn't help it. We'll find new prey."

Though she didn't know where or when.

It had been three days since they'd eaten, she reminded herself; the bongo was a distant, taunting memory. Seek's ribs were visible through his baby fur, and Chase's anxiety wasn't helping her hunt. *I was too rash with the pig. I should have been warier. If I'd been killed . . .*

Alone, Seek would be entirely defenseless. He would never have seen another sunrise.

She was seriously considering returning to the tainted monkey corpse when she caught a familiar, unwelcome scent on the night air. Halting, she felt her hackles bristle, and she peeled back her muzzle from her fangs. Seek stopped behind her.

Silent, a black shape emerged from the trees ahead of them. "Good night to you, Chase, and good hunting."

"Good night to you too, Shadow," she told him through gritted teeth.

"But if I may make a suggestion," he growled mockingly, "I'd leave hunting bushpigs to Prowl. She's bigger than you, and they're dangerous."

So he'd been watching them again. But Chase's irritation was blunted by a jolt of sadness.

"I can't," she said shortly. "Our mother is dead."

Shadow took a pace toward her, his eyes widening. "Truly? Chase, I'm sorry." All the mocking levity was gone from his voice. "I noticed her scent marks had faded in the last couple of days. I thought it unlike her to neglect them. How did it happen?"

"Gorillas," grunted Chase. Her throat felt tight.

"Surely not?"

Her anger stirred. "You doubt it? I saw them with my own eyes."

"I . . . No, I don't doubt you. It's just, Prowl . . . she was so experienced, and strong. It's hard to see how she could have—"

"It happened," said Chase.

Shadow kept his distance but lowered his head submissively. "Then let me help you hunt," he said gently. "You have the cub to feed, and I can—"

"No!" she snapped, recoiling with a curl of her muzzle. "Seek and I will manage on our own."

She thought she heard a whimper of objection from Seek, but it was very muted. *Sorry, little one. I can't let Shadow interfere in our lives.*

Shadow hunched his shoulders. "As you wish, Chase. But be careful. The prey is jumpy, not least because that other leopard's still around. With your mother gone, others may move in too. And you know what will happen if a new male finds . . ." His voice trailed off, and he glanced meaningfully at Seek.

"We'll be careful," said Chase, swinging her haunches protectively in front of the cub; Seek shrank behind her, quivering under Shadow's stare. "We'll be fine."

Shadow nodded, looking unconvinced, and turned without another word to slink into the night. Chase shook herself and turned to lick Seek's nose.

"Come along," she murmured. "We'll find something to eat, even if it's not until tomorrow night. No leopard should rely on another for help, Seek. Once you have learned to hunt, you must trust only yourself."

He nodded and followed her obediently as she retraced her steps toward the den. She had to find something soon, she told herself bleakly; Seek's faith in her was almost too much to bear. *What if I can't feed him?*

"Chase!" he exclaimed under his breath, and she turned, flicking her ears.

Seek nodded at something in the bushes, transfixed. Following his gaze, Chase saw a small rock python, its coils wrapped around a small creature that looked like a rat.

"Well spotted, Seek!" she growled. She pounced forward and slapped her paw down close to the snake.

It was unintimidated. Clearly it couldn't flee without

releasing its prey, but it seemed strangely unwilling to make the sacrifice. Its yellow eyes glared at Chase with a cold hatred.

It's a youngster. I can take both, she thought hopefully. *Snake and rat!* She slunk cautiously forward.

But the python at last seemed to accept its position. With a look of contempt, it released the rat and slithered with lightning speed into the low vegetation.

Chase nudged the rat toward Seek. "Go on. You spotted it, and it won't feed us both. I'll find something else."

He looked doubtful for a moment but was clearly too hungry to argue. He fell on the rat, ripping it into smaller pieces and gulping it down. The smell of fresh blood made Chase's stomach tighten, but she ignored it. "Come along. We'll go back to the den and rest."

She could smell that rotting monkey again, though. Almost against her instincts, she beat a path back toward it, trying not to flinch from the acrid, sweet stench. It wasn't hard to track it down once more, to say the least. Chase stood over it, flicking her tail.

It didn't seem right to eat what she hadn't killed, but it wouldn't be the first time. Even Prowl had occasionally resorted to carrion, in lean times. And Chase was a lot bigger than Seek; if there was something wrong with this monkey, it would affect her less.

And if I don't eat soon, I won't be strong enough to hunt at all.

"Don't touch it, Seek," she growled to him. "In fact, don't even look."

He hardly needed to be told. The cub hung well back, his eyes pitying as Chase ripped mouthfuls of soft, unpleasant flesh from the maggot-ridden corpse. She choked it down, almost gagging at the taste. Well, she thought, trying to close her nostrils as she ate: her stomach at least would thank her.

But maybe I should have accepted Shadow's offer after all.

CHAPTER TWELVE

It had been days since Prance had last seen her herd, but somehow it felt a little easier this way. *Out of sight, out of mind*, she told herself as she plodded across the shimmering plain. It wasn't actually true—her thoughts drifted back to them constantly, making her long for their company, their protection, the comfort of the Us. But at least she did not have that aching visual reminder of all that she had lost.

They must be far away by now. Prance had lingered close to the collection of small watering holes she had found. It wasn't just the nearness of water in this heat—after all, she could manage on fresh grass for a good while—but being close to other Bravelands creatures made her a little more hopeful and positive.

She hadn't forgotten the words of the elephant Boulder, though so far it wasn't working as he had predicted. Prance would mingle for a while with another herd, only to see them move on quickly, casting her strange glances. Some were sympathetic—zebras, wildebeests, and giraffes had all asked her why she was alone and offered to help find her herd. But when Prance explained that she'd lost her herd for good, that there was no going back, they would look at her with incomprehension, shake their heads, and trek on, leaving her alone. Some, of course, noticed her absence of shadow—especially when, as was so often now, she stood apart. Those sharp-eyed creatures would make even greater haste to get out of her presence.

Only one creature seemed unwilling to leave her, but Prance wasn't grateful for its staunch presence—it was a solitary vulture that watched her with black-eyed fascination. Once or twice she had tried to charge it, to scare it away. But it would hop a couple of paces at most, before flapping back toward her, so she had given up. She thought she recognized it; she was sure it was the vulture from the flock around Leap's remains, the one that had lunged toward her and caused her to flee in panic. But perhaps she was imagining the connection; how could she possibly know?

All Prance knew was that the bird frightened her. Taking a deep breath, she paced toward it now, her nostrils trembling.

"Get away from me!" she demanded, a quaver in her voice. "I'm not going to die. You're wasting your time!"

The bird just stared at her. Its eyes glittered.

"And *you're* wasting your breath," laughed someone nearby. "Those things only speak Skytongue. You might as well talk to a rock."

Prance glanced around, surprised, but grateful as always for a friendly voice. "I know that," she told the zebra beside her. "But this one keeps tracking me."

The zebra shook his bristly mane. "Vultures don't waste their energy following living animals. Well, unless you look thoroughly doomed." He brayed a laugh, though Prance shivered. "Mind you, I've heard of stranger friendships. Look at the story of the Three Heroes, for one thing!"

At last, Prance chuckled. "Maybe you're right. It's possible that bird just wants company! Maybe it doesn't want to eat me. I'm Prance Herdless, by the way." Each time she had to say the name, it was becoming a little easier.

"Herdless?" He laid his ears back in surprise. "Oh, that's bad luck. Did you lose them? How awful for you."

Prance took a deep breath, preparing herself to explain the wearisome story all over again. But the zebra simply shook his head and sighed, then went on talking.

"I'm Grassfriend, and it's a pleasure to make your acquaintance. I came over here to ask you your opinion, actually." He jerked his head at a cluster of zebras nearby. "That's Dawnfriend, and we're having an argument. You look like a gazelle who's seen many things."

Prance had no idea which of the seemingly identical zebras was Dawnfriend, but she nodded encouragingly. "Go on. Though I don't know if I can help."

"It's about the sun. Dawnfriend says it's the same one that rises and sets each day, but that's ridiculous! How can it set over *there*"—he tossed his mane and nodded at the western horizon, then twisted to look the other way—"and then reappear *there*? I don't think the sun can tunnel underground."

Prance tilted her head. "What's your theory, then?"

"I say the sun is like an egg. A new one gets laid every day. That makes *much* more sense."

"Um." Prance thought it sounded just as unlikely as the sun that burrowed beneath the land overnight. "I'm sorry, but I don't know myself. Have you tried asking one of the really wise creatures? An elephant, maybe?"

"No, but that's a good idea. Next time I see one, I'll do so." Grassfriend seemed satisfied with her answer; at least, Prance guessed, she hadn't told him he was wrong. "Why don't you come and graze with us for a while? Some of my herd are right over there, by the trees."

Her spirits lifted, Prance wandered after him to join the little group that included Dawnfriend. She grazed with the zebras contentedly as the sun—whether egg or tunneling ball of flame—rose higher in the morning sky. *Perhaps these will be the creatures who take me in*, she thought hopefully.

Maybe, she thought with amusement, she would be with them long enough to find out which zebra was Dawnfriend—because the sun argument seemed to have been entirely forgotten.

After a long, peaceful time, Grassfriend stretched out his neck and shook his mane. "Time to move on, it seems."

Around him, the other zebras nodded. Other small groups were also raising their heads, glancing toward one another, and moving off in a steady walk. It was almost like the Us,

Prance realized, and suddenly she couldn't help herself.

"Could I come with you?" she blurted. "At least for a while?"

Grassfriend turned back to her, startled, and his friends exchanged surprised looks. "Don't you want to find another gazelle herd?"

"Eventually, I'd like to," muttered Prance, pawing the earth nervously. "But just until then?"

The zebras drew together, heads lowered as they whispered among themselves. At last Grassfriend tossed up his head and came trotting back to Prance.

"Yes, we don't see why not," he said cheerfully. "My friends think it's a little odd, but I don't mind in the least. Come along, then."

Gratefully, Prance walked at Grassfriend's side as the zebra groups merged together and set off westward in a great mass. It felt strange to be surrounded by striped bodies instead of golden ones, but simply being part of a herd was a blissful sensation, even without the buzz of the Us. Prance found herself relaxing, her muscles loosening and her stride becoming easier, less effortful. *Safety in numbers, even when they aren't mine.* Some of the zebras cast her curious glances, but none questioned her; they simply seemed to accept that she was with Grassfriend now.

The only niggling worry that remained was the vulture. Prance couldn't help looking over her shoulder for it. And there it was, hopping and flapping along in the wake of the herd. Sometimes it was hidden by the mass of black-and-white bodies, but every time Prance caught sight of it again, the bird was still watching her with those bright, relentless eyes.

The moving zebras around her had shifted, and though Grassfriend was now a little ahead and to her right, a smaller, more gangly zebra had trotted to her side. A foal, she realized, perhaps only a few months old. It was quite a relief to be on an eye level with her neighbor, and she turned her head to the youngster.

"Hello," she said, "I'm Prance Herdless."

"You're not herdless right now," observed the filly, eyeing her with mild interest.

"No, and I'm grateful to Grassfriend for letting me join you for a while." Prance dipped her head a little.

"Anyway, it's nice to meet you," added the filly. "I am Breezefriend."

There was a faraway look in the foal's eyes that might, thought Prance, be sadness. "Is everything all right, Breeze-friend?"

"Oh yes. Now that my father, Mistfriend, has decided the herd should move on—he's the alpha stallion, you see."

"You didn't like it by the watering holes back there?" asked Prance.

"It was nice enough," sighed Breezefriend. "But there were bad times there. Two foals were lost. They were my friends, born about the same time as me."

"I'm sorry to hear it," said Prance softly. "Life is hard for grass-eaters."

"So Father keeps saying," murmured the filly. "It's kind of sad."

"Were they . . . did predators take them

"Probably," said Breezefriend, her exp

blinked her long lashes. "We didn't see any

strange. Normally foals stay close to our mo

thing we're taught. And we always know

mothers are, so it isn't hard. We can't get l

we just *know*."

"I'm beginning to realize that zebras have y

of the Us," said Prance.

Breezefriend flicked her ears curiously. "W

"It's . . . hard to explain." Prance wrinkled he

ing. "The gazelle herds—we're not one singl

sometimes it *feels* like that. It comes over us in

when we're threatened or hungry or tired, and

knows what to do. Without even thinking about

it's not a constant state of mind, but it's there when

Except for me, now. But Prance didn't say that part out lou

Breezefriend was nodding slowly. "Yes, we feel somet

the same. I've never really thought about it. My mother ta

about the Friendship, and she doesn't just mean the herd.

suppose it's our *Us*."

"It sounds like it." Prance glanced ahead. "There, everyone

is coming to a halt now."

"That's just how it happens," agreed Breezefriend. She

seemed to have cheered up since the beginning of their con-

versation, and Prance was pleased to have distracted her from

thoughts of her lost birth-mates. "See, dusk is falling, Prance.

So we'll stop for the night."

or us." Prance nodded. She wanted to ask
ons, but Breezefriend was striding on, her
d Prance followed her curiously.

le twilight, the zebras seemed to be mill-
as she and Breezefriend joined the surging
ld make out a pattern to their movements.
fact wheeling, slowly but in quite a precise
st they raised turned the last rays of sunlight
e.

the zebras lose its shadow?" asked Prance sud-
ense of familiarity came over her. This felt so
g of the gazelles when one was Chosen . . .

?" Breezefriend looked startled.

zelle is going to die," explained Prance, "it loses
the Great Spirit's way of marking the one who
ate next."

y? Wow! Oh, nothing like that happens to us."
friend gave a small shiver and stamped her hoof. "No
ra is *chosen*. My mother says that we always know death will
ome to one of us, and it hardly matters which. So we ready
ourselves as a herd."

The great circle of zebras continued to move, trotting and
walking, and as Prance skipped to keep up, she could hear
a whinnying murmur. At first she didn't understand it, but
gradually, as her ears adjusted to the strangeness, she could
make out some of the phrases they chanted.

"In ancient times and with us still, Death takes who and when it will."

"*Comes Death to me, or to my friend; always we recall their end.*"

"*Peace tonight and peace tomorrow, whether dark hours bring life or sorrow.*"

Prance felt a thrill of wonder tingle along her spine; how much stronger must that sensation be for the zebras who were bound up in the Friendship? She found herself in awe both at the strangeness and the familiarity. The ritual, the whole attitude of the zebras was so unlike the gazelles' . . . yet it had strong elements in common. Acceptance even in sadness; honor and respect for those who would fall . . .

I never accepted it. I deserved to lose the Us. Prance's horns drooped as the remorse and guilt returned in a sickening surge.

But at that moment the zebras halted all around her, flanks heaving, nostrils flaring and blowing. They stamped and pawed the dust, shaking their manes and turning to one another.

Grassfriend stood next to another zebra she recognized from the earlier group, and Prance heard what he said to her. "Dawnfriend, I am sorry if my words were harsh today. Let us forget our quarrel."

So *that* was Dawnfriend! Prance had seen her with the others, of course: a slim-shouldered young mare with a torn ear.

"Of course, Grassfriend," the mare whinnied. "And I too regret any sharpness! What does it matter who brings the sun? If it rises tomorrow, we are happy."

Little Breezefriend was talking to an adult zebra, who

was grooming her neck with her blunt teeth. "Thank you, Mother," said the filly, blinking her lashes. "For taking care of me today."

"Thank you for being a good foal, Breezefriend," murmured the mare.

All around Prance, the same conversations were happening, till the air was filled with the soft neighing and murmuring of the zebras. Apologies for squabbles, thanks for help and companionship, reassurances of love and protection.

Breezefriend nudged Prance and nodded toward the big zebra stallion at the center of the circle. "That's my father," she said, her eyes shining. "Mistfriend. He'll finish the ritual now."

Sure enough, the stallion reared up, striking the dusty ground with his huge hooves.

"Thank you, Great Spirit," neighed Mistfriend, his whinny ringing out across the plain. All the other zebras joined in his cry:

"For keeping us safe on the plains today, and leading us to fresh grass!"

The circle dispersed, though the zebras stayed close to one another as the shadows stretched out across the grassland. At last a strip of fading yellow on the western horizon was all that was left of the daylight. Prance settled to rest, her eyes half closing.

She felt safer than she had for many days, protected by the strange Us of different creatures. Somehow she knew that, even if her death was still tracking her, it would not find her tonight.

* * *

The zebra herd was already moving on as dawn lightened the eastern sky, and they had settled into a steady pace by the time the sun spilled over the horizon to light the savannah with gold. Prance walked with Grassfriend and Dawnfriend, who had already resumed their argument despite their ritual dusk reconciliation.

"I tell you, it's an egg, and I suspect the moon lays it," insisted Grassfriend. "Look at how solid the land is!" He paused to strike the grass with a hoof. "How could a piece of light burrow underground from west to east in those few hours, Dawnfriend? It's not possible!"

"You're being very silly," neighed Dawnfriend, rolling her eyes in exaggerated disdain. "Maybe it doesn't burrow at all. Maybe it switches off its light somehow and rolls right along the horizon till it's back in the east. The sun's round, isn't it?"

"That makes more sense than your original point," admitted Grassfriend. "So I see you've changed your argument *completely* since yesterday. . . ."

The squabble, Prance had already realized, was really quite good-natured; it was clear these two friends spent most of each day debating unimportant matters in such detail. She understood completely—it was no doubt more fun than contemplating the next imminent death and wondering when a predator would strike.

"Oh, look," announced Dawnfriend gloomily, abandoning the debate for a moment. She nodded ahead. "Mistfriend's come to the Gully River already. I didn't realize we were so close."

Grassfriend pricked his ears forward. "Oh, I always hate this part," he muttered.

The zebra herd had slowed; as they milled and stamped hesitantly, Prance could make out the landscape ahead. The line of a steep escarpment was quite clear in the morning sunlight, its far bank hazier. Between those two shallow cliffs, she remembered, lay the Gully River; it was one the gazelles too had to cross, on their own Great Grass Trek.

The crowd of zebras was growing denser, as the leaders paused on the embankment and the others caught up. Mistfriend was trotting back and forth on the edge of the bank, peering down in concern.

"It's fuller and faster than usual," he neighed. "The rains in the early season must have swelled it." The big stallion placed his two front hooves a little down the slope, but he seemed to change his mind; he reared back onto the cliff edge and cantered farther downstream. The rest followed, whisking their tails in confusion.

"There are bound to be crocodiles," whinnied Grassfriend. "There always are."

"I think Mistfriend saw them already," said Dawnfriend. "Look, he's searching for a better place to cross downstream."

"I doubt he'll find one. He needs to make a decision soon."

"He needs to make a decision *now*," Prance put in. "See the longer grass behind us? Lions!"

As soon as Grassfriend and Dawnfriend turned toward the prowling big cats, the message spread instantly through the herd. The zebras began to neigh in panic, whirling and galloping in short bursts, before twisting and cantering back toward their leader. Mistfriend, too, had registered the threat; he brayed a warning and seemed to make a decision at last. He plunged down the steep bank, vanishing from sight, and the herd began to follow him, one by one.

A tight crowd had built up behind Mistfriend, and only one or two zebras could follow his path at once. They were streaming down into the river now, but many were still on the grassland, and they were beginning to panic. Bucking and rearing, galloping in all directions, they churned the grass into mud as they eyed the approaching lions.

Prance at least had experience of being unable to sense a herd's movement. She tried to stay close to the bank, her legs trembling as she waited her turn, trying to ignore the panicking zebras. The sun was high enough now to dazzle her, and her heart raced as she tried to keep the tawny hunters in her field of vision. The lions picked up speed, trotting faster and faster toward the zebra outriders. Two big lionesses broke into a run.

They were too close for comfort now, and the zebras were scattering. Prance spun and leaped away, but almost collided with Breezefriend. She stumbled to a halt, glancing back.

"Little one, run!"

"I can't!" neighed Breezefriend in panic. "I've lost my mother! I've lost my mother! How can this happen? I can't feel her!"

The filly was too distressed to listen to reason; Prance knew it straightaway. Nudging Breezefriend hard with her shoulder, she brayed, "Run with me!"

She and the foal ran together, galloping full tilt toward the embankment, but already Prance could make out a blur of lion fur at the edge of her vision. She veered, shoving Breezefriend with her, but another lion was cutting toward them from the left, his loping strides lazy and confident.

"Breezefriend," she panted. "We have to cross the river. *Now!*"

That seemed to get through to the foal; Breezefriend's muzzle was flecked with foam, and her eyes were so wide, the whites showed in complete circles. But the filly ran at Prance's command, heading straight for the bank between the two approaching lions.

There was no way of seeing the right path; Mistfriend's original track was lost in clouds of dust, and zebras were pouring down the cliffside now with little regard for their footing. Prance skidded to a halt and darted along the edge. The lions altered their course slightly, and their paws hesitated; they seemed unsure whether to follow Prance or go after the foal.

"Go, Breezefriend! Cross!"

The angry lions swerved and came after Prance. She saw Breezefriend take a breath and leap over the edge, crashing down onto slippery mud and only just keeping her balance. But the foal was galloping headlong into the water now, throwing up spray.

Prance twisted, stotting and leaping to disorient the lions.

As they turned clumsily, she too sprang from the escarpment, trusting her footing to the Great Spirit. Her hooves slithered wildly in the churned mud, and she slid most of the way down on her haunches, but she was safe.

For now.

The irate lions were tumbling down the bank after her; she had no choice but to keep going. Prance made a wild leap for the water. Her hooves splashed down in the murky river, but she barely let them rest; the yielding mud sucked at her feet, so she went on springing, desperate, her breath rasping and her chest aching. Three huge leaps, then a final exhausted stumble, and she crashed forward onto the mud of the far bank. She had been too quick for the crocodiles.

Terrified, she risked a glance back. The male lion was on her tail, plunging through the water, his eyes blazing with hunger. Prance scrabbled wildly in the mud, her hooves sliding from under her as she tried to stand. *My death, it has found me—*

There was no bite of fangs in her rump. Exhausted, she slithered another couple of paces, then rolled onto her flank. Surely he must catch her now—

The lion's jaws gaped, so close to her hind legs. But he wasn't pouncing; his roar was one of shock and fear, and he was being dragged back into the water. Staring aghast, Prance saw him pulled abruptly under in a vast splash of bloody foam. Something huge and scaly rolled with him, twisting, its pale belly and scaly tail exposed as it sank the lion in the deepest central current of the river. Lion and crocodile disappeared together; all that surfaced was a spreading stain of dark blood.

Panting, Prance dragged herself up the sheer bank, hauling herself at last over its crest. Her whole body shook violently. She could hardly bear to look back over the river, but when she risked a glance, she saw the rest of the lions fleeing back across the trampled grassland. Their muzzles were unbloodied.

Staggering onto safer ground, away from the riverbank, Prance walked on shaking legs toward a line of trees. A familiar high voice whinnied to her, weak and still terrified, but alive.

"Breezefriend!" Prance trotted unsteadily to the little zebra.

"I can't find my mother! I still can't find her!" There was unbearable panic in Breezefriend's whinny. "What's happening, Prance? Why am I lost?"

"Come, Breezefriend." Prance forced herself to take deep breaths, to steady her rapid heartbeat. "We'll find her together." Gently she nudged the filly's flank.

"How?" cried Breezefriend. "How, when I can't feel her? What's happening?"

I don't know, thought Prance. *It sounds almost as if my fate is overtaking your whole herd, and you're losing your Friendship, just as I lost the Us.*

Was some strange curse affecting all the herds?

But she didn't want to utter those thoughts aloud to the young zebra. "Let's find your mother together," she said firmly. "The rest of the herd is gathering again; she'll be among them."

Her sternness seemed to give Breezefriend strength, who

shook off her frenzy and plodded obediently after Prance.

But Prance herself couldn't help looking back once more, because there was one herd-follower she hoped to have lost. Surely, in all the chaos, it had given up its obsessive pursuit of her?

No such luck. A black speck on the wind that grew swiftly larger, the vulture soared over the gully and banked, flapping down to the ground. Prance almost thought it smirked at her as it hopped to a halt and folded its wings.

Shaking off that bird was too much to hope for. Prance sighed and closed her eyes briefly. The Great Spirit would not let her forget, then: death had missed her once. Perhaps, after her narrow escape from that lion, she had now dodged it twice.

And one day soon, death would catch up with her and right that wrong.

CHAPTER THIRTEEN

Parting the foliage as cautiously as he could, Bramble peered out from his hiding place in a big mahogany tree. Beneath him, in a shallow valley dotted with scrubby bushes, another gorilla troop went about their daily business: grooming, eating, relaxing.

What was there that could possibly interest his father? Gorilla troops kept to themselves; they rarely bothered one another, and no one wanted to instigate trouble.

Still, the very mystery of Bramble's purpose gave him a thrill. If it was such a puzzle, it must be important—and Burbark had entrusted the job to Bramble.

Shaking off his uncertainty, he focused once again on the group in the valley. It wasn't a large troop. There was a Silverback, of course, but only two Goldbacks and two youngsters—and one of those was still suckling. Burbark's troop was much bigger, but still, the family dynamics looked familiar. The big Silverback was entertaining his older daughter, roughhousing and play-fighting.

The sight gave Bramble a pang of nostalgia. That was how Burbark had once played with him, but it had been a long time since their relationship had been so relaxed, and he could barely remember the last time they'd had this much fun. The whole family looked carefree, and Bramble wondered whether this troop had visited their own Spirit Mouth the day the mountain shook. It didn't look as if they'd had the same dreadful warning as his own troop.

Bramble was bored; he couldn't help it. There was nothing to see here. Gorillas being gorillas. He gave a vast yawn, peeling back his lips; he'd thought, if he'd thought at all, that he could do it silently. Instead a squeaking growl escaped with the yawn.

One of the Goldbacks craned her head around, frowning. Her eyes met his through the leafy branches. "Hey!" she barked.

Scrambling hastily down from his perch, Bramble loped away as fast as he could through the forest. Behind him he could hear the desultory sounds of a search, and the voices of the gorillas. He couldn't make out their words, but they sounded unconcerned; the troop would probably assume he was nothing more than a curious youngster. They were unlikely to harm him, but still—his father had told him to be secretive. Bramble was determined to make Burbark proud of his first mission.

There was nothing much to report, but he would track down his father straightaway. As he padded on, he mulled over what he had seen. None of it seemed important . . . although now that he thought about it, a few things stuck in his mind. Had one of the Goldbacks looked jealous of the other? Had the Silverback shown too much preference for the older infant?

Maybe he *had* found useful intelligence, without even realizing it. Bramble's heart lightened. Yes, he was sure now that he'd observed something vital; his father would soon find out what it was. Pride swelling in his chest, Bramble loped a little faster.

Beneath a twisted fig tree, he hesitated, glancing around. He was sure he'd heard something. Narrowing his eyes, Bramble listened harder. Yes, there it was—a mewling, muffled cry that came from between the fig tree's roots.

Pacing over to the base of the tree, Bramble peered over the blade of the biggest root and into the hollow behind it. His eyes widened. It was a tiny leopard cub, alone and vulnerable. Why did he keep running into leopards these days? Three of them in less than half a moon!

This one, though, was nothing like Chase Born of Prowl, or the massive dead leopard that had killed his brother. He couldn't even feel resentment toward this tiny cub. *Poor thing.*

Bramble's heart softened as he gazed down. Its eyes were huge and scared, and its little whiskers trembled. Its mother must have abandoned it. Or perhaps she had left it here for safety, but something bad had happened to her?

At any rate, Bramble shouldn't interfere. It was really none of his business. Still, he hesitated. And in the sudden silence, he heard a vicious, spitting snarl.

He whipped around and instantly tumbled back as a far bigger leopard hurtled toward him, fangs bared in fury. Its eyes blazed as it leaped, and Bramble barely had time to panic. There was the faint, numb knowledge that he was as good as dead, and then—

The leopard stumbled, one forepaw giving way beneath it. It collapsed forward, falling hard onto its shoulder, and lay stunned, flanks heaving. Still it snarled, lashing a weak paw at Bramble.

Now Bramble felt his heart lurch into a delayed hammering. He panted in shock but crept toward the leopard. It didn't look like a threat anymore, despite those extended claws and the savage bared fangs. And though its coat was dull and its ribs protruded, he had the impression he recognized this creature.

He edged forward. It *was* the same leopard, Bramble was sure of it. The one who had challenged him for that bird and had lost it for both of them. The one who had helped him drive away the hyenas . . .

She was struggling to rise; she propped herself up on her forepaws, swaying. Her muzzle was still curled in menace, but she was so thin and weak, Bramble couldn't even bring himself to be nervous.

"Are you all right, Chase Born of Prowl?" he asked. "What's wrong?"

Her eyes narrowed. She seemed to have trouble focusing on him.

"It's me," he added. "Bramble, uh . . . well, I'm Bramble Brightback now, at least." He grinned, but she could only stare at him in confusion. "You don't look well."

"She's sick," came a small voice. The little cub crept forward from his hiding place behind the root, its paws trembling. "Chase ate bad rot-meat. I think the monkey was sick when it died."

Chase's eyes had widened again in panic, and she lurched forward. "Get away from my cub!"

Bramble rose up and backed away a little, raising his hands defensively. "I don't mean any harm, I promise."

The cub slunk to his side, gazing anxiously at Chase. She looked from him to Bramble and back again, but she was clearly too weak to protest.

Bramble stared at her, torn. She'd helped him once; perhaps he should ask for help from the Goldbacks? They knew about sicknesses of the forest. But would they be willing to help a leopard, after what had happened to Cassava? The Blackbacks might even kill Chase in revenge. All the same, he had to do something. . . .

Bramble turned and shambled back into the undergrowth. He was sure he'd seen bromeliads, and it had rained recently . . . there. Bramble peered into their stiff splayed leaves and picked the one with most water caught at the base of each leaf. Uprooting it as carefully as he could, spilling only a few drops as he yanked the last roots free, he carried it back to Chase.

She bared her fangs again as he approached. "I don't need your help!"

"Yes, you do." He squatted by her head and tilted the plant awkwardly toward the corner of her mouth. Clearly unable to resist, Chase turned her head to catch the rainwater as he dribbled it into her parched jaws.

Much of it spilled, trickling down her fur, but she sighed in relief and licked droplets from her whiskers. "I'll get you some more," he told her.

"No," said Chase hoarsely. "I told you, I don't need your help."

"I didn't need *yours* with the hyenas, but you gave it to me anyway." Bramble grinned.

She glared back. "You don't . . . understand. It was . . . your troop . . . that killed my mother!"

Bramble sucked in a breath, stepping back. Suddenly, it made sense. That was why he'd seen so many leopards lately; Chase was born of Prowl. And Prowl must have been the dead cat the troop had found near Cassava's body.

"No!" he exclaimed angrily. "It was your mother Prowl who killed my brother!"

"Don't lie to me," snarled Chase. "My mother would never have been stupid enough to attack a grown gorilla!"

"Cassava would not have attacked *her*. He walked away from trouble when he could!"

Chase's fury must have given her a surge of strength; she staggered to her paws, swaying, her hackles raised. "Your troop killed her, and they desecrated her body!"

Bramble blinked. So Chase had seen that happen? It had been wrong of the Blackbacks, he knew, but understandable.

"He was our Brightback!" he snapped. "Every gorilla loved him. Your mother took him from us!"

"Get away from my cub, and get away from me," growled Chase. "Gorillas are Codebreakers! I never want to lay eyes on you again."

She jerked her head, and the little cub ran to her, following her as she crept unsteadily into the trees. Bramble glared after them, speechless, as they vanished. *I can't believe we helped each other just a few days ago.* And she had accused gorillas of being Codebreakers, after what her mother had done to Cassava?

"*You're* the Codebreakers!" he barked at last, though probably too late for her to hear him.

As he made his dejected way back to the troop, Bramble kept turning the encounter over and over in his mind. *I know Cassava didn't attack that leopard.* He knew it as surely as he knew the sky was blue or that the rains would come.

But . . . something didn't seem right. Chase had seemed equally certain of her mother. And why *would* a leopard take on a powerful gorilla like Cassava? The story didn't make sense.

There is more to those two deaths than meets the eye. Bramble was sure of it now. He rather wished he could retrace his steps and find Chase so that they could get to the bottom of the mystery together.

But they'd never help each other again, he was certain.

Sudden weariness weighted his limbs. Dusk was falling, Bramble realized; he had spent the whole day on his mission. *I just need to report to Father, and then I can get some sleep.*

He halted, stiffening. A fallen tree lay between him and a shallow dip in the forest; its vast roots had been torn from the earth and now formed an almost-vertical shield between him and the small valley below. He could see gorillas down there in the dusk, and he tried to breathe quietly. Like the other troop, he doubted they'd attack him—but here was yet more intelligence he could bring back to Burbark. Narrowing his eyes, Bramble crept close to the earthy tangle of roots and peered around their edge.

No, it *was* Burbarktroop—or at least some of them: Goldbacks, Blackbacks, and their leader himself. Bramble's eyes widened in surprise. What was his father doing so far from the nests as night fell? And the others—Woodnettle was there, and Apple Goldback, and Bindweed.

Bramble did not hurry forward to greet them; they were acting too strangely. They stood in a rough circle around Burbark, rearing up on their hind legs and stamping their feet rhythmically. Bramble squeezed his eyes, trying to focus in the twilight. He was sure his father was holding something. A small branch?

No. Bramble gave a silent gasp, putting his hand over his mouth. In Burbark's hands was a snake, a live one. It coiled around his fingers and arm and raised its head, swaying to the same beat as Burbark. The snake and the big Silverback seemed mesmerized by each other. The sight of their weird dance made Bramble's blood run cold.

The rhythm of the stamping feet grew faster. Burbark gripped the snake by the middle of its body, and it uncoiled from his arm, rising and swaying in time.

Then it struck, too fast to see. Its fangs were buried in Burbark's wrist, right where he had already been bitten. Bramble stared, horrified, but his father did not fling the snake away. Instead he threw back his head, closing his eyes almost blissfully. Then he opened them again, staring skyward. He gave a great shuddering sigh, of pain and pleasure combined.

Bramble's heart hammered; he could not repress a stifled cry of shock. At once the stamping halted. Burbark's head snapped around in the silence.

"Is someone there?" he called.

He should reveal himself, Bramble thought. He should creep out from behind the root cluster, greet his father, express his amazement, talk to him and to the other gorillas. He would find out what was happening, realize what it was all about, find the answers that would after all be perfectly rational and understandable. They would all laugh about it together.

Yet something held him still and quiet in his hiding place. Breathing as silently as he could, Bramble crept backward, and as soon as he dared, he turned and loped away.

A cold, confused fear settled over him. It was a dread born purely of some instinct inside him, Bramble knew, because he did not understand what he had just witnessed. If only he knew why his father was behaving like that, it might make sense. It *would* make sense.

Yet he would not ask. *Could* not. Better by far not to know. Actually, best of all for Bramble would be to forget he had seen anything at all.

CHAPTER FOURTEEN

Day and night meant nothing. Chase drifted in a world of shadows and occasional, sudden flashes of light. They hurt her head, and she was afraid to open her eyes. Yet she desperately wanted to, because she could hear Seek's voice, and she wanted to help him. He *needed* her.

"Chase? Chase, please wake up. *Please*. I'm scared."

Her eyes creaked open. She was lying curled; she could see her own scrawny flanks rising and falling with jerky irregularity. It did not look right, so she squeezed her eyes shut again, letting herself float back to the darkness.

"Chase, I don't know what to do. Tell me what to do."

If Seek would just leave her alone to rest for a while, she would be fine. That was all she needed: a long, long sleep. Her head whirled, and she sank farther below the surface. That was it: she was underwater. She liked the water. *Leave me be, just for a little bit longer.* . . .

"Chase?" That was not Seek's voice.

She woke again, abruptly. A big male leopard stood over her. There was something wrong about him—yes, that eerie pelt, dappled black like a midnight forest. Chase lashed out a paw and felt one of her claws catch flesh. "Go away!"

Her growl sounded slurred, but he must have understood her. Yet he still waited there, peering down, Seek crouched anxiously at his forelegs. "What's wrong, Chase?" asked Shadow gently. "How can I help?"

"You can't! Go 'way. 'M fine. *Go.*"

He must have gone this time, because the next time she looked, Shadow wasn't there and the sunlight had faded. Gratefully she fell back into unconsciousness.

When she wakened again much later, the moon bathed her with its cooling light. An adult leopard was once more at her side—but this one she was happy to see. More than happy.

"Mother!" Chase sprang to her feet, completely fit and rested. "Mother, I thought you were dead!"

But Prowl curled back her muzzle and snarled, bringing Chase's joyful dash to a halt.

"Stop being lazy, Chase! You have work to do."

"No, Mother." Suddenly she was a cub again. "I've been sick, that's all. But I'm better now."

"No, you're not. You're still lying around here while Seek has gone!"

"What?" Chase spun around. She stared hopelessly around at the patch of crushed foliage where she'd lain for far too long. The cub was nowhere in sight. "Where is he? Mother, where has Seek gone?"

"That's for you to find out, not me. I am dead, daughter."

"No, you're not!" Chase twisted desperately back to Prowl. "What happened to Seek?"

Her mother hunched her shoulders, sadly. "Perhaps a predator took him while you were asleep?"

"I'm sorry, Mother! I tried to care for him." She trotted toward Prowl. "Mother, don't go. Please! I'm scared. Stay with me!"

But Prowl had turned and was walking away, her elegant tail flicking. "Seek was scared too, I daresay. I don't have time to look after you, Chase. That's not something I can do anymore."

"Wait! Mother!" Chase sprang after her, but Prowl was gone, dissolving into the misty morning.

"Come back . . . please . . ." Chase stumbled into the trees, her paws slipping and sliding, but the mist was growing darker and thicker, coiling around her like clinging vines. "Mother?"

The darkness swallowed her entirely, and the world vanished.

Chase did not know how long it was before she woke again. But she knew instantly, when her eyes blinked open, that what she had seen was a vision. *Mother was never here.*

And Seek still is!

The cub was curled against her belly, snoring hard. He was

safe and alive. Was this another dream, though? Her heart
lurched.

Weakly, Chase leaned her head down and licked the crown
of the cub's head. The taste and smell of him was vividly Seek,
sweet and leafy. *It's not a dream.* Relief washed over her. *Thank
the Great Spirit.*

Seek wasn't gone, but he might easily have been. Perhaps
that was what her mother had tried to tell her. Groggily, her
jaw clenched in determination, Chase clambered to her paws.
She swayed but kept her footing. Perhaps it was the water
Bramble had brought her, or perhaps it was just a lull in the
sickness? But she felt just a little better.

Not ready to hunt, she knew, but what choice did she have?
Seek must eat, or she really would lose him. They would *both*
die, curled up here together.

Stop being lazy, Chase. Get up and hunt.

She nudged the cub with her nose. "Wake up, little one,"
she said hoarsely. "We need to find food."

"Chase!" His eyes went wide, and he jumped to his feet and
spun in delight, chasing his tail. "You're better!"

"Yes, much better," she lied. "Back to my normal self."

It had always been a lost cause, Chase thought some time later,
as the two young leopards padded back toward their den. She
did feel as if the sickness had passed, that was true; but after
their failed hunt, she was footsore and wearier than ever. She
and Seek had found not so much as a rat or a beetle. Chase's
body felt as if an elephant had trampled it, and hunger clawed

at her stomach. Seek trudged at her side, ears drooping, eyes half-closed with exhaustion.

Then, suddenly, his head jerked up with renewed alertness. "Chase, what's that?"

She blinked, trying to focus on the tree above their den. There was something odd about the shape of its foliage, as if a fat new branch had grown in their absence and was already broken and drooping. And now she could smell something very fine: fresh blood and meat.

"It's a bushpig!" cried Seek. "How did it get up the tree?"

It really was a bushpig, a big one. Chase blinked in astonishment. She had a sneaking idea of where it must have come from, but she was not going to take offense, not this time. Reaching down, she clasped her jaws around Seek's scruff. She took a deep breath, and with the last reserves of her strength, she clawed and dragged her way up the tree.

Hooking the bushpig with her claws, she dragged it into a safer position on its branch. She and Seek fell on it, tearing into the soft flesh and sinew, gulping down mouthfuls. They ate and ate, each of them seeming afraid to stop in case the bushpig vanished into thin air.

Their muzzles were blood-drenched by the time Chase flopped along the branch, her stomach distended and aching slightly. It wasn't the pain of sickness, though; it was the fullness of a belly that had been empty too long.

Seek was already snoozing on his back, his paws in the air and his head resting against the bushpig's exposed rib cage. Chase rolled carefully over and sniffed at the corpse. She couldn't catch Shadow's scent, but it was hard to make out any distinct presence, with the reek of pig meat filling her nostrils.

Dry leaves rustled at the foot of the tree. Her ears pricking up, Chase rose to her paws and balanced on the branch, lashing her tail.

She peered down through the foliage, her hackles springing erect. There was a huge male leopard on the ground beneath her, but it wasn't Shadow; it was Range. He sat down, coiled his tail around his rump, and gazed up at her with those unsettling eyes.

"If you didn't want us to eat it," she growled, "you shouldn't have stashed it in our tree."

"But I did want you to eat it." He licked a paw. "It was a gift." His blue eyes met hers once again.

Chase glared down at him, but he didn't look away. At last she swallowed hard.

"Thank you," she told him gruffly.

"It's not a problem." He hunched his shoulders. "I can kill much more than I eat. Leopards should help one another out, after all."

"Leopards should look after themselves," she replied.

"And each other," Range insisted, "once they've taken care of their own needs."

His words went against everything her mother had ever taught her, yet she felt a deep, if reluctant gratitude to him. *If he hadn't done what he did, Seek and I would both be dead now.*

"Well," she grunted after a pause. "It was kind of you."

Seek had woken up; he was staring down wide-eyed at the

big male. Chase hesitated, but only for a moment. She scrambled backward down the tree trunk, and the cub followed her.

She moved deliberately between Range and the cub, lashing her tail warningly. But Seek squirmed past her and trotted up to Range, who batted at his ears with a paw. Seek began to chase the big leopard's twitching tail.

"He's got plenty of spirit," remarked Range, gazing at the capering cub. "You've done well to keep him alive so long."

Nodding, Chase allowed herself to relax a little. "Thanks. I have a responsibility."

"And you've been sick. That's obvious." He nodded at her flank, where the ribs still protruded despite her rounded belly.

"Yes." Exhaustion washed over her again. The stress of Range's reappearance had worn her down, she realized; she was nowhere close to full fitness yet.

"Why don't you sleep?" Range's eyes were kind. "I promise I'll watch over the cub. I'll protect you too, Chase. When you wake, perhaps we can hunt together?"

Chase did not have the energy to refuse. She realized that for better or for worse, she trusted this blue-eyed leopard; for the first time in many long days, she felt her muscles relax.

Maybe, Chase thought as she slunk wearily into the den and curled up to sleep, *just maybe things are looking up at last.*

CHAPTER FIFTEEN

Prance's heart beat fast as she walked to rejoin the zebra herd, most of whom had crossed the river by now. She wondered how many losses there had been.

Prance glanced nervously at the foal who paced beside her. Breezefriend's ears were pricked forward, her hooves stepping high; she looked every bit as excited as Prance had felt, the day she cheated death and ran back to her herd.

What if the zebras react the same way as Runningherd did? Worry twisted in Prance's gut. *What if they think Breezefriend was marked for death and should have submitted to it?* Prance didn't think she could bear to see her own crushing disappointment reborn in the young filly's face.

Some of the zebras were already turning, taking trotting steps toward Prance and Breezefriend. One of them broke into a delighted gallop. "Daughter! You're safe!"

"Mother!" whinnied Breezefriend. She bounded forward to meet the mare, and the two tossed their stiff manes and grazed each other's necks gently with their teeth. More zebras joined them, bucking and pawing the earth with joy. Relief flooded through Prance, together with a deep sadness that her own herd reunion had been so different.

But she was happy for Breezefriend. The zebras were clearly delighted at the filly's safe return. After a moment, Breezefriend and her mother came cantering over toward Prance, followed by their herd-mates. The filly was talking high and fast, the story spilling out of her.

". . . Prance who saved me," she neighed. "She told me to jump, and she drew the lions away. And was nearly killed herself! She would have been, if the crocodiles hadn't got the lion that was after her."

"This is a wonderful story," exclaimed Breezefriend's mother, trotting to a halt in front of Prance. "And I thank you for my daughter's life."

"Prance saved Breezefriend!" Another zebra had turned to whinny the news back to the rest of the herd.

"What a brave gazelle you are." Dawnfriend's eyes glowed.

"I knew she would make a fine herd-mate," declared Grassfriend. "Didn't I say so, Dawnfriend?"

"For once you were right about something." Dawnfriend rolled her eyes and snorted. "I say we call this gazelle—Prancefriend!"

"Prancefriend! Prancefriend!" More zebras took up the cry,

stamping their hooves and tossing their heads. "She is Prance-friend!"

A warm glow filled Prance, from her nose to her tail tip. *Do I have a new herd after all? Perhaps the elephant was right! I am Prance-friend now. . . .*

The sense of joyful contentment stayed with her throughout the morning, as she grazed with her newfound herd. She would never experience the Friendship, just as no zebra could feel the Us, but this was more than enough. She had a home, and friends, and as much safety as a grass-eater could ever expect. *Maybe I belong here.*

Chewing on a mouthful of sweet grass, Prance raised her head, eyeing her surroundings. There was no sign of lions or cheetahs or hyenas; for now, the herd was at peace. And she would take her turn watching for threats, just as any herd member should.

She narrowed her eyes. Something was approaching from the shimmering grassland, something brown and furred, but far smaller than a lion. It was a baboon, she realized; it padded purposefully toward the zebras, its tail held high.

A quiver of nervousness ran through her stomach. Baboons would not tackle a zebra, but they had certainly been known to kill young gazelles. Ears flickering, she drew back farther into the shelter of the herd; she would stay out of sight, but she could still keep an eye on the baboon.

The baboon halted on the edge of the group and rose onto its hind paws. It turned its head slowly, scanning the zebras.

"I'm looking for your herd leader." She was a female; her voice rang out clear and strong.

"That would be me." Mistfriend paced toward them through the parting herd, his head stretched out to examine the baboon. "What business do you have with us?"

"My name is Fig Highleaf." She sat back on her haunches. "I am an emissary for the Great Father himself."

There was muttering among the zebras, and neighs of curiosity and disbelief.

"Then you are welcome, Fig Highleaf," announced Mistfriend, with a glance at his herd to quieten them. "How is the Great Father's health?"

The baboon dipped her head. "Thank you; he is well. His body grows weaker, as it must, but his mind remains as sharp as ever. He is deeply concerned about some rumors that are spreading in Bravelands."

"Go on." Mistfriend twitched his ears.

Fig gazed around at the herd. "Great Father has received reports of strange happenings, things that go against the natural order of things in Bravelands."

Prance's hide bristled. *Could she mean me?*

"We've seen nothing like that," said Mistfriend. "Though a crocodile did take a lion just this morning, as we crossed the Gully River. That's something I've never seen before. The lion was overconfident and foolish, but the crocodile's nerve was unusual, especially with many zebras around. I love and respect my own kind, but we would be far more easily taken than a full-grown lion!"

"May I speak?" Prance crept forward on trembling hooves.

"Of course, Prancefriend." Mistfriend glanced down at her in surprise.

"I spoke to an elephant not long ago," she said. "I've always trusted the elephants. I don't think they tell tall stories."

Fig Highleaf nodded. "Great Father would wholeheartedly agree with you."

"This elephant, Boulder—he too said that the crocodiles were becoming more aggressive. Unusually so. And that would fit in with—with what happened in the river earlier."

"It would indeed," said Fig thoughtfully. "But tell me, Prance—why are you so far from your own herd? Which is it? Skippingherd?"

Prance swallowed hard, suddenly very self-conscious. Every zebra in the herd seemed to be waiting for her reply. And so was that wretched vulture. She could see it in the shadows of a lone acacia, its wings hunched and its black eyes as piercing as ever.

"I'll be heading back to my own kind soon," she said, forcing cheer into her voice. "I'm traveling with Mistfriendherd for now, that's all. I'm with Runningherd."

"Well, good luck to you, Prance Runningherd." The baboon grinned. "You clearly have an adventurous streak. The Great Father himself would approve."

Overcome by embarrassment, Prance could only nod and mutter her thanks and farewell, as the baboon dropped onto all fours and padded back the way she had come. Prance backed away, merging with the herd again. What had possessed her to speak up like that? All she'd done was pass on some gossip, elephant-given or not. It had probably been of little use, and Fig Highleaf was only being polite. *Do not draw attention to yourself, Prance!* Her own mother's words came back to her vividly. *Gazelles should not try to be special! Mortal danger finds the special ones first!*

Just as she thought it, a swift flash of black reared up from the long grass nearby. Prance started, with a sharp cry, and skittered back. It was a black mamba, and it ignored the zebras beside Prance, slithering swiftly straight toward her.

Prance wanted to pronk, to bound away and outrun the snake, but her legs seemed frozen to the spot. She could only stare as the lethal serpent shot toward her, lightning-fast.

A wild buffeting of broad wings, the crunch of powerful talons striking the ground, and the snake was suddenly whipped into the air, gripped in the vulture's claws. The bird flapped away gracefully, alighting on one of the acacia's lower branches. With a challenging look at Prance, it began to rip the snake apart with its savage beak.

Prance stared in disbelief as the vulture gulped down lumps of snake meat. Zebras were cantering toward her, shaking their heads and whinnying with concern.

"Are you all right, Prancefriend?"

"That was a close one!"

"That's twice today you've cheated death!"

And I've cheated it more often that you know, she thought with a sinking heart.

They were bustling around her, excited and breathless.

"You're a very lucky gazelle, Prancefriend!"

Yes, and I doubt I'm supposed to be lucky. That heavy feeling of dread in Prance's chest grew worse, and the sun's rays seemed dimmer and colder. *I'm still defying my fate and the Great Spirit.* This could not end well.

The crowd of zebras around her had grown quieter, and Dawnfriend gave a sudden bray of horror. "Look, Friends! Prancefriend has no shadow!"

Prance blinked, her heart clenching in horror. Tearing her attention away from the maddening vulture, she focused again on the zebras who surrounded her. She was alone in the center of them, and the sun hadn't faded at all; it hadn't even moved behind a cloud. It shone down fierce and bright on her, and the truth was painfully, horribly obvious.

"What kind of creature has no shadow?" gasped an old zebra behind her. "Is she cursed?"

"Curses come only from the Great Spirit," whispered a young mare.

Mistfriend was backing slowly away from Prance; even Grassfriend stared at her in shock.

"This is not right," neighed the leader. "Prance, you must explain yourself. Quickly!"

Prance's throat tightened. They'd stopped calling her *Prancefriend.*

But she needed her new herd. She had to convince them she had done nothing wrong, because only then would she be allowed to stay; she saw that in their keen, suspicious gazes. Even if she herself feared she had committed some great sin against Bravelands, she must tell the zebras the truth. They must decide for themselves if she was worthy of the Friendship.

She lowered her head, then raised it to gaze pleadingly at Mistfriend.

"There's something I haven't been honest about," she whispered, and cleared her throat. "A truth I need to tell you . . ."

CHAPTER SIXTEEN

"It's true, I tell you," whispered Bramble to Moonflower. He darted his eyes to left and right, afraid another gorilla might overhear. "A snake, I swear. Held in his hands, like this." Bramble raised his own arms. "And Burbark *let* it bite him."

He hadn't meant to tell anyone else. In fact, he'd convinced himself that he'd forget the sinister little scene in the forest, so long as he didn't talk about it. Instead, Bramble had found that *not* telling made it worse. The confusing images gnawed away inside his head, like a wasp larva in a soft fruit.

"You're the only one I've told," he added, giving Moonflower a beseeching look. "Please don't reveal it to the others."

She shook her head. "Don't worry, I won't. Because I'm sure you imagined it, Bramble. You were so very tired when you came back from your patrol. . . . Perhaps you ate the wrong flower, or a bad mushroom, and it made you see things?"

"I don't . . ." He frowned and hesitated, pursing his lips. "I don't *think* so. . . ."

"Burbark wouldn't pick up a snake," Moonflower reassured him. "Gorillas stay clear of snakes, you know that."

"Yes." He nodded slowly. "I know, but . . ."

"It could have been a branch," suggested Moonflower. "Honestly, the number of times I've almost jumped out of my skin, and then I've realized the green mamba that was after me was a new spring twig!"

A branch? Bramble summoned up his memory of the scene as best he could. *Burbark gripping the snake . . . it uncoiled from his arm . . . it rose and swayed in time . . .*

Then it struck.

"No," he said firmly. "I'm sure of what I saw. It was definitely a snake."

She stared at him for a long time, her amber eyes burning into his. At last, Moonflower gave a resigned sigh.

"All right, then. But there has to be a rational explanation. Burbark wouldn't do that for *fun*. He's far too responsible a Silverback." She scratched thoughtfully beneath her arm. "Though I've no idea what might explain it."

"Well, quite." Winning the debate didn't give Bramble any pleasure at all.

"I'll tell you what." Moonflower creased her brow in thought. "I have noticed a few odd things about Burbark myself. Just recently, I mean."

"Such as?" he asked with trepidation.

"Nothing specific, really." She twisted her mouth. "He's

just got into a habit of muttering away with particular gorillas. Some of the Goldbacks, and a certain group of Blackbacks—not my favorite ones, either. Woodnettle, Pear, that arrogant crowd. He never used to approve of those kind of little gangs."

"He's certainly been very quiet. Sort of withdrawn."

"Of course he's feeling low," said Moonflower. "With . . . well, with Cassava and everything. And that awful confusion and argument about the Spirit Mouth prophecy."

Cassava's death didn't seem to bother him as much as it should have, Bramble wanted to say, but he clamped his jaws firmly shut. "Maybe," he muttered, and bit his lip. He scratched at it with a fingernail, then rubbed at his arm. His whole skin seemed to be prickling all of a sudden.

"And what are you two whispering about?" Groundnut shambled into the clearing and slumped back against a tree trunk, scratching at his chest. The old gorilla looked perfectly relaxed, but his eyes glittered with curiosity.

"Nothing." Bramble began to shake his head, then hesitated. He glanced keenly at Groundnut. He could be grumpy, but he was the most senior of all the Blackbacks, and Bramble trusted the forthright old gorilla.

"I . . . I saw something happen in the troop. Something very strange," he ventured as Moonflower gave him a surprised look.

Groundnut's gaze was kind, curious, open. "Tell me what you saw, then."

Bramble bit his lip. But the decision was already made, he told himself; he'd confessed that he'd seen something.

Taking a deep breath, Bramble composed his thoughts. Then, patiently—and choosing his words far more carefully than he had with Moonflower—Bramble described once again the extraordinary scene in the forest.

Groundnut would want nothing more than the bare facts, Bramble knew. He must do his best to sound dispassionate and rational; he *must* convince this wise elder, because there was no one else he could turn to for advice.

". . . So then Burbark lifted the snake—like this—and swayed. It swayed with him. That was when he let it bite him. Right here, on his wrist." Bramble pointed.

Groundnut lifted an arm sharply to silence him. His gaze was very steady, and his jaw moved slightly, as if he was actually chewing over his words. Bramble held his breath.

"All right, Bramble. Listen: it was just a snakebite. Those little serpents can't kill a gorilla."

"But he let it—"

"You see here? I've been bitten." Groundnut held out his arm and turned his wrist upward so that Bramble and Moonflower could see. On a raw patch of skin were two neat, scabbed-over puncture marks.

Bramble felt the shock like a punch in his gut. Groundnut's wound was in exactly the same spot as his father's.

His throat felt choked with dismay, but Groundnut only shrugged. "A bite is a daily risk when you rummage in the bushes. No harm done."

"But—" Bramble began again; then he fell silent. Groundnut's gaze was still level and intense . . . almost too intense.

Around his dark brown eyes a thin circle of white gleamed, and something burned deep in his pupils. It gave the big gorilla an almost crazed look.

Bramble heard Moonflower draw in a hissing breath. Surreptitiously, she touched Bramble's elbow, then squeezed it. It felt like a warning.

"Burbark is a good leader," said Groundnut after a moment. "A fine leader, and I hope you are both proud to be his offspring."

"Of course," said Moonflower meekly.

"You mustn't question the Silverback's judgment like this," Groundnut scolded. "We are all lucky to have him."

"Yes," rasped Bramble. His throat felt tight with the beginnings of anger at the old gorilla.

"So tell me." Groundnut relaxed back against the trunk again, scratching at his belly. "Did you see anything interesting when you went out scouting, young Bramble?"

"Not much." Bramble shrugged, giving Groundnut a guarded look. "There was some jealousy among the Goldbacks of the other troop. And the Silverback seems to have a favorite infant." He searched his memory, dragging up and relating all the other details he had already told to Burbark. "That's it, really. Why do you need to know?"

Groundnut rose to his feet with a dismissive grunt. "Thank you, Bramble. Interesting indeed." Without another word, he shambled off into the shadows of the forest.

"Now that," said Moonflower, staring after him, "was *really* odd."

* * *

Perhaps it was only that he was paying more attention, but in the following days Bramble realized that the oddness in the troop was not confined to Burbark and Groundnut. Everywhere he looked, he seemed to see a gorilla with a snakebite on their wrist. Why had he never noticed? Had he really been so careless and happy-go-lucky that he hadn't used his eyes?

Apple. Bindweed. Woodnettle and Pear. Spiderwort and Mallow. All of them bore more or less fresh wounds on their arms and wrists. Were they really letting the snakes bite them? What kind of weird craze was affecting the troop?

Bramble was certain that the other gorillas were avoiding him much more than usual. They would eye him as he approached, fall silent, and shamble away. He'd wake in the night and hear muttering among small groups, but if Bramble made a sound to show he was awake, they would glance sharply in his direction, then roll over and go back to sleep. *Or pretend to . . .*

Bramble found he didn't want to think about it too hard, because the madness of it made his head spin. Despite his new status as favored son, he did his best to avoid Burbark and spent most of his time in Moonflower's company. At least she wasn't involved in this snakebite nonsense—and of that he could be sure, because each of them checked the other's wrist every single day. It had become their secret greeting, thought Bramble sadly—the thing that separated them from their own troop.

"Don't ever be tempted to join them, will you?" Moonflower

begged him again as they shambled through a heavy fringe of vines one cool afternoon. "Even if you're unbearably curious."

"I was going to say the same to you," admitted Bramble, swinging himself down over a mossy rock. "Why in the endless forest are they doing it? That's what I don't understand."

"It must hurt," agreed Moonflower, "and snake venom can make you so sick!"

Bramble shuddered. "There's no chance I'm letting a snake bite me for fun, that's for sure."

Moonflower jumped down to his side. "Well, don't let it happen by accident, either." She pointed into the dense foliage close to his head.

Bramble turned. A slender snake was coiled around a narrow branch, gazing at them with huge black eyes. Its scales were bright green, rimmed with black.

Bramble eyed it warily. He'd have expected it to dart away, but it stayed where it was, its head swaying slightly from side to side. It seemed to find the two young gorillas of immense interest.

"I'm sure that's the one that bit my father," he murmured. "Or one just like it."

"Boomslangs aren't uncommon." Moonflower shrugged. "But don't get too close. That one doesn't look timid at all."

As they watched, the snake coiled around on itself. Strangely, it still seemed to watch them as it retreated along the branch. It paused, twisted its head to gaze at them directly, then slithered into the shadows.

"It seemed like it was taunting us, don't you think?"

Moonflower scratched at her lip.

"I'm going to follow it," announced Bramble, clenching his fists against the forest litter. He loped forward. "Come on."

"Don't get too close," called Moonflower as she bounded after him.

Bramble's heart beat hard as he scrambled over rocks and through brush after the snake. It moved quickly, yet he couldn't shake the feeling it was enticing him on. He could have sworn it cast him sly glances now and again.

Clambering down a short blade of rock and letting himself drop to the soft ground beneath, Bramble turned and stared. Where had the snake gone? Moonflower jumped down beside him and pointed across the small open glade.

"There," she whispered.

"I see it." Bramble didn't know why they were suddenly speaking in hushed voices, but there was something unsettling about the glade. The sky, unobscured by dense treetops, was a brilliant, glaring noonday white. Beyond a tangle of dry grasses and shrubs, and a few skeletal trees, lay another stumpy rockface. One of its slabs was cracked into a long, jagged slit that broadened toward the ground. The boomslang was right next to that crack in the rock. It gave them a last, cold glance, then vanished into the darkness.

"It's a cave," murmured Moonflower.

Bramble was about to bound after the snake when she grabbed his arm. "Wait! Be careful."

He jerked back. Another snake, a yellow one, rippled

through the parched grass at his toes, following the booms-lang into the crack in the rock. No sooner had it disappeared than Moonflower gave a sharp cry and yanked Bramble back even more violently.

Another boomslang dropped from a spindly branch above them, hitting the ground right where Bramble had stood. It gave them a glare before flicking away into the cave with the others.

"Not just snakes," whispered Moonflower, pointing at a pair of agama lizards that hopped and darted over the rocks toward the slit. "It seems to be a gathering place for Sandtongue-speakers."

"I think we could just about fit through that gap," growled Bramble, shutting one eye to examine the cave mouth.

"I don't care if we could. We definitely *shouldn't*." Moonflower backed away a few paces, fists dug firmly onto the dry ground.

Bramble nodded. "Yes. You're right." He felt a shiver ripple through his fur. "Let's go back to the troop. We've seen enough for now."

"I'm not sure I ever want to see more than that," remarked Moonflower, gesturing over her shoulder. "I hate to think what it's like in that cavern. Full of lizards and snakes, by the look of things."

The two young gorillas scrambled back up the lichen-draped rocks and made their way once more toward the green heart of the forest. Bramble realized that the closer they came to the troop, the slower their progress became. It was as if, he thought, he and Moonflower were only really comfortable in each other's company.

But that's silly. Our troop is our family. Yes, some silly snakebite-madness had swept through the gorillas, but the fad would pass as quickly as it had appeared.

Dark shapes loomed through the shadows—familiar gorillas were feeding and grooming, stripping the dry sheaths from bamboo or padding idly from one tree to tug fruit from the next. All was calm and normal, thought Bramble with relief.

"Bramble Brightback!"

He started and turned as his name was called. Apple Goldback was lumbering toward him, but then she sat back on her haunches and sucked at a shoot of bamboo. "Bramble, your father was looking for you. Where have you been?"

"Just wandering," he muttered.

"Well, you've wandered enough. Moonflower! Come help me groom my back. . . ."

Bramble left the reluctant Moonflower picking at a spot between Apple's shoulder blades; the Goldback stretched blissfully and closed her eyes. There was an opportunity now, Bramble knew, to dart away and get pleasantly lost in the forest on his own. . . .

No. He was the Brightback, and he couldn't ignore a summons from Burbark. *I have responsibilities now.* Bramble sighed deeply and padded off to find his father.

Burbark wasn't far away, but he wasn't alone. On either

side of him were Spiderwort and Groundnut, glaring at each other and punching the ground. Huffing and grunting, they hopped and fidgeted and scratched at their wrists. As Bramble drew closer, he realized both Blackbacks had been fighting—probably with each other, he thought disapprovingly. Spiderwort had a nasty cut over his left eye, and the socket was swollen; it gave him an even more sullen and brooding look than normal. Groundnut was favoring one hand as he thumped the ground, and Bramble saw that one of his gnarled fingers was angled badly, most likely broken. Yet even as Bramble watched, Groundnut reared back onto his legs and hammered at his chest, as if that fractured finger barely bothered him at all. Spiderwort mimicked him, pounding his own slabs of chest muscle.

As he edged warily into the glade, Bramble caught his father's eye. Burbark perked up and clapped his huge hands together.

"You two. Leave us!" he grunted.

Without so much as a huff of objection, Spiderwort and Groundnut dropped forward onto their fists and lurched off into the trees. Bewildered, Bramble stared after them.

"Well, my son! My Brightback!" Burbark slapped his hands together again. "What have you been up to? Seen anything . . . of interest?"

Bramble hesitated. There was something about the gleam in his father's eyes that set the hairs prickling on the back of his neck. Suddenly, he was sure of something.

The snake ceremony. He knows I saw it. Groundnut must have told him.

He swallowed hard. Too cheerfully, he said, "Nothing much today, Father."

Burbark's eyes narrowed. "Mmph."

Bramble could not go on meeting his father's gaze; he averted his eyes, staring at the ground. Around Burbark's feet were scattered frail things that looked like long, skeletal leaves, pale brown and wizened. Bramble couldn't help frowning in puzzlement.

Abruptly the big Silverback's eyes widened. "Oh, these!"

He snatched up one of the fragile leaves; Bramble saw that it was curled, nearly translucent, and patterned with a delicate lattice.

He sucked in a breath. Of course they weren't leaves; they were the discarded skins of snakes. He'd never seen so many in one place.

Burbark closed his eyes. He carefully stroked his own cheek with the desiccated snakeskin, then rubbed harder. He wore a blissful expression as he blinked his eyes open and offered the crumpled snakeskin to Bramble.

"A gift for my heir." He smiled, his eyes distant.

Bramble knew he couldn't reject it. Stifling a shudder, he reached for the dangling thing. His father hooked it ceremonially over his fingers; Bramble forced them not to tremble.

He peered down at the hideous skin. It must be his imagination, but its feathery touch was as cold as a mountain stream: one that had never seen the sunlight.

"Thank you, Father," he said hoarsely.

Burbark nodded and sat back, smiling in satisfaction. "You may go now."

Bramble backed away. At the edge of the glade he turned his back on his father and padded deep into the trees. Finding a thick tree stump, he clambered onto it; the canopy was thin at this spot, and it was a good place to bask in the sun.

And I need to feel the warmth. Bramble stared at the snakeskin; he could swear it had tangled itself more tightly around his fingers. Despite the sunlight, a clammy coldness spread through his body from its touch.

Bramble flung it aside. It was swallowed up by the long grass, but he imagined it hissed out a breath, a slithering rasp.

Father won't know, he told himself. *And I don't want that thing anywhere near me.*

Or, he thought, anything like it. *Ever again.*

CHAPTER SEVENTEEN

Range was a wonderful storyteller: Chase had to admit it to herself. Her ears couldn't help but flick toward him as he entertained Seek, who sat enthralled between his paws. The little one's eyes were wide and bright, and he looked not the slightest bit intimidated by the huge adult leopard looming over him. Range's deep rumbling growl sounded soothing to Chase's ears, but Seek didn't look remotely sleepy.

"So there I was," growled Range, "my claws hooked into this huge wildebeest's rump, but I couldn't bring him down. And I certainly wasn't going to let him go. *Wait till I shake you off, cat,* he said. *I'll show you sharp, when you're on the end of my horns!*"

Seek gasped. "I didn't know grass-eaters would dare talk to us like that!"

"This one certainly did. And he was a big one, Seek, so I took him seriously. I went bouncing along, clinging to his rump, while he bucked and twisted and swung his head at me. And there we might still have been, both of us hopping and springing across the savannah, if he hadn't tried to whack me hard against a tree. I saw it was coming, and that was the moment I picked to let go. Great Spirit, did I jump up and run fast!"

Seek shut one eye, wrinkling his muzzle. "You got beaten by a *wildebeest?*"

"I got beaten by a noble Bravelands creature who was bigger and more determined than I was." Range gave a roar of laughter. "Every leopard should know when to swallow his pride, little one."

Chase couldn't help but be amused and choked back a laugh of her own. Range was charming and fun to be with, but she had to remember what Prowl had told her, about a strange leopard encroaching on other territories. *Trust only yourself, Chase. . . .*

"Where is your territory, Range?" she asked suddenly. "Why have you left it?"

He swung his head toward her, his blue eyes keen and appraising. "Left it? I haven't. I simply don't consider myself *bound* by it. I am Range Born of Sprint, and I go where I please."

Chase flattened her ears. "And roam freely on others' land?"

He hunched his shoulders. "It's not as if I want to take it. My own territory is large and fine."

Seek jumped up and spun in an excited circle. "Aren't you

worried another leopard will move in? While you're gone?"

"Is that what you're planning, cub?" Range batted Seek's ears with a paw. "I'd better be careful."

"No, I won't! I wouldn't!" Seek stopped spinning, to gaze earnestly up at Range. "I was thinking about Shadow."

Range huffed another laugh. "Shadow doesn't worry me, youngster. I think you'd be a bigger threat than he is!"

Seek giggled in delight as Range rolled him onto his back, but Chase stared thoughtfully at Range. *He's absolutely right*, she thought. *Range is far more imposing than Shadow. He's got nothing to fear from him.*

As if he felt her gaze, Range turned to her, his ears twitching forward. "You should come and live in my territory, Chase Born of Prowl. I could protect you better there. Stay with me, and you will never regret it."

Chase sucked in a breath, silenced for a moment by the blatant request. *He wants me for his mate. If not immediately, then once I move to be under his protection.*

The thought was hugely tempting. He was right: few creatures would dare to threaten Chase if she lived as Range's mate. *I would be safe, for a long time. But Seek?*

She shook her head slowly. "I cannot leave Seek. Not yet, Range."

The big leopard raised his brow. "I would do this cub no harm," he murmured. He bent to lick the top of Seek's head. "I agree it's neither normal nor traditional, but I would be willing to treat Seek as my own family, until he's grown and independent."

"And I could help!" Seek butted in eagerly. "I could hunt too. I'd earn my keep, I promise!"

Chase could feel herself yearning, her muscles tightening as she leaned almost imperceptibly toward Range. *Strength and protection, and our bellies would never be empty. . . .*

But something within her resisted. Perhaps it was no more than her natural suspicion. "Let me think about it," she heard herself say. "It's a lot to consider."

Range inclined his head in acceptance. "That's reasonable, Chase, and wise. I had a great deal of respect for your mother Prowl, you know. And you take after her in many ways."

The tension flowed out of Chase's body, and she sagged a little in relief. She hadn't realized just how anxious she had been about his response. But Range looked as relaxed and friendly as ever, jumping to his paws and beckoning Seek with a jerk of his head.

"Let's hunt," he suggested. "All of us."

"Yay!" exclaimed Seek.

"I caught the scent of a dik-dik earlier," said Chase, glad of the change of subject. "In the brush to the west."

"Then let's find it!" Range nuzzled her affectionately, and her whiskers tingled at his touch.

"I'll show you," she said quickly, turning and trotting toward the dense undergrowth.

The scent was only a little stale, and as the three leopards padded in its trail, it grew stronger. Chase halted, flaring her nostrils, and changed direction slightly; Range nudged Seek and followed her. They moved quietly and steadily through the brush, halting often to test the air, to peer keenly into the dense foliage.

Chase did not hold out much hope of finding the dik-dik now, despite the newer scents, but she was glad of the distraction of the hunt. And she couldn't help enjoying Range's company, though she had always hunted alone. The big leopard didn't interfere, he didn't offer unwanted advice, and he let her take the lead.

"You're good at this," he murmured as they walked abreast along a broad gully. "Tracking, I mean. I'd have lost that scent many times by now."

His flattery warmed Chase, despite her reservations. "My mother taught me well."

"It's no more than I'd have expected from Prowl." Halting for a moment, Range sniffed the air. "I think there are bongos nearby too. Shall I scout from that ridge?"

The fact that he asked her permission gave Chase a flush of pleasure. "Good idea," she said. "Then we'll have another option, if we can't find the dik-dik."

Range nodded and turned to spring up the side of the gully. Lithe and quick despite his size, he vanished instantly in the shadows.

Seek nudged Chase's forepaw. "You like him," he said mischievously. "Don't you, Chase? *Don't you?*"

She gave a low, irritated growl. "No, I don't. He's a good hunter, that's all."

"Yes, you do. You do like him!" Seek gave a giggling growl. The cub was right, though Chase had no intention of admitting it. *I do like Range. He'd make a fine and protective mate, and our cubs would be strong and healthy.*

So what was holding her back? For a moment she imagined her mother at her shoulder, offering her wise counsel in that familiar low rumble.

Caution, Chase. Always caution. Trust no one but yourself. . . .

Chase shook her ears, almost angry. Didn't she deserve an easier life? She hadn't expected to be orphaned now, or to care for a cub before she'd even had a litter of her own. *You're gone now, Mother, and I have to live on in this world. You're not here anymore to protect us.*

Maybe caution was not as important as security. Yes, thought Chase; she *should* accept Range's offer. Any female leopard would be grateful to have such a fine mate. And how many males would tolerate another's cub? Range didn't just put up with Seek—he actually *liked* him.

I will accept his offer. I will!

"Whoa!" Seek exclaimed, his ears pricking forward. He pounced on something just ahead of Chase.

She had been too preoccupied to notice the lizard, but Seek now had it pinned firmly beneath his paw. It was pale brown and skinny, and it wriggled in terror.

Seek batted at its tail with his free paw. "Look, Chase! I caught it!"

"Yes, you did," she told him proudly. He was still teasing it, half lifting his paw from the trapped lizard, only to slam it back down. "You're a hunter."

"Not a proper hunter," came an angry growl. Range was

back, leaping down the gully slope. "Let it go!"

"But I—" Seek flinched beneath Range's angry blue stare. "I caught it by myself and—"

"And you're playing with it," snarled Range. "If you're hungry, kill what you catch. Let it go right now! You don't deserve to eat it."

Chase stared at Range, stunned, but he was still glaring at Seek.

"Let it go!"

"Why should he?" demanded Chase, moving in front of Seek and lashing her tail in anger. "It was his prey. He caught it fairly!" She bared her fangs.

"Yes," growled Range, "and if that had been a bushbuck or a wildebeest, he would not have had the chance to toy with it. It would be gone, and he'd starve, and all because of a silly game." He turned on Seek again. "It's a lesson you must learn, cub!"

Looking chastened, Seek released the lizard. It skittered into the nearest tumble of rocks and vanished.

"I guess Range is right," whispered Chase to Seek, as Range turned and stalked away. "But you did well to catch it. You really did."

"I know." There was an edge of resentment in the cub's voice, and he glowered at Range's retreating tail and haunches.

"You'll catch another, and next time you'll get to eat it, I promise." Chase licked Seek's ear, but he looked surly as the two of them padded after Range.

Much of the fun had gone out of their hunt, but the night

had barely begun, and after all, Chase thought, they did not seek prey for fun. That must have been what Range was trying to teach Seek, but she couldn't help feeling sorry for the cub. Now Seek trailed a little behind Chase as Range forged ahead.

The large male halted suddenly, the black tip of his tail twitching. Cautiously, Chase slunk abreast of him and followed his gaze down into the shallow ravine ahead. Starlight picked out huge, broad-shouldered shapes that plodded through the grass and rocks of the ravine floor, their fists thudding into the ground as they advanced up the mountain. Their movement was slow and steady, but every high-domed head was raised and alert as they scanned the gully around them for threats.

"Gorillas." Chase's hackles sprang up. "Why are they moving in the dark?"

Range shook his head in perplexity. "They should be in their nests," he murmured.

Chase's hide prickled all over. Already she mistrusted gorillas, and these could be the very ones that had desecrated her mother's body. She glared down, narrowing her eyes, searching for recognizable features: hard black eyes, a scarred nose, a bare patch of hide . . .

She could see little at this distance, and her tail-tip flicked in agitation. It wasn't natural for gorillas to travel at night, so they must be up to something.

Cautiously, Range placed his paws on the slope and slunk a little way down. Chase turned to Seek with a whispered "Wait here," then followed Range, her body low to the ground.

The night was very still, but for the chirruping of crickets and the rasp of cicadas; Chase could soon make out the low, rumbling conversation of the gorilla troop. She halted, her ears twitching, and ahead of her Range glanced back and stopped too. Both leopards lowered themselves even flatter against the grass. They were close to the troop now, and they'd have to be careful.

The leading gorilla stopped, snuffling the air. He scowled, scratched his chest, then moved on.

"It's nothing," he muttered to the nearest female. "Cats hunting. They won't bother us."

"So long as it isn't that other troop." The female paused, touching the baby that was nestled against her stomach. "I don't know what made them so hostile, but I don't want to run into them again."

"It was bizarre behavior," grunted the male. He halted and sat on his haunches, looking back the way he'd come. That was when Chase noticed some of his troop were lagging behind. Two young males were limping badly and had to be assisted by other gorillas.

These were not the gorillas that had desecrated Prowl's body, Chase realized. But they had clearly been involved in a bitter fight not long ago. It was quite possible these gorillas had had the misfortune to come across that other, aggressive troop. . . .

The Silverback leader waited for the laggards to catch up a little, then moved on again. "We'll be safe higher up the mountain," he rumbled. "Out of harm's way, till that lot come to their senses. We'll fight them again if we have to, but I'm not going to go looking for trouble."

The gorillas' voices faded as they progressed on up the shallow valley. Chase and Range exchanged a look.

"What do you suppose that was about?" murmured Chase.

"Sounds as if they've had a squabble with another troop," said Range with a flick of his head.

Chase nodded. "The mountains are changing, I think. But the fewer gorillas in our part of the forest, the better I like it." After what happened to her mother, she'd be happy never to see another gorilla in her life.

"I could not agree more," agreed Range with a growl. "Let's go back and get Seek, and keep moving. And we'll steer clear of any more gorillas, I promise."

The sound of water began as a distant, rushing whisper, but by the time Range led them across a series of ragged gullies, the noise had grown to a thunder. Chase and Seek halted beside Range, staring up at the waterfall that crashed down into a river below. The cliffs looked precipitous, and the torrent raged far too wildly to cross.

"Where do we go from here?" Chase had to raise her voice to be heard, and she laid her ears back in discomfort. The pool at the foot of the waterfall was a turmoil of white water and fountains of spray, glowing in the light of the stars; from here, the river flowed on steeply down the hillside through savage-looking rocks and swirling eddies of foam.

"I'll show you," declared Range loudly. "This is one of my dens, and it's a good place to hide, Chase. If you ever need to."

She started. "It is?"

"Watch." Range twisted and leaped down from the boulder where he stood.

Chase gave a gasp. From her vantage point, it seemed he had sprung directly into the raging torrent. But when she leaned forward, trembling, and peered down, she saw Range gazing back up at her, his whiskers twitching with amusement. He stood safely on a wide slab of glistening black rock, and his fur sparkled with droplets of spray.

"Jump," he called. "You can't miss."

Her heart rose in her throat. "But—"

"Jump," he called again. "And follow me!" With that, he turned and bounded straight toward the waterfall.

Seek gave a squeal of shock and fear. Chase's fur stood up straight all over her body. She expected to see Range's body tumble in the crash of water and plunge into the pool below. Instead, he vanished completely; the last she saw of him was a cocky flick of his black-tipped tail.

Chase swallowed hard. Surely Range would not have jumped if there had been any true danger? Yet the prospect of making the leap herself was terrifying.

Life is terrifying. Much of the time, at least. We've never been safe. Neither Prowl and I, nor I and Seek.

She tilted her head, her ears twitching as she stared at the spot where Range had vanished. The blue-eyed leopard had jumped with such confidence. He had offered them security, a refuge. How relaxing it would be to be safe, if only for a little while. . . .

Chase bent her head down to Seek, her heart beating hard.

"I'm going to go after him. I'll tell you if it's safe."

"But Chase—" The cub's eyes were wide with terror.

"I must." She licked his nose gently. "If I don't return for you, run to the forest. Hide somewhere. Catch lizards, like you did so well just now! Grow strong, and big."

Seek's little whiskers trembled. He pressed his cheek to hers. "Please don't leave me," he whispered.

Inside her chest, Chase's heart wrenched. Could Seek survive a third bereavement?

Probably not. But this was her chance to find a safe place for both of them. *I have to take the risk.*

"I'll come back for you, Seek." She drew away, gazing into his frightened eyes. *"I promise."*

She had to jump now, or she never would. Twisting around, she took a breath and leaped.

Cold spray stung her eyes, and she felt for a moment as if she would fall forever. Then her paws thudded hard onto the flat slab, and her legs shuddered as they absorbed the impact. Chase stood up straight.

She stared at the vertical cascade, her tail lashing. Above and a little behind her, she could see Seek, leaning over the edge and blinking down. She could not hesitate for a moment longer. Chase gave the cub a reassuring nod and sprang toward the waterfall.

She still half expected the water to crash against her like

falling boulders, to drive her down into the foaming pool to her death; instead there was only the cold shock of light spray along her spine. She hurtled into wet, cool darkness, somersaulted forward, and skidded to a halt on her flank. For long moments she could only lie there, flanks heaving as she gasped in shock.

In the darkness, she felt Range's breath on her cheek, then his quick tongue.

"See? I said you could trust me."

Chase rolled over and staggered to her paws. Her breath was still harsh and fitful as she blinked around the blackness of the hidden cavern.

"It's an illusion, see?" Range's voice held fond amusement. "You have to jump through at the right spot, though. The falls are thin right there. Anywhere else and you'd be swept to your"—his voice lowered to a dramatic growl—"your watery doom."

Chase shook herself, sending droplets splashing all over him. There was a faint silvery glow here after all, from the spray of the falls, and her eyes were adjusting.

"And now you'll have to be patient for a moment," she told Range. She swung around haughtily, just to prove he hadn't scared her *too* much, and padded back toward the cavern mouth and the waterfall that shielded it. "I'll fetch Seek. Before the poor cub really does think I'm dead and runs away to the forest."

Despite the frightening jump to the wet slab, and the even more terrifying leap through the deceptively thin veil of water,

Seek hung limp and obedient in her jaws. It seemed to Chase that he had been so afraid after being left alone on the ridge, he was now willing to go with her anywhere, simply to keep her at his side. When she set him down within the cavern, he jumped quickly to his paws and glanced around, sniffing. It seemed his dignity was more or less intact, Chase thought with inner pride.

There was a scuffing, dragging noise from farther back in the cavern, and Range emerged from the deepest shadows there. He was tugging a carcass—some kind of antelope, Chase reckoned, though it was half-eaten already. All that was identifiable were its haunches, and she knew she'd never seen such an animal before.

"That looks good." She licked her chops, feeling hunger growl in her stomach. "I'd almost forgotten how long it's been since the bushpig."

"My goat is yours to share." Range dropped the prey at her paws. It reeked deliciously.

"A goat-antelope? Is that what it is? Thank you." She nudged Range's cheek gently, before tearing a strip of meat from the carcass. "Come on, Seek; you must be hungry."

She glanced back at the cub. He seemed hesitant and unusually quiet, though he couldn't help approaching the prey on trembling paws. He settled down at her side and pulled at a tatter of flesh on the rib cage.

"It smells strange in here," he muttered through his mouthful of food. "I don't think I like it, Chase."

The poor cub—he must still be smarting from Range's

scolding earlier. It might take Seek a long time to forget and forgive; he was only a baby, after all. Chase bent her head to him.

"The food is good, and we're safe. That's all we can ask for in a refuge, Seek. Don't be afraid." She licked his ears lovingly.

"Eat and sleep, little cousin. I won't let anything bad happen to you."

CHAPTER EIGHTEEN

"Well, I don't understand gazelles one bit," neighed Grassfriend. He stamped his hoof crossly. "You survived a lion attack, Prancefriend! Your herd should have welcomed you back as . . . as a hero! That kind of luck—and skill—why, it means good fortune for a whole herd!"

"I agree," whinnied Dawnfriend, tossing his head. "And they *really* won't take you back?"

"They won't." Prance sighed, her head sagging from the effort of telling her story all over again. "I do understand, you know. It is the way of the gazelles."

"To reject you, when the Great Spirit has smiled on you like that?" Grassfriend snorted. "The gazelles' way is *silly.*"

Prance didn't bristle at the insult to her kind. All she could feel was warm gratitude for her new friends' understanding and sympathy. The herd surrounded her in a dense circle of black and white, their ears pricked forward in excitement at her story. Now that the tale was told, the zebras murmured and exclaimed among themselves, retelling the best parts for herd-friends who hadn't quite managed to hear.

"Have you ever heard the like?"

"So that's why she has no shadow! What a story."

"What was the bit about the lion?"

"If you'd *paid attention*, Stonefriend—"

"Well, I'm listening now! Tell me again, because that gazelle had a *very* soft voice."

Relief washed through Prance. *I really shouldn't have worried. The zebras are kind. They accept that I don't have a shadow, that I can't help it, that it wasn't my choice. . . .*

Or rather, most of them did. As the zebras dispersed, ripping casually at the grass, Prance's large ears caught other, less sympathetic voices among the chattering throng.

"How long do you think that gazelle will stay with us?" she heard an old mare murmur.

"Not too long, I hope," replied her companion. "Have you noticed that vulture who follows her around?" The zebra shook his neck.

"I've seen that," put in a third, younger mare. "It doesn't behave like a normal vulture, does it? But it seems sure that Prancefriend is headed for death."

"It's *very* unnerving," declared the first, with a toss of her mane.

Prance backed away out of earshot and moved closer to Grassfriend and Dawnfriend to walk beside them. *Most of the zebras accept me*, she told herself firmly. *I could never have expected all of them to be delighted. . . .*

The herd was moving at a leisurely pace across the grassland, heading for the shimmer of a watering hole in the distance. The lakes and rivers had gradually shrunk over the last moon, and Mistfriend seemed even keener than usual to keep moving. The constant search for sweet grass grew ever more challenging as the dry season progressed. The zebras raised clouds of yellow dust as they followed their old Grass Trek ways. Alongside them walked herds of antelopes and wildebeests, and always, at the margins, predators lurked hopefully in the longer grass.

Prance could not see far ahead, her vision obstructed by the dust and by the masses of striped rumps. But she became aware that they were moving downhill now, into a long and shallow depression in the plain. There were marks and swirls and ridges that showed it had once held water, and not so long ago. Prance recognized the signs of a former lake bed, and as always, she found herself yearning for the return of the rains. But how could it be so dry already? The Gully River had been full and fast, and that had been barely days ago. She frowned in confusion.

"What by all the plains' grass—" exclaimed a zebra a few lengths ahead of her.

A curious murmuring and neighing rose around Prance. She realized she had moved closer to the front of the herd as they traveled. There were only a few ranks of zebras ahead of her now, and she could see Mistfriend at the head of the horde. He was sidling past something on the ground, his ears laid back and his lip flared back from his teeth in an expression of disgust.

In moments, Prance saw what had caused the excitement. There, at the lowest point of the dip in the grassland, lay the skeletal remains of four hippos, three adults and what might have been a yearling. The carcasses were picked almost clean; only a few scraps of fly-blown rot-flesh remained, and tatters of leathery skin stretched over the bones.

"Well, that's unusual," remarked Dawnfriend, wrinkling her muzzle. "Hippos that died of thirst? It's not as if all the lakes are gone. Why didn't they go find new water when this one dried up?"

"Maybe a predator killed them." Grassfriend tilted his head in curiosity.

"Four hippos? Don't be silly," neighed Dawnfriend. "Though there's a lake right on the horizon, so dying from lack of water doesn't make sense either."

"Maybe they were lazy," suggested Grassfriend. "Though if they were waiting for rain here, they were idiots. It looks as if this lake's been dry all year."

Prance shivered. There was something sinister about these remains, so far from where hippos should be. "They might have had no choice. Maybe there are crocodiles that wouldn't let them share another lake?"

"Crocodiles can't make hippos do *anything*," sniffed Dawnfriend.

"It's a mystery, all right," said Grassfriend. "Let's see if we can solve it, Dawnfriend...."

The two zebras walked on, already arguing over new and fantastic theories about the hippos' fate. Trailing after them, Prance realized it was the sun debate all over again, with a new and thrilling subject.

But she couldn't bring herself to listen closely. She glanced back over her shoulder at the rest of the herd. Zebras were skirting the hippo remains with expressions of distaste, but as the dust clouds rose and thickened, the corpses were swiftly hidden from Prance's vision.

She was glad. The carcasses had been more than unsettling. How could four hippos have died like that, stranded in a dried-up lake? One hippo alone was an intimidating enough target for even the largest predator. How could four—three of them adults—have met their deaths together here?

Prance found herself thinking about the Us, and of how it had left her—without apparent reason, since she had not died. She remembered how the zebras' Friendship had seemed to fray and fracture during the lions' attack at the Gully River; Breezefriend had been unable to locate her mother for a long time. Perhaps the hippos had their own version of the Us and the Friendship? It could be that it, too, had been knocked out of balance by some strange affliction. Maybe that was what had led these four hippos so badly astray.

Prance picked up her feet and trotted more quickly, almost without meaning to. It seemed to be an instinctive desire to move as far and fast as she could from the hippo carcasses. So she was near the front of the herd when her big eyes picked out a line of golden bodies trekking to the southeast, in the same direction as the zebra herd.

"Gazelles," remarked a zebra close to her. When she turned to him, she recognized Mistfriend; she was right at the front of the herd now. "I hope those hyenas in the scrub decide to go for one of them, and not us. You see the big brutes, between the two lines of acacias? They think they're being surreptitious." He whinnied in amusement.

Prance swallowed hard. She couldn't help hoping the same—every creature hoped another would be the chosen victim—but she felt a twinge of guilt too, because she recognized those gazelles. *Runningherd.*

And now another fear began to creep through her. If the gazelles and the zebras came abreast of one another, if the animals on the outer edges began to mingle, one of the zebras might talk about the strange, shadowless gazelle who traveled with them. Might? No, they definitely would: Prance already knew how the zebras loved to gossip and trade news. The gazelles of Runningherd might even spot her without being told. *And if Runningherd start to chatter and spin stories, they're bound to turn more of the zebras against me. They'll tell the zebras I'm dangerous, that the loss of a shadow is a terrible thing!*

Prance came to an abrupt halt, and Mistfriend glanced at her quizzically. "What is it?"

"Cheetahs," she blurted. Her blood ran hot with shame and guilt, but it was the only way she could think to turn the zebras aside before they merged with Runningherd. "They're lying in wait below that kopje, and if we keep going this way, they'll intercept us."

"I've always admired gazelle eyes," said Mistfriend. "Well spotted, Prancefriend!" He spun around and whinnied, "East! East and south."

Almost as one, following their leader and the subtler urging of the Friendship, the zebra herd swung slowly, steadily toward the southeast. Glancing over her shoulder and down the long slope behind her, Prance could see the angle of the dust cloud change as the herd turned. Despite her guilt at her lie, she was glad. Now Mistfriendherd would not come into contact with Runningherd, and her new allies would not be turned against her.

At least, not immediately. Inwardly Prance sighed. She could hardly force the zebra herd to turn aside every time she spotted a familiar gazelle.

"We steered clear of the cheetahs," rumbled Mistfriend at her side, "but this doesn't look good."

Prance's heart leaped into her throat, and she felt a thudding remorse. Ahead, they stared out over a grassy ridge, toward a precipitous downhill slope that was scattered with rocks and boulders.

"I suppose we can get down there." Mistfriend shook his mane. "It's not as if we have a choice now." He planted his front hooves carefully over the ridge and began to make his cautious way down the slope.

It was unnervingly steep, but they could not turn back now.

It's my own fault, thought Prance. She had directed the zebra herd to this dangerous terrain, however unintentionally. She had no choice now but to follow Mistfriend, her slender legs trembling.

Stones rolled beneath her hooves, bouncing and dancing down the hillside. Behind her surged the whole herd, driven on and guided by the Friendship as much as by Mistfriend's beckoning neigh.

"Oh," said a mare beside her, "this is *very* high. Careful, everyone!"

"Whose brilliant idea was it to come this way?" grunted an old stallion as he slithered and almost fell.

"Prancefriend saw cheetahs," called a younger mare behind them. "That's why Mistfriend changed course."

Prance did not dare look around; she could almost feel the resentment in the zebras' gazes. She gulped and focused on keeping her footing as the gradient grew alarmingly steeper.

"Whoaaah!" The squealing whinny of fear came from right behind her, and Prance only just dodged in time as Grassfriend slid helplessly past her.

"Grassfriend!" Aghast, she watched him tumble over his forehooves and thud hard onto his flank, then slither wildly down the slope, picking up speed. His baying terror was almost unbearable. *Not Grassfriend! Not when it's my fault!*

She could not breathe. There was nothing anyone could do. Grassfriend's hooves scrabbled as stones tumbled down around him, but he could not find purchase on the dry ground. He swerved wildly again on a hummock, and this time he slid rump-first backward, his terrified eyes locked on Prance's.

With an abrupt, sickening jolt, Grassfriend came to a halt. For a moment there was absolute silence, but for the skittering of small stones as they bounced past him and plummeted out of sight.

The zebra's whole body was trembling, but his hooves were still planted firmly on solid ground. Mistfriend, Prance, and the others picked their careful way down the slope after him, and soon Prance realized with horror what had so nearly befallen her best friend and ally in the herd. Just beyond Grassfriend's rump, the ground fell away into a perpendicular cliff. Had his haunches not caught on another stumpy tussock, he would have fallen helplessly through thin air, to smash against the rocky plateau far below.

"Come on, Grassfriend, don't be afraid. Pull yourself up," commanded Mistfriend.

"Yes, Grassfriend. Come back to us!"

"All will be well. You've stopped falling."

The voices rose around Prance in a whinnying murmur, and she knew suddenly what was happening: the Friendship was at work, encouraging and heartening Grassfriend. He scrabbled forward, dragging himself on his front hooves away from the edge. At a slightly safer distance, he rose shakily to his feet and edged up the slope toward the rest of his herd. Sideways, sideways he walked, until with a last surge of panicked energy he propelled himself up onto the less precipitous ground.

"Carefully, everyone," neighed Mistfriend. "Keep going, and support Grassfriend."

And once again, the herd began to move, slow and steady and cautious; this time, Grassfriend was comfortingly hemmed in by warm striped bodies.

Prance felt a pang of longing for the Us. The Friendship was very different, but it came from the same sense of togetherness and unity, she knew. Along with the yearning for what she'd lost, there was the sharp claw of guilt and shame. *Grassfriend wouldn't have fallen, if not for me. I lied about cheetahs to spare myself embarrassment, and my friend almost paid with his life.*

She knew that more and more of the zebras were doubting her. She couldn't help but notice their sharp looks and their hostile mutters as they supported Grassfriend down the rest of the hillside.

"Cheetahs, she said . . ."

"I didn't see any, did you?"

"She must have seen them. Why else would she turn us this way . . . ?"

"You know gazelles: paranoid."

When the ground leveled out, the zebras bounded forward, stretching out their long forelegs, bucking and stamping and tossing their manes. The peril and constraint of the slope were over, and their relief was obvious. They gamboled like foals, kicking with their stiff legs to loosen the tension.

Prance could not join in. She still felt terrible. Her head sagging, she plodded up to Grassfriend. Even he seemed to have recovered from the trauma of his fall; he reared up joyfully and kicked out his hind legs.

"That was a close one," he neighed cheerfully.

"You were a bit *careless*," scolded Dawnfriend, gently nipping his friend's withers.

No, he wasn't. It was all my fault. Prance could bear it no longer. She stepped close to the two zebras and gazed up into their dark, friendly eyes.

"I . . . I am sure I saw my herd back there," she stuttered. "You've all been so kind to me, but I think I should go to them."

"But—" Grassfriend blinked with shock. "I thought you couldn't go back?"

Young Breezefriend picked her way toward them. "What did you say, Prancefriend?" she whinnied anxiously. "You can't be going back to your herd?"

"I have to try," said Prance hoarsely. "I won't forgive myself if I don't make one more effort. They're . . . they're my family."

"*We're* your family now," said Breezefriend indignantly.

But other zebras were thronging around Prance. Some looked hurt and disbelieving, but there were some who exchanged relieved glances. Prance even heard a few mutters of "Thank the Great Spirit."

"Thank you, all of you." She turned slowly, gazing into the zebras' faces, whether sorrowful or hostile. "You took me in when no one else would, and I'm so grateful for that. But it's time to return to my herd, however they greet me." She stretched out her muzzle to Grassfriend's, and he blew sadly against her nostrils. "Farewell, my friends. I won't forget what you did for me."

She had to go now, before she thought too hard and

changed her mind. Turning determinedly, she paced through the zebras, who parted before her, nodding and murmuring their goodbyes.

Not all of them are fooled, she thought. *Some of them know this is hopeless. They know I'm lying again. But at least this time I'm doing it to protect them.*

Of course Runningherd would not take her in. It was pointless even to try. Prance knew that all she could do was walk to meet her inevitable fate, wherever it caught up with her.

She glanced to the side as she strode; she had already left the zebra herd behind, but not that wretched vulture. It hopped and flapped along, distant but always present.

It still knows. I've said goodbye to Mistfriendherd.

But I'm really saying goodbye to my life.

CHAPTER NINETEEN

Bramble was so preoccupied with thinking about his father and the snakeskin, he almost tripped over Dayflower. The old seer was crouched in the shadow of a huge clump of bamboo, picking delicately at a shoot to find the tender core. As Bramble stumbled to a halt with a muttered apology, she glanced up and smiled.

"Hello, Bramble Brightback. You seem distracted!"

"Sorry!" He blinked.

Moonflower leaned around her mother; she too had been sitting in the dappled shadows. "Bramble's head is always somewhere else these days. Isn't that so, brother?"

Embarrassed, Bramble shrugged. "There's a lot to think about."

"I know." Moonflower gave him a sympathetic smile.

Bramble shambled around and sat down, facing the two of

them. He chewed at his lip. "Can I talk to you both?"

"Always, Bramble." Dayflower looked at him kindly. Moon-flower's eyes narrowed in curiosity.

He took a deep breath. "Before I do . . ." He paused.

The two female gorillas glanced at each other. Moonflower said, "What, Bramble?"

"You know what," he blurted.

Dayflower's wrinkled brow furrowed even more deeply, but Moonflower held out both wrists in front of him. He was relieved to see she hadn't been bitten.

"I . . . I need to check you too," said Bramble to Dayflower. "For snakebites."

Dayflower smiled. "Moonflower told me about the snakes. I can't say I think it's much to worry about, but go ahead." She proffered her arms.

Respectfully, Bramble picked through her fur. Besides the usual thorn scratches and everyday scrapes, she was clear of any sinister puncture marks. Bramble let out a deep breath of relief and sat back on his haunches.

"Something strange happened with Burbark today," he began.

"Again?" Moonflower said.

"This time, it was weirder." Now Bramble almost wished he'd held on to the dried-up snakeskin; why should these two believe him, after all? But summoning all his courage, he told Moonflower and her mother about the sinister conversation with his father.

"And . . . I'm afraid I threw it away," he finished, staring miserably down at the ground. "I should have kept it to show you, but I couldn't bear the touch of the thing."

Moonflower's eyes were wide with consternation. Dayflower, on the other hand, seemed thoughtful. "This does trouble me," she said softly. "It's odd behavior, I grant you. But he is our leader, and he deserves our trust and respect."

"And if we're worried about him?" Bramble gazed at her beseechingly. "Terribly worried?"

"I do understand." Dayflower sighed. "I just don't know what you want me to do."

Bramble rubbed his teeth with a finger, then scratched at his lip. "I want to consult the Spirit Mouth." The words came tumbling out in a rush. "There's no one else to ask. Only— only the Great Spirit has the authority to reassure us about Burbark. Don't you see?"

Dayflower drew back, her breath hissing. "Oh, Bramble. That would—I think that might be sacrilege. It is the Silverback's role to remove the stone, to let the Spirit Mouth speak. It would be rash folly to go behind his back!"

Bramble clenched his jaws in renewed determination. He leaned forward, gazing into her anxious eyes.

"There's no other way, Dayflower."

"We can consult with some of the other Goldbacks." Dayflower nodded firmly. "That is our path for now, Bramble Brightback. Many of the older Goldbacks are wise."

"No! I saw many of them at the snake ritual!" Bramble wrung his paws together, desperate. "I swear to you, Dayflower: I don't know who I can trust. I can't tell this to *anyone* else. The Spirit Mouth is my only hope."

"Mother," said Moonflower quietly. "I think Bramble's right."

Dayflower stared at her in surprise, her lips parted.

"What's happening with Burbark is unnatural and worrying," Moonflower went on, gazing at her mother. "But it's not confined to him. Any of our troop could be involved. And Mother . . . I think it would be dangerous for Bramble to ask advice from another. We don't know who might report back to Burbark. Groundnut and Apple are wise, but they are wholly loyal to the Silverback."

"As are we!" exclaimed Dayflower in indignation.

"Yes," agreed her daughter, "but our loyalty includes concern for him, and fear. That's why I think, Mother . . . you must consult the Spirit Mouth for Bramble."

Dayflower lowered her head, rubbing at her brow with her fingers. She was silent for a long time, and Bramble and Moonflower eyed each other nervously; Bramble felt as if his heart might explode with the tension.

At last, the old gorilla lifted her head and blinked at them. "I can't allow it. I'm sorry, both of you. I know why you worry, but I cannot go against my Silverback, and I cannot consult the Spirit Mouth on behalf of anyone else. I'll be alert for any more changes in Burbark; I will listen carefully for rumors in the troop, and if I can I will ask subtle questions of gorillas I feel I can trust. But I will not speak to the Spirit Mouth for you, I'm sorry. I can't, and I mustn't."

Disappointment flooded Bramble, his heart heavy as a

fallen tree. There was no point arguing with the Mistback once her mind was made up; she had clearly thought hard. Yet he couldn't help opening his mouth to make one last effort to convince her.

Then he caught the slight shake of Moonflower's head. Her eyes burned into his, as if she were trying to tell him something silently. Bramble closed his mouth again, gave a nod, and sighed.

"I understand, Dayflower Mistback," he said quietly. "Thank you for considering it, anyway."

He trudged away from them, his steps sluggish and his fists heavy in the forest litter. He had no idea what to do now. He'd told Dayflower the truth: there was no troop member he could confide in. Grief rose in his throat as he remembered the one gorilla he could have trusted with his life. *Cassava, my brother. I miss you more than ever.*

There was a crunching of leaves behind him, and he turned to see Moonflower padding quickly after him. "Bramble," she whispered.

He stopped. She was glancing to right and left, as if making sure they could not be overheard. Bramble furrowed his brow curiously.

She came close to him and gave the forest a quick last scan.

"I know why my mother turned you down," she murmured, "but I can't agree with her. This is an emergency, Bramble, and our father the Silverback will never consult the Spirit Mouth about it."

"But what can we do?" He shrugged helplessly. "Your

mother won't change her mind."

"We'll do what no gorilla has ever done." Moonflower's amber eyes glittered with fierce determination. "We'll go to the Spirit Mouth tonight—and we'll ask for its guidance ourselves."

It was forbidden, this thing they were doing. Indeed, Bramble could think of nothing they could do that would be more taboo, more sacrilegious, more *wrong*.

But Moonflower was right: they had been left with no choice. There was no saying whether the Spirit Mouth could, or would, tell them anything. Neither he nor his half sister was a Mistback; neither had experience of communing with omens. But Bramble saw no other way. If the Great Spirit wanted to tell them something, he trusted it would find a way.

His limbs trembled as he followed his half sister through the forest in the darkness. They were climbing sharply uphill, and the Spirit Mouth had to be close. Nervously, Bramble glanced into the shadows. He could hear the skitter of small creatures, the shriek of a hunting owl, and the ever-present chorus of the cicadas, but there was no crunch of leaves from a larger body, and no cry of angry summons from a member of the troop. Every other member of Burbarktroop would be asleep in their nests.

He almost wished he could be there with them, sleeping the sleep of a gorilla with a clear conscience. But no: this had to be done. And ahead of him, Moonflower was already scrambling up the last ridge, toward the slab of rock that concealed the Spirit Mouth.

She laid her hand against it and turned to him with wide, nervous eyes. "This is it, Bramble. Are we certain about this?"

She seemed suddenly far less sure of herself, Bramble thought, but perhaps it was his turn to be confident. He nodded. "Let's do it, Moonflower. As fast as we can."

Yet as Bramble, too, touched the rock, he gave a yelp and flinched back. "Where did that come from?"

A chameleon was perched on the rim of the slab. Against the dark gray stone, its bumpy scales shimmered as blue as an azure sky, and though its eyes swiveled with seeming randomness, one of them was always staring at Bramble.

Moonflower gave a nervous laugh and flicked a hand at it.

It didn't move. Angrily, Bramble batted its tail. It gave him an intense glower, both eyes at once, but at last it crawled away out of sight behind the rocks.

It's not an omen, Bramble told himself. *Just a particularly brave lizard . . .*

Moonflower and Bramble were both young, but they were strong, and there were two of them. Still, as they tensed their muscles and heaved, Bramble felt not so much as a tiny shift. He bunched his shoulder muscles and grunted with effort as he pushed harder, but it was no use. He stumbled back, panting and rubbing his gritty hands.

Moonflower shook her head. "It's a lot heavier than I thought. Our father is strong!"

"Come on, try again." Clenching his jaws, Bramble put his shoulder to the stone. Moonflower took her place again facing him, and with a deep breath, she nodded. Gathering all his strength, Bramble heaved and shoved.

At last, with a groan, he tumbled back and lay flat. Moonflower too staggered away, gasping.

"It's hopeless," muttered Bramble.

Her breathing still rapid, Moonflower took another step back and eyed the stone. Twisting his head to watch her, Bramble could almost see her mind working. She padded around the great slab, feeling its edges with her fingertips. *My sister's always been clever at this sort of thing*, Bramble thought. If anyone could find a way to move this enormous rock, it was Moonflower.

"Grab the stone right there," she said softly at last, pointing at a jutting corner where the boulder must have broken long ago. "And I'll hold it here." She patted a bulge on the lower left of the stone. "Then, on three, we push it a *little* toward the vent and to the right. All right?"

Bramble nodded. He took a deep breath, flexing his muscles and clenching his fists. Moonflower nodded as she gripped the slab, and Bramble seized the corner she'd shown him.

"One. Two. *Three.*"

With a grunt and a deep breath, they both shoved as hard as they could. Bramble felt his muscles burn with the effort. Moonflower was trembling, and her jaws were clenched tight, but she wasn't giving up, and neither would he.

"Keep going!" he gasped.

From deep within him, he summoned an extra surge of energy, heaving with all his might. And suddenly, the stone gave a jolting scrape to the right.

It was only a small movement, but it gave Bramble new heart. He angled his shoulder against the widening gap to shove farther, jamming the soles of his feet against the ground. If the stone slipped back now it would crush his arm, but that only gave him greater reason to keep trying. He could hear Moonflower's harsh breaths, but he couldn't look to see how she was doing, because his eyes were shut tight. *Push! Push!*

There was another rasping scrape, and a tremor that seemed to run through the entire mountain. Then the stone rocked back, thudding violently against the vent.

How had his father tossed this thing aside so casually? Bramble felt a new and nervous respect for Burbark. But Moonflower had been right about how to target their efforts, and the two young gorillas had not striven in vain: the stone had shifted. The black vent seemed to sigh, and its hot breath curled out through the gap as a tendril of smoke.

Moonflower was gasping for breath, but her eyes shone. "That's wide enough for us," she whispered. "Let's go. Carefully!"

"Follow me," said Bramble softly. His fur was standing up all over his body, but he couldn't let Moonflower go into that darkness first. Not on the most starless night in the deep forest had he seen such impenetrable blackness.

Rising up on his hind legs, he squeezed behind the boulder, then dropped to all fours. For a long moment, as Moonflower wriggled after him, he stayed very still, breathing in the hot odors of the Spirit Mouth.

The impact of the smoke was instant; it seemed to seep through his nostrils into the farthest parts of his bloodstream, and his head spun. Despite the dizziness and the utter darkness, he had a clear sense that the cavern where he stood was vast. It was almost as if he was floating in a void as huge as the night sky; he curled his fingers and toes tight against the rock to ground himself.

"Do you see?" whispered Moonflower. Her awed voice could have been right beside his ear or at the farthest point of the cavern; it swirled in his head like the smoke.

But despite the disorienting heat and stench and smoke, Bramble realized he *could* see something. Not the walls of the cavern; he still had no idea where those were, and where this lightless emptiness ended. But shapes moved in his vision, smoky and vague, leaping and bounding and spiraling. The shapes coalesced, flared, and dissipated once again into the smoke.

Two coils of ethereal white twined around each other, separated, and solidified for a moment. Bramble gasped. His brother Cassava sat there, a creature of smoke, talking earnestly with a fully grown leopard. Before Bramble could cry out to his brother, Cassava and the leopard were gone.

What am I seeing? Ghosts? The past? The future?

Shapes swirled again, more like gaps threaded in the darkness than actual light. A slender creature formed, long-legged, its horns swept elegantly back as it gazed at the sky.

Nothing here was natural. Bramble suddenly, violently, wanted to leave this place. "Moonflower, I think we should get out of here."

His words didn't seem to come out as he'd planned; they drifted like the smoke, lost and confused, swallowed by the oppressive silence. But his sister must have heard him, because she gave a cry of distress.

"Bramble." Again her voice seemed to come from everywhere and nowhere. "So many messages. I hear too many! I don't understand. . . ."

"What? What are they saying? What do you see?"

"I don't know. . . . I've never done this. . . . I can't see, just hear. . . ."

"Tell me! I can't see you but I'm here, I promise."

Moonflower gasped again. "It said *speak* and *plains* and *blood*. I don't understand, it's just words. *Blood on the plains*."

A huge shudder went through Bramble. He turned desperately, searching for her, but apart from the smoking shapes, he could see nothing.

"It said," cried Moonflower, "it said, *Speak to the dead one on the plains*."

That made no sense. None of this made sense. How could they speak to a creature that was already dead? Bramble's throat felt tight with terror and confusion. He was desperate to be out in the open air once more.

He spun, dropped to all fours again, and tried to run. But another smoky form reared up right in front of him, looming out of the blackness. And this time, the shape was monstrous.

It was the head of a snake. Bramble cowered, helpless, trying to cover his face with his arms. But there was no escaping it. The snake's eyes glittered like black stones in the silvery wisps of smoke. It opened its jaws wide—then wider again, exposing muscle and membrane that glistened in the eerie mist-light. Rows of tiny teeth lined the impossibly wide maw; Bramble could almost feel the bite of those curved fangs, could imagine them piercing his flesh, drawing him remorselessly into that crushing, smothering throat.

It's only a vision, he told himself. It was made of air and smoke and his own fears. Still, he flung his arms out to fend it off, reared up on his hind legs, then twisted and bolted for the vent mouth.

His body crashed into Moonflower's. Together they wriggled and tumbled from the dark cavern into the star-lit freshness of the hillside. Night on the open mountain no longer seemed sinister; it felt once more like their true and welcoming home. *Where our family are—*

Their family. Panting, his muscles limp as he sprawled on the dewy grass, Bramble raised his head and felt his stomach plummet. Beside him, Moonflower too peered up, and she gave a frightened gasp of shock.

Around them stood the Blackbacks and Goldbacks of the troop, glaring in silence. Burbark loomed right at the front and center of the group, his eyes glittering with fury, his fists resting deep into the grass as if he was fixed to the mountain itself, immovable as a rock. To Bramble, the great Silverback seemed suddenly bigger than he had ever seen him. It was as if a strange light—not quite the moon and stars, but perhaps the lingering glow of the cavern's ghosts—cast his shadow up into the sky, and Burbark and that massive shadow were as one.

Even the cicadas seemed to be silenced; there wasn't the chirp of a cricket or the cry of a bird. There was only the heavy, menacing breathing of Burbark Silverback. Bramble clambered to his feet with Moonflower. A cold ripple of fear and remorse flowed through his blood.

"Explain yourselves," snarled Burbark, his voice resounding from the rocks. "And do it *now*."

CHAPTER TWENTY

It had been a long and arduous trek, dragging the remains of the kill Range had given them, but Chase had been unwilling to abandon any of the precious meat. Who knew when she and Seek would next be lucky enough to hunt successfully?

I could have stayed with Range. He would not have harmed Seek. . . .

But Seek had been impossible to convince. When scolding him had proved as useless as pleading with him, Chase had finally been overcome with embarrassment. She had no idea what had turned the cub against Range so abruptly and completely. That scolding Range had given him, for toying with the lizard, was no excuse for Seek's sullen moodiness. Range had tried to reassure her, to say he understood about cubs— he had even tried to placate the brattish Seek, for the Spirit's sake! But it had all been too much for Chase to bear. Range had been so kind, so welcoming; he had offered them shelter and protection, and Seek had rewarded him with rudeness. Mortified, she had taken Seek home in disgrace.

"You had better enjoy what's left of this goat-antelope," she growled at the cub now. "Who knows when we'll eat so well again?"

"At least we'll have caught the next kill ourselves," came the surly reply. "Even if it's just a *lizard*."

Chase was about to snap at him again, when she caught a scent on the air. Her hackles sprang up: it was the musky reek of another male leopard. Freezing where she stood, her fangs still sunk in antelope haunch, Chase flared her nostrils and growled. "Quiet, Seek."

The cub, too, went still.

Her whiskers tingled. The scent was familiar: it was only Shadow. He came pacing out of the night and halted before her, his forest-green eyes glowing.

"I'm glad to see you've made a full recovery," he murmured.

Releasing the goat-antelope, hunching her shoulders protectively over it, she glared at him. There was a scabbed-over claw mark on his face, and Chase vaguely recalled putting it there. *I didn't dream that I lashed out at him when I was ill. And that means he was no hallucination. . . . He really was here, looking out for me.*

"That's a good kill, if a little tattered." Shadow nodded with amusement at the remains. "How far did you drag that?"

"Very far," snapped Chase. "And it's ours." She edged closer to Seek.

"Of course it is," murmured Shadow. "I wouldn't dream of

touching it, and I can hunt for myself. It's good to see you have prey, that's all. These are worrying times."

"The times are always worrying," said Chase. She grabbed the corpse again, tugging it to the foot of her tree.

"True, but right now they're strange as well as alarming." Shadow licked a paw. "The gorillas are behaving oddly, and so are other animals. And there are snakes everywhere, haven't you noticed? They move around freely and fearlessly."

"I've noticed," she admitted, thinking of the snake that had been so unwilling to release its rat for Seek.

"Perhaps it's time to leave the mountain, at least for the time being," suggested Shadow. "Especially now that you have Seek to care for."

"Don't talk nonsense." Chase glared at him. "The mountain has always been my home. *Our* home."

Shadow shrugged. "When times change, leopards should change with them," he said. "You've already come close to death once, and if you'd died, it would have been the end of Seek, too. Face it, Chase. You're not experienced enough to care for yourself *and* a cub that isn't yours."

Anger coiled inside her. "Oh, and you are?" she snarled. "Who else will take care of him? A coward like you, who wants to run away from our rightful home? Look at this kill." She slapped a paw onto the dismembered haunch. "I can provide for both of us!"

"What is it, by the way?" Shadow, ignoring her insult entirely, tilted his head. "I've never seen an antelope like that before. Where did you find it?"

Chase opened her mouth to reply, but she didn't get the chance.

"Range says it's a goat, not an antelope," Seek piped up. "He's the one who caught it."

Shadow went quite still. He stared at Seek, and Chase noticed that the sardonic glint was gone from his eye. He looked sober and serious, for once.

"Range? Oh, Chase, be careful. That leopard isn't . . . he isn't *right*."

"Range is a fine leopard, he's kind, and he doesn't mock me!" growled Chase. "Yes, he gave me this carcass! So what? I *could* have killed it myself."

"Listen to me, Chase." Shadow took a couple of paces toward her, his tail swinging low. "Range has strange hunting methods. It's just one more of the odd things that have been happening on the mountain. You think he brought food for you because he likes you? Because he wants you for his mate?"

"What if he does?" she snapped.

"Would it surprise you to learn," said Shadow quietly, "that he has also brought kills to me?"

She opened her jaws and closed them again. At last she grunted, "Why?"

"I don't know." Shadow hunched his shoulders. "To flatter me? To get me on his side in some dispute I know nothing about? He's not normal, Chase, that's all I'm saying."

"If he looks out for us—brings us kills—I'm fine with that." She glowered at Shadow, her tail tapping in irritation. *What proof does he have of any of this?*

"You're thinking of what Range can do for you—and not of what he *could* do *to* Seek." Shadow wrinkled his muzzle. In the uncomfortable silence that followed his words, he pressed his point. "You think Prowl would approve? That she would want you to trust—"

"Leave me alone!" Chase snarled, lashing out with a paw to make Shadow jump back. "And leave Seek alone! I don't want to hear any more of your jealous gossip, Shadow."

He looked surprised, but nodded. Reluctantly, the black leopard turned with a flick of his tail. But as he left their clearing he paused and glanced back over his shoulder.

"Pay attention to his behavior, Chase; that's all I'm saying. Don't ever let your guard down." He curled his muzzle in a half smile. *"Trust no one but yourself."*

Chase shook herself. She was more irritated than she'd thought she could be by that interfering leopard. Gripping the antelope—the *goat*—she clutched the tree trunk with her claws and began to haul it up to safety.

"I think Shadow has a point," said Seek in a small voice. He seemed to have lost all his grumpiness.

"What?" she mumbled through the haunch.

"I'm not sure about Range, either," said the cub, watching as she climbed higher. "I told you that, didn't I?"

"You made it perfectly clear! That's why we had to leave!"

"Chase . . . I know he was friendly and helpful, and I'm grateful and everything. But he's *weird.*"

"Does this antel—does this goat smell too *weird* to eat?" she snarled down. "Range has every reason to try to help us.

You're too young to understand, Seek, but one day you will. There's nothing irrational about what he's doing."

"Shadow's always been there for us, too," muttered Seek. "And I know *exactly* what you're talking about, and Shadow's *nice.*"

Chase flicked her ears in anger. She dumped the goat half on, half off a low branch. "Shadow wants our territory! That's all he's ever wanted. He thinks he's better than us."

"Chase—"

"That's enough. I won't listen to any more nonsense about Range and Shadow. I told you, you're too young to understand!"

"No, Chase, I—"

"What?" she roared, and twisted to glare down at him.

She gasped in horror. Three hyenas were prowling into the glade, their snouts lifted to snuff eagerly at the scent of a fresh kill. Seek was staring at them, backing against the tree.

"Seek, get up here!" cried Chase. *"Now!"*

The cub broke out of his frozen state, spun around, and scrabbled up the tree, claws digging desperately into the bark. His flight, in turn, sparked the hyenas' hunting instincts; their eyes snapped away from the dangling remains of the goat, and they lunged for the cub.

"Climb!" shouted Chase in horror. She stretched down the tree toward the clambering cub, reaching down as best she could without losing her balance.

The hyenas' slavering jaws were right behind him; they had their forepaws up against the bark of the tree and were shrieking and yapping to scare him into falling. The noise was deafening to Chase's sensitive ears, and she couldn't imagine how terrifying it must be for Seek. Urging him with her eyes, she stretched down her neck to grab him. The cub reached up a paw, grabbing for a thin branchlet—

The twig snapped. Losing his balance and his grip, Seek plummeted to the ground.

"No!" screamed Chase.

"Yes!" yelped the biggest hyena, and let out a squeal of glee.

Just as Chase coiled herself to leap down herself, something large and black hurtled into the midst of the hyenas. Claws slashed and fangs bit, and green eyes flashed with fury as Shadow fell on one hyena after another. Taken by surprise, they yelped and scattered.

If they had been better prepared, Chase knew, they could have torn Shadow apart—but his attack was a complete shock. Tails between their legs, the hyenas bolted, dripping blood trails where Shadow's savage claws had caught hide and flesh. Chase sprang down the tree in three elegant leaps and stood over the trembling Seek as Shadow roared a warning to the last hyena and trotted back to the tree.

"Th-thank you—" Chase stammered. "You didn't have to—"

"Yes, I did!" Shadow's growl was harder now, devoid of his usual humor. "Seek is too small to be left alone, Chase. You need to be more careful!"

Anger bristled along her spine, and Chase's hackles sprang up.

"You interfered again! If Seek hadn't stood there arguing with me, the hyenas wouldn't have caught him at the bottom of the tree!" Chase found herself spitting with resentment, and suddenly she was too tired and angry and worn down to care about anyone's feelings but her own. "I can fend for myself, *Shadow*! I wouldn't have a problem if I didn't have to take care of some other leopard's mewling *infant*!"

As soon as the words left her mouth, bitter remorse clutched at Chase's gut. She spun to face Seek, hoping against hope that he had not heard.

But he was gazing at her, his eyes wide with hurt. Before Chase could form the words to make it right, to apologize, to pretend it had all been a joke, the little cub turned and slunk miserably into their den.

CHAPTER TWENTY-ONE

She was not meant to live alone. She had thought she could find a
way of living with others, even if they were not her own kind;
but that had proved impossible, and she should have realized
it from the start. The elephant Boulder, despite the wisdom of
his years, had been wrong.

Prance kept walking across the plain, placing one hoof in
front of the other, staring at the grass that stretched out all
around her; her horns and her head were too heavy to lift to
see the horizon. She didn't know what waited for her there, at
the eventual end of her journey, and she didn't care.

Yet again she told herself: *No gazelle should walk alone.*

It was no good. She hadn't *wanted* to give up. She could
still remember the ferocious love of life that had swept over
her as that lion attacked; her determination that *today she
would not die.* She remembered it had happened . . . but she no

longer recalled how it had felt.

Back then I didn't want to give up, Great Spirit. And I've kept trying, I really have. But now you've left me no choice.

And that meant that the gazelles of Runningherd had been right all along; her death waited for her, and she should go to it. Prance drew a painful breath.

The sooner the better, Great Spirit. I promise I'll accept it this time. Please don't let me wait too long.

So why was she walking at all?

The thought struck her very suddenly. Why exhaust herself with weariness and thirst and hunger? Prance came to an abrupt halt and raised her head to gaze at the whole of the plain and the sky.

The undulating grassland was clear of all but occasional trees; it stretched into a hazy blue distance where it met the lilac clouds of twilight. She was so exposed here: a lone antelope, herdless and utterly vulnerable. *If I am to be taken, Great Spirit, make it now.*

She closed her eyes. At once the sounds of the savannah seemed louder to her swiveling ears: the rustle of a mouse on the stony ground beneath her, the skitter of a lizard, the breath of the warm wind through the savannah grass. She heard the first piping calls of the crickets as they prepared for a night of song; she heard the beat of egrets' wings as they flew toward their roost.

Prance wanted very badly to open her eyes, but she refused to. *Three times I've escaped death, Great Spirit. If that was wrong, prove it! Answer me!*

There was another sound now, of heavy, soft paws on dry earth. And more, there was the dark, overpowering smell of carnivores. Prance couldn't help herself anymore; she snapped her eyes open, her breath coming shallow and fast.

And there was the Great Spirit's answer: a pride of hunting lions, padding straight toward her across the grassland. At their head walked a huge lioness, one ear torn and one eye scarred. Her tail lashed as she stalked toward Prance.

Thank you, Great Spirit. At least she had her reply, and it was an honest one. *I won't run from death again. I promised I wouldn't. I* WON'T.

She stood firm, her hooves barely trembling on the flat ground. She could see each lion's face now: the scars, the white line beneath each fierce yellow eye, the streaks of black and brown and gold in each individual mane.

She could see their yellow teeth, the tongues that came out to lick their muzzles as they approached her.

It wasn't the Us that sparked her panic, but it felt not dissimilar. A thrilling shiver of blood through her veins, a tingle in her limbs like the buzzing of bees. Every part of her, every muscle and nerve and sinew, screamed at her to *run.*

It was the basest of instincts, she knew. She had promised the Great Spirit she would not run. She had vowed her acceptance, her submission to the Spirit's will. She could not run. *I must not run!*

The pulsing energy of that inborn imperative filled her veins and bones, intensifying with every step the lions took toward her. Prance's head spun and reeled with the effort of resisting it.

And suddenly, it was too powerful for her. With a gasp of despair and defeat, Prance ran.

She could not help it. The instinct came from a place far deeper than conscious thought. *I'm sorry, Great Spirit. I broke my promise, I'm sorry—* Yet still she kept running, pronking, dodging in desperation. The lions were in her peripheral vision; they too had begun to run, and now they were fanning out on each side of her, their strides long and powerful and almost lazy as the foremost of them drew abreast of her.

Prance picked up speed, her light hooves flying across the plain. *Don't look back, don't ever look back—*

She had to; she couldn't help it. A quick glance over her shoulder and she saw that the lions surrounded her now on both sides and the rear, keeping pace, their strides still loping and easy. It was as if they weren't in any hurry, as if they knew already what would happen, because it was ordained by the Great Spirit, and they didn't even have to make much of an effort. . . .

She was sure the pride was bigger now. More lions had appeared, running at her flanks. She saw them as tawny blurs as she raced, but still they didn't angle closer to her. For a panicky, fanciful moment, she felt as if she was not running from a pride of lions, but leading them. They were following in her hoofsteps, not hunting her—

Then she saw why. Rising up from the twilit plain, she saw

a huge, tawny-maned male directly in her path. There was nowhere to run, nowhere to dodge; she was hemmed in at the rear and on the sides. This time, death was taking no chances. It had her trapped.

The lion was colossal, and she could see nothing but his fierce jaws and mane, but she jigged and pronked high. With the last of her energy, she leaped over his head.

She had a fleeting glimpse of his roaring jaws, the frustration in his glittering eyes as his paws swept thin air. She fancied she even heard his rumbling curse: *"Oh, stars! What in the Great Spirit's name—"*

Prance landed hard. The ground sloped abruptly and unexpectedly, and her hind legs went from under her; tumbling onto her flank, she skidded down a sheer grassy slope, then was flung into a helpless somersault. She had a vague impression of her own slender legs flailing above her, and then she thudded to a painful stop against a rock.

When she could breathe again, Prance rolled upright onto her belly and shook her head. She stretched out one foreleg, then the other. Her pounding heart in her throat, she pushed herself up onto her front hooves.

She glanced down. She could still walk, if she had to; miraculously, her bones had not snapped. But down her right fetlock trickled dark blood, from a deep gash above her knee.

Prance had seen such a wound before. Small, but deep: the kind that made an animal weaken and sicken, until even the smallest rot-eaters could take it down. They would begin to eat before she was even dead. . . .

So this really is my time, Great Spirit. You might not have made it so cruel. . . .

Above her, on the ridge from which she'd fallen, she heard a bellowing roar. She glanced up. The big male lion glared down at her, his pride around him. He began to pick his way down the escarpment, followed by the others.

Not the cruel death, then. She had no strength to rise to all fours, let alone run farther. *You are merciful, Great Spirit.* Prance closed her eyes, then blinked them open. For the Great Spirit's sake, she would meet her end with courage. Soon—perhaps in moments—she would run among the stars that were even now blinking into life in the purple sky above her. Lowering her head, Prance breathed deeply. Then she lifted it to directly face the approaching lion.

He halted. He cocked his head and shook his mane. He narrowed his yellow eyes, quizzically.

"You really do have luck on your side, don't you?"

She stared at him. *Get it done. Get it done!*

The lion stalked closer, his pride holding back at a short distance. He stood over Prance, massive and powerful; she had to strain her neck to keep her eyes fixed on his. His jaws lowered toward her, so close she could smell the old blood on his breath.

"I said, get it done!" This time, she brayed it out loud, right in his face.

He looked to the side, then to the sky, then back at Prance.

"There is nothing to be *done* here, Gazelle. Today is not the end for you."

The huge maned head brushed her flank, and she realized he was nudging her, urging her to her feet. Bewildered, she began to tremble violently. *He's taunting me.*

"Didn't you hear me?" He butted her, then took one horn gently in his jaws and pulled her to her shaking hooves. "Be brave. It's not as if you don't know how." He huffed a laugh. "There's someone who wants to meet you. . . ."

CHAPTER TWENTY-TWO

Bramble barely knew which way was up and which was down; he had been tossed and shoved between the Blackbacks for so long, he had lost all sense of balance. His head whirled and ached from their blows. Distantly, he thought he could hear Moonflower's voice, pleading for the troop to stop, to leave him alone; but they ignored her. Groundnut seized his arm again and sent him flying and tumbling across the earth toward Woodnettle's waiting fists.

"Sacrilege! Dishonor! Treason!" The yells of the gorillas surrounded him, and the voices were those of the Goldbacks as well as the Blackbacks. There were plenty of females here too, but not one of them intervened to stop the beating. Indeed, they seemed to be cheering the Blackbacks on.

"Blasphemy!"

"Shame!"

"Stop, *please stop!*" That was Moonflower again; she tore herself from Apple's grasp and bounded to Bramble's side. He could only lie there in her shadow, limp and gasping for breath.

"Father, listen to me! It was all my idea, and *I* went into the vent first! Nothing happened! I got stuck, and Bramble was only trying to help me get back out!"

In his haze of stunned pain, Bramble felt a pang of gratitude. Moonflower hated lying; the fact she was willing to do it for him, now, was oddly touching. Even if she was *very* bad at it . . .

Unfortunately, Burbark knew it too. "Liar!" he hollered at his daughter. "Tell me what really happened, Moonflower. Tell me what you saw in the Spirit Mouth!"

As his father bounded forward to loom over Moonflower, Bramble blinked, thinking he was imagining things. But no; that odd shape on his father's shoulder was the chameleon they had seen earlier, he was sure of it. He squeezed his eyes, trying to see better. The chameleon balanced there, shimmering dark green, its tail curled around a clump of Burbark's fur.

It was too much. Bramble dragged himself to his feet, flinching as Woodnettle lunged and grabbed his arm, but holding his ground this time.

"What's going on? Father?" He licked his dry lips. "What is happening between you and the Sandtongue-speakers?"

The jeering troop fell silent and looked toward Burbark. The big Silverback turned slowly away from Moonflower and stared at Bramble. So did the chameleon. Burbark glanced at it fondly and stroked its head with a finger; then he looked at Bramble once again.

"A new age is coming, Bramble Brightback," intoned his father. "It is time for you to recognize it. It is time for *all* of us."

As he raised his head to gaze around the troop, the gorillas rose to their hind feet. As one, they brandished their arms high. Every single wrist was marked by the livid scar of a snakebite. Some of the wounds still appeared to be weeping.

Bramble stared at them all, stunned. Moonflower put her hands over her mouth.

"What is happening?" she whispered.

Her quiet croak was echoed by a clearer, firmer voice as Dayflower pushed through the troop, her face full of bewildered anger. "What is going on here? Moonflower, what's happened? Explain yourselves, all of you!"

Moonflower gave a gasp of relief and dashed toward her mother. But she was instantly seized by two of the Goldbacks, who held her firmly back. As she struggled, uselessly, other females stepped forward to block Dayflower's path to her daughter.

"Burbark!" exclaimed Dayflower, trying and failing to push past them. "What is the meaning of this?"

Burbark's resounding voice rose above the cries of the mother and daughter. "Bring the Mistback to me. *It is time.*"

Dayflower gave a disbelieving yell of shock as Groundnut seized her arm. "How dare you?"

Groundnut took no notice. He tugged her forward as the line of Goldbacks drew apart and dragged the Mistback, still protesting, to Burbark's feet.

"Burbark. *Burbark!* Stop this at once!"

But the Silverback took no notice of Dayflower. He reached back over his shoulder, and when his hand reappeared, it held a coiling, swaying snake.

"No!" screamed Moonflower. The two Goldbacks pushed her mother to the ground and held her there.

Dayflower was silent, gaping in mesmerized disbelief as Burbark lifted the snake high above her. Around the eerie scene, the gorillas of the troop began to stamp rhythmically and sway in time with the snake. There was a rising hissing noise that hurt Bramble's ears, and he glanced around in panic, expecting to see thousands of snakes emerge from the forest. Then he realized it was the troop themselves who were making the sound. They hissed through their teeth, as if mimicking snakes, and as the noise of it rose, their stamping gained speed. Groundnut forced Dayflower's arm out in front of her, and Burbark brought the snake closer and closer to her exposed wrist.

It was his father doing this. *His Silverback.* All the same, Bramble knew he couldn't just watch. Twisting, he bit hard into Woodnettle's arm.

As the big gorilla yelped with shock, he released Bramble. Bramble bounded forward, ducked between Groundnut's splayed legs, and sprang at his father.

He was too weak even to make contact, let alone strike Burbark; he staggered and collapsed. But the big Silverback was shocked enough to stumble back a pace, and the snake darted from his hands to coil around his upper arm.

Burbark recovered fast. *"You,"* he bellowed. He seized Bramble by the neck and dangled him off the ground.

Bramble clutched at his father's hands, but the Silverback's grip was unshakable. His breath rasped in his constricted throat, and forest and troop spun in his vision. He could barely hear Moonflower's cries of protest through the buzzing in his ears.

His father's eyes were close to his as that awful grip tightened. "You have fight in you," growled Burbark, "but you are not worthy of serving Her. Not yet."

Abruptly, he released his hold, and Bramble thudded to the ground. Aching all over, pain shooting through his head and throat, Bramble managed to stumble to all fours. He stared at his father.

"Her?" He panted, shaking his head in confusion. "Who is that?"

"You will know soon enough," Burbark intoned.

"Will we kill these traitors for Her?"

The yell came from Apple Goldback, who had always been so kind to Bramble. He stared at her in shock, but his father was shaking his head.

"No. Throw them into the vent and seal it."

"Father! No!" The thought of being trapped in that terrifying darkness was worse than being beaten to death. "Father, please!"

"You cannot," cried Dayflower, struggling against her captors. *"This* is sacrilege, Burbark!"

Moonflower was screaming in incoherent fury as the two Goldbacks dragged her toward the vent. Bramble gasped in horror. "Father, don't let them do this!"

At last, Burbark looked directly at Bramble, but there was no softness or mercy in his eyes, and no change of heart. "Ah, my son. And my daughter, too. To think it was my own offspring who failed to recognize the new world and welcome it. All three of you let me down."

All three of us? For a moment, Bramble was speechless.

"Cassava too, yes. He could not, would not understand." Burbark shook his head sadly.

Bramble's words clogged in the back of his throat. *What does he mean? What is he saying?* It was Moonflower who spoke, finding utterance to his own confused thoughts. "The leopard didn't kill Cassava!"

"Ah, daughter. I wish Cassava had lived. He *could* have lived, if he'd made the right choices."

"It was you!" screamed Bramble.

"He was warned of the consequences."

"You killed my brother!" cried Bramble. His heart felt torn in two. "Your *own* son!"

Burbark looked directly into his eyes, frowning. "I will have other sons."

Bramble was dragged toward the vent after Moonflower. Grief, horror, and fury burned inside him, but he knew suddenly that there was no point fighting and no point begging. Almost effortlessly, Burbark was shoving the great slab away from the black vent, releasing swirls of that foul smoke.

Bramble's eyes blurred with tears of rage and grief, but all the same, he made out Moonflower being flung into the mouth of the cavern. He saw a larger shape dragged toward the vent; Dayflower too vanished into darkness, with an echoing cry of despair. Bramble himself did not struggle as he was yanked forward. A powerful hand slammed into his back, and he tumbled into the enveloping darkness.

The stone slab rumbled back into place with an echoing crash; when the reverberations died away, there was only a menacing, total silence.

Bramble edged forward, feeling the rock with his fingertips. In moments he touched warm fur, and there was a stifled gasp.

"Bramble." A hand found his in the darkness.

Bramble flung himself forward and was caught in strong gorilla arms. Dayflower's familiar scent enveloped him; a moment later someone else clutched at him, and he heard Moonflower whimper, felt her shaking arms go around him and hold him tight. The three gorillas clung together, shivering with fear as the reeking smoke billowed around them.

"Can we get out? Can we move the rock again?" Bramble's voice sounded too loud in his own ears, and he ended on a whimper of fear.

Dayflower's arms released him, and he felt her draw reluctantly away. "Not from this side," she whispered. "There's nowhere to grip it. This is known by every Mistback. The vent and its seal were chosen for this very reason; it can be opened only from the hillside."

"Then we're doomed," came Moonflower's voice, cracking with terror.

"There are ways out of here that the troop doesn't know," Dayflower murmured. Bramble felt her grip his hand and squeeze it. "Don't be afraid, either of you."

"Mother . . ." Moonflower gulped audibly. "If the troop doesn't know it, how can you?"

"Other troops consult the Spirit, all over this mountain," said Dayflower softly. She coughed and sucked in a harsh breath before going on. "The Spirit has many mouths. . . . We just have to find . . . one of them."

Bramble's heart gave a jolt of hope. "Of course—" But his next words were lost in a fit of hacking coughs. The air in his lungs and throat burned. He gasped and spat out the taste of ash. "Moonflower, Dayflower. The fumes are getting worse."

"Then we must start searching right now. Finding the other vents won't be easy," warned Dayflower, "but we will. Follow me as close as you can."

Bramble gripped the old Mistback's hand even tighter, terrified of losing contact. In turn, he felt Moonflower's fingers twine into his and hold them fast. Bramble squeezed his sister's hand.

"Don't let go," he murmured. "Nobody let go. . . ."

As Dayflower moved away from Bramble, he followed her, his feet sliding and stumbling on the uneven rock. It was the oddest, most unsettling feeling, walking into absolute darkness, trusting only to his fingers and toes, and to the old gorilla who walked ahead of him, her fingers wrapped firmly around his.

But with his eyes useless, Bramble found himself reaching out to his surroundings with his other senses. Every fumbling step the three gorillas took, every slip and slide, echoed eerily and distantly around them. His own rapid breathing sounded disconnected from his body, and he began to realize that his earlier sense of this great cavern had been correct; the space truly was enormous. They seemed to creep in the darkness for a long time before the echo of their shuffling and breathing began to sound closer. Bramble gave a hesitant grunt; this time it did not resound into a vast emptiness. Now he was sure of it: the walls had narrowed into what felt more like a tunnel.

In the constricted space, the stench of smoke was worse. All the same, Bramble could hear something above their rasping breath and their frequent hacking coughs.

"There's something else down here," he said, before clearing his throat and trying to sound less terrified. "Something moving around?"

"I didn't hear anything," said Dayflower, but she sounded wary.

"Me neither," added Moonflower.

As she said it, the darkness brought the skitter of disturbed gravel and tiny stones. It was hard to tell which direction it came from, but it sounded close. Then another noise, a rasping hiss like the wind through wet leaves.

"We mustn't panic," whispered Dayflower. "Try to stay—"

Her voice was abruptly cut off. Bramble, who was gripping her hand, felt it go absolutely rigid.

"Dayflower?" he gasped. "What is it?"

Moonflower's body eased past him in the narrow space, and Bramble felt her let go of his hand.

"Mother?" she whispered.

Bramble grabbed wildly for his sister's arm and caught it. Moonflower halted.

Dayflower's voice, when it finally came, was feeble and breathy. "I don't feel . . . quite right . . ." She slumped down.

Moonflower's arm went rigid in Bramble's grip. "Mother!"

Dayflower did not answer her daughter. But after a moment's terrible silence, Bramble heard her quiet, rhythmic muttering. The words were incomprehensible, but Dayflower sounded calmer. Almost too calm, in fact: there was an eerie serenity about the sounds.

All the same, Moonflower's arm muscles relaxed quite suddenly.

"It's the Great Spirit," she whispered. "I think Mother's having a vision."

That was unnerving, thought Bramble with a shiver, but perhaps it was a good sign. At least something was happening, and if the Great Spirit was willing to guide them—well, they might just have a chance of getting out of here. . . .

He had hardly allowed himself to relax, when a booming voice echoed all around them, familiar yet weirdly altered.

"Go to the plains." The words were Dayflower's, if Dayflower spoke like low distant thunder. *"You must go, or it will be too late."*

Perhaps it wasn't Dayflower at all, Bramble thought with a tremor of awe. It was more as if something spoke through her.

"Go to . . . the plains."

"The plains?" whispered Moonflower hoarsely.

"The . . . plains. Let them swallow you or . . ."

"Swallow us?" Bramble squeaked.

"Be immersed in the great seas of grass. Let it be so. . . ." For a long moment, the intense monotone fell silent. Then Dayflower rasped again:

"Or let evil swallow Bravelands entirely."

The Mistback's rigid body went suddenly limp, and if Bramble and Moonflower had not grabbed a wild hold of her, she would have collapsed onto the floor. Bramble heard her confused, rapid panting.

"What happened? I—"

"You had a vision, Mother!" Moonflower reassured her.

"I have *never* experienced a vision in that way!" gasped Dayflower.

At that moment, something dry and smooth slithered across Bramble's hand. He gave a shriek and flinched back, losing his grip on Dayflower.

"What was that?"

"What was what?" Moonflower's scared voice already sounded farther away.

"It—" Bramble sucked in a terrified gasp. The thing, whatever it was, coiled around his hand once more. Reflexively he tightened his fist, and the creature hissed and pulsated, slipping out of his grasp.

"A *snake!*"

"Bramble, don't panic!" That was Dayflower, her voice level. "It can't hurt you."

"Bramble!" cried Moonflower. "It's all right! Calm down!"

But it was all too much: the darkness, the fumes, the sounds, and the booming voice that had possessed Dayflower. And now, the dry, cool body of a serpent that writhed around his fist, refusing to be shaken off. With a shriek of panic and disgust, Bramble staggered away.

He had no idea which way he was fleeing; he knew only that he had to run, to escape the evil of the darkness. *I have to get out!*

"Wait, Bramble!" Moonflower's frantic plea sounded distant. *"Stop!"*

Bramble could neither wait nor stop. His feet and hands fumbled and slipped, and he almost hurtled head over heels. His shoulder crashed hard against stone, but he recovered, flailing wildly in the darkness, and bounded on.

He was aware of his two friends following. They were some way back, but they were loping after him with pleas and gasps and cries of terror. Far behind him in the blackness, Moonflower gave a cry of pain, and then another. Her knuckles, like his, must be slamming into sharp rocks. Bramble no longer had breath to cry out, though. There was only one thought in his head, one overwhelming need. . . .

Great Spirit, get me out of here!

The walls were narrowing. Bramble felt both his flanks crash and scrape against hard rock. Perhaps he was fleeing right into the belly of the deepest part of Bravelands, he thought wildly. Perhaps this tunnel was the throat of some great beast that would swallow him. Even as Bramble pounded through the narrowing darkness, a terror filled his body, driving him into despair.

I'll never see daylight again. . . .

His foot caught a sharp lip of rock, and the world tipped. He threw out his arms to find some purchase, but there was nothing. Then his head struck something hard. For a moment, there was pain.

Then nothing at all.

CHAPTER TWENTY-THREE

Chase woke with a start in her den. And instantly, the awful moments came back to her: the fury that she had turned on Seek, her angry roars, the cub's wounded face as he stared at her. Aghast, she rolled over and propped herself up on her forepaws.

"Seek?"

The den was empty but for her. Chase's heart twisted violently.

"Seek!"

Oh, Great Spirit . . . had the hyenas returned and taken him while she slept? Chase scrabbled up out of the den and stood in the open air, her tail lashing, her nostrils flaring wide.

There was no hyena-stink close to the den, she was relieved to find. But she could smell Seek himself; he had left the den not long ago, though he was nowhere in sight. Oh, if something had happened to the cub because of her . . .

How could you, Chase? She didn't know whether the inner voice was her own or her mother's. Perhaps it was both.

I have to find him.

Seek was not yet skilled in hiding his tracks, so the trail was easy enough to follow. Chase picked up speed, bounding over branches and fallen logs, her heart thundering with fear. *Please, Great Spirit. Please let me find him before something happens—*

She recognized this part of the woods. Chase slowed and halted. She began to pad forward again, her fur bristling. This was the glade where Shadow had his den. . . .

Lowering her head, clenching her jaws, she paced forward. At the tree that hid the den, she caught a strong whiff of Seek's scent—but instinctively she looked upward, into the branches.

There was the cub, sprawled contentedly along a bough as he chewed idly on the remains of a small impala. He seemed entirely relaxed, as if he did not realize or care how much he had alarmed her. Chase choked back her cry of anger; she must not scare the cub again.

She narrowed her eyes, staring. Shadow could be very difficult to spot, but no: there was no sign of the black leopard.

Chase clawed her way up the tree, toward the branch where Seek sat. Now there was no way for him to flee again without her catching him. He caught sight of her and stopped chewing.

His eyes widened as she climbed toward him, and for a moment he looked guilty, but then he scowled.

"Did Shadow bring you here?" Chase demanded. "Did he make you leave the den, Seek? I've been so worried!"

Seek averted his eyes. He scratched at the branch with his claws. "No, Chase. You didn't need to worry. I came by myself."

"*Why?*" Even as she asked the question, she had a horrible feeling she knew the answer.

"I didn't want to be a burden. I know I'm a problem." He scowled, but when he spoke again his voice was plaintive, and he ripped obsessively at the bark. "I know I make things harder for you, I know that anyway, and then you said it yourself."

Chase's heart flipped painfully inside her. Guilt and remorse tightened her throat.

"Seek, I didn't mean it. I'm so sorry. I was angry with Shadow, not with you."

"It's true, though, isn't it? That's why you want to go and be with Range." The cub's ears drooped. "It's fine if that's what you want. But I'm not coming with you."

Chase took a deep breath. "We'll talk about it, back at the den. I never meant to hurt you, Seek. Let's go home."

The cub didn't move. She saw his claws dig deeper into the branch.

"I don't want to go back. It's safe *here*, Chase. Can't we stay with Shadow?"

"No!" growled Chase, laying her ears back in shock. "No, we are *not* giving in to a leopard who's after nothing but our territory!"

"That's not true!" exclaimed the cub angrily. "He's really

kind, and he wants to protect us—"

"That's enough." With a quick glance around for Shadow, Chase bounded forward onto the branch and grabbed Seek by his scruff.

His claws were still lodged in the wood. "You can't make me!"

"Yes, I *can*." With one good yank, she dislodged his claws, and his body went limp in her jaws.

His submission was only a reflex, and it didn't stop him complaining. He yowled as she carried him down the tree: "Leave me alone! I want to stay with Shadow!"

"What's going on?" said a grim voice behind Chase.

She set the cub down and spun around. Shadow stood right at her haunches, and his defiant stare locked with hers. His tail-tip flicked warily. There was no spark of amusement or fondness in those familiar green eyes.

"You had no right to take him, Shadow! Seek is under *my* protection, not yours!"

"And you think you can defend him against hyenas?" growled Shadow. "There are still some around, you know. This is foolish behavior."

"Back off," she snarled. "Our lives are nothing to do with you, Shadow. Seek and I will live in our own territory!"

"Really? And have you asked Seek what *he* wants?"

"Yes," put in the cub, his tone surly. "And I told her—"

"It doesn't matter!" cried Chase in a fury. "Seek is *my* responsibility!"

Snatching up the cub by his scruff, she sprang out of the

clearing and sprinted for her own territory and den. Behind her, she could hear Shadow roaring at her to stop.

"Don't be stupid, Chase. Don't be selfish. Think of the cub!"

She ignored him and ran on. How *dare* Shadow accuse her of selfishness, after all she'd done to raise and protect a cub who wasn't hers?

The arrogance! She didn't trust him not to chase her and force her to bring the cub back, though she couldn't hear any sound of pursuit yet. *Best to take the roundabout way back to the den,* she decided. *He could still come there, but we'll be on our own home ground. I can see him off!*

Loping uphill, she realized indignantly that she'd been right. She *could* hear the crunch of paws following her. Couldn't he just leave them alone?

Except . . . that wasn't one set of paws she could hear; there were at least four or five. And they were not as light or quiet as the footfalls of a leopard.

A chill ran through her. They were back. The hyenas. They must have been lurking close to where they knew the cub was. They must have known Shadow would have to leave Seek and hunt, that he could not protect him every moment of the day and night. . . .

Any more than I can.

Chase's heart plummeted. She could hear more hyenas off to her flank; the foliage rustled and cracked, and she made out flashes of brindled hide through the trees as they fanned out left and right. They were trying to hem her in. Their yips

of excitement were horrible, and she was weighed down by
Seek's limp form.

The little cub was breathing hard in her jaws; he must be
terrified, but he didn't speak. Desperation flowed through
Chase as the hyenas gained on her. In their hunting frenzy,
they could easily kill her and the cub. Just off to her left, dark
shadows were drawing closer; she caught glimpses of yellow
eyes, hungry jaws, lolling tongues.

But on her right . . .

I know that stream. It was one that fed into the river Range
had showed her. Changing course, she bolted toward the
sound of fast-flowing water. As she leaped and bounded over
a stack of flat rocks, she heard the thunder of the waterfall
itself, cascading down above her.

"Can't cross that river!" yelped a hyena's voice, far too close.

"Watch your footing, cat!" laughed another. "You might
slip!"

Growling in her throat, Chase forced herself to slow down
for the steep ascent. The hyenas were taunting her, but they
were right: she could not afford to fall now. Seek still dangling
from her jaws, she struggled up the rocky bank toward the
torrent of the falls.

The hyenas seemed more hesitant. Risking a glance down,
she saw that they were prowling and trotting among the scattered boulders by the pool. One licked his lips and grinned up
at her.

"We can wait, cat," one chuckled. "Watch you don't fall!"

There, beyond a ridge and below her, was the flat slab she

recognized. Leaping onto it, her paws slipped and she almost tumbled off. But she steadied herself and stared at the sheets of water cascading down the cliff. She gathered her courage.

I made the jump easily before, even carrying Seek. I can do it again.

The hyenas were all laughing now, and some of them, impatient, had begun to climb the steep rocks to drive her down. *Now or never.*

Taking a deep breath through her nostrils, Chase tightened her grip on Seek and sprang from the slab.

A spray of cold water hit her spine, but this time she was expecting it. She landed hard, but on all fours, within the dank cave behind the falls.

Setting Seek carefully down on the damp cavern floor, Chase edged back toward the waterfall. Through that thinnest part of the water, she could make out the disappointed hyenas far below. They were hunting around the pool and along the riverbanks, snuffling in bushes and pawing the water's edge. They looked bewildered and more than a little annoyed; perhaps they thought the two leopards had vanished into thin air, or that they'd been drowned deep by the force of the falling water. It wasn't long before the hyenas gave up and trotted off.

Breathing out a long sigh, Chase lay down at Seek's side. He was wet and trembling, and despite his anger at being taken from Shadow, he pressed against her flank for warmth and comfort.

"I really am sorry, Seek. For what I said yesterday." Chase licked the crown of his head. "And I'm sorry I ran into those hyenas."

"But you got away from them," Seek whispered, cuddling even closer. "I thought they were going to eat us."

Chase's heart turned over with pity and love for the bedraggled cub. "We'll be safe here. Range will be back soon, I think."

"Range is back already," came a soft voice from above her.

She glanced up, surprised. There, on a high ledge, lay Range. His body was in shadow, but his blue eyes burned bright in the dimness.

"I'm glad you came, Chase." He rose to his paws.

"I had to!" she growled as she went over the events of the day in her mind. "That arrogant fool, Shadow—he took Seek from me. He stole my cub! I had to get away from him *and* the hyenas. He'll never touch Seek again!"

Seek gave a muffled whimper against her rib cage.

"I can help you," murmured Range. "If you trust me. Do you trust me, Chase?"

Yes, she wanted to say, loud and firm. But something held her back. His blue eyes were so very bright, so very intense: it was a little unsettling.

"What are you doing up there?" she called. "Why don't you come down?"

He didn't answer that. "The mountain is a perilous place, Chase. It's full of threats and traps for the unwary. We creatures who make it our home: we need a strong leader. Why didn't I realize that before? It makes life sweeter and easier, to be led and protected by a powerful creature." His gaze grew dreamy. "I have found that leader."

Chase licked her jaws in confusion. "What are you talking about? There's nothing more powerful than a leopard!"

"I used to think the same." His voice was low and smooth. "Don't be afraid, Chase."

She did not have time to ask him what she should not be afraid of. The walls of the cavern seemed to come alive at that moment, and she leaped to her paws with a growl. The rocks were moving: rippling and undulating in a way that shouldn't be possible.

Then she realized that it wasn't the rocks; it was the snakes that slithered out of every crack and hole and crevice in the stone. Hundreds of them, silent and purposeful, crawling toward her and Seek in the center of the cavern.

Seek gave a squeal of terror and hid beneath Chase's legs. She should look strong for him, she knew, but she couldn't help the trembling of her own limbs.

What is going on? Had Range drawn these snakes here? How could he do that? *Why* would he do it?

Slowly, making sure Seek stayed between her legs, Chase backed toward the waterfall. Already there were tiny snakes between her paws, coiling over and through one another and striking out with their fangs. Seek darted out with a courageous snarl, seized a snake in his jaws, and crushed it; but another swiftly bit at his paw. As the long fangs sank into his flesh, he squealed in pain and terror.

"Chase!"

"I see it!" Chase spun and struck the snake away. It tumbled down, twisting as it fell away from the cub, but it didn't skitter into the shadows as she expected. Coiling up, its eyes locked with hers. Then it drew back its head and struck out at Chase's own paw.

The attack was too fast to see, and far too fast to dodge. The snake drew back, unhurried, a look of satisfaction in its sinister eyes. Chase stared at it in horror.

They'll kill us both. There was no avoiding more bites, she realized; more snakes writhed around them, darting and drawing back, rearing up and lunging forward, and Chase couldn't watch them all at once. The bite on her paw burned.

Yet strangely, the snakes had stopped biting. They writhed in their dance, advancing and retreating, coiling erect before twisting back down, but no more of them tried to strike. And every yellow eye watched Chase and Seek.

"Join us, Chase!" Range's voice echoed over the hissing, slithering mass. "There's no way out, beyond dying in the falls. Join us willingly and serve the Silent One!"

He was mad, she thought. Mad! *He's talking nonsense!*

"I don't know what you're saying," she snarled. "Why would we serve anyone?"

"It is the only way now," said Range. "Please, Chase—open your eyes and see what your mother could not."

"What?"

"I tried to warn her, truly I did," said Range. "I offered her safety—safe haven for you *all*—but she was too proud to listen."

Chase reeled, sick to her stomach, trying to make sense of his words. *I was wrong about Range. So wrong.* The horrible knowledge struck her like a giant paw in her gut.

"It wasn't the gorillas that killed her. . . ."

Range did not answer her directly, but turned half away, his voice a low growl. "It would break my heart if you were to meet the same fate."

Chase licked her jaws and forced herself to speak her words clearly and defiantly, with her eyes fixed on the snakes.

"I am Chase Born of Prowl. And I serve *no one!*"

"Then I cannot help you either," said Range.

The waiting snakes stuck as one, and Chase felt their fangs across her legs and flanks. One or two bit Seek as well, eliciting squeals of pain. She seized him by the scruff, turned, and bolted toward the waterfall. There was no time to look for the right spot; she could only coil her muscles and hurl herself blindly into the torrent. So this time, there was no tickle of cold spray on her back; the water hit her like a gigantic gorilla fist, smashing her down. She heard Seek cry out briefly, and then she lost hold of him. Now she was alone in the torrent, her mouth and nose filling with water, choking and drowning.

An instant later, she smacked through the surface of the pool, her impetus driving her deep beneath the water. Her paws scraped rock, and wildly she pushed against it, driving herself back to the air. But the force of the waterfall was enormous, shoving her under every time she tried to rise. Bubbles leaked from her nose. *I have to find Seek, I have to!*

Again the power of the falls drove her down. It was hopeless trying to swim upward; frantic with desperation and the longing to inhale, she flailed her paws and paddled weakly along the bottom of the pool. Her lungs ached to suck in air, and the water around her seemed to be darkening with every passing moment. *I'm sorry, Prowl. I failed Seek. . . . It'll be quick, at least—*

And suddenly, she was drifting upward, the force of falling water lifted; she had swum free of its current. With one last push, Chase breached the surface and gasped in a great lungful of air.

She had come up at the edge of the pool, where water eddied and swirled, tinged with brown foam. Chase dragged herself onto the bank, but she could not allow herself to lie down. If she had escaped the terrible suffocating weight of the waterfall, perhaps Seek—

She gave a cry of distress. There, a little way along and bumping against the bank in the current, floated a limp and sodden bundle of dark yellow fur. She raced to Seek's side, plunged her forepaws into the water, and hauled him out.

Oh please, Great Spirit, PLEASE don't let him die!

She couldn't allow it. She would never forgive herself. It was all her fault. She rolled him over onto his back and licked frantically at his face.

"Wake up, Seek! Get up! Please!"

There was no response. Grief surged through her. *You have to wake up!*

She rolled him again, onto his belly, and shoved her nose under him, trying to force him to stand. Seek's body arched, hanging limp over her muzzle, his paws dangling.

And then, miraculously, Seek's whole body gave a violent

jerk. He gave a hacking cough, and muddy river water poured from his mouth and nostrils.

Chase jerked away in shock, and he flopped to the ground. Then she nuzzled him, urging him up. "Seek! Seek! You're alive!"

He staggered groggily to his paws and fell over again, coughing up more water. Once again he made himself stand, as Chase licked and licked at his pelt, cleaning him of river mud and warming his shivering bones.

At last, they collapsed back onto the bank together, curled up around each other for warmth. Chase went on licking at the cub's ears and head. She sniffed at the double puncture wounds on his forepaw and washed them with her tongue. There were more higher up his leg. She didn't know how many times he'd been bitten, or how venomous the snakes were.

"I thought we were dead," whimpered the cub.

"The Great Spirit must be smiling on us, Seek. We survived the snakes *and* that fall. I don't know how." Chase's voice grew soft. "But there's something I do know for sure."

"What's that?" Seek mumbled into her chest fur.

"You're not *someone else's cub*. I was stupid to think that. You're my cub. *Mine*. I'm not going to protect you because I owe it to our mothers."

She nuzzled his nose and lashed his face with her tongue.

"I'm going to protect you because I *am* your mother now."

CHAPTER TWENTY-FOUR

"Moonflower? Dayflower?"

Bramble was almost afraid to whisper, but he had to. His head throbbed, and reaching up he felt a lump under the skin. He had no clue where his headlong flight had taken him, in the bowels of this terrible mountain. The mindless panic had faded at last, draining all the energy from his body, leaving him bereft and utterly lost. He *must* find the others.

How far had he come before his accident? Perhaps Moonflower and Dayflower weren't even together anymore. It could be that the three gorillas were all alone now, fated to wander solitary in the darkness until they died miserable and thirsty and starving.

Panic almost choked him. He cried out louder: *"Moonflower!"*

"Bramble! Bramble, where are you?"

"Moonflower!" He turned, then twisted again. It was so hard

to tell the direction of the sound. It didn't sound close.

"Bramble! *Brother!*" The echoes reverberated in the darkness, ricocheting and dwindling to silence.

He must move, he realized. He could not stay here, lost forever and alone, yet afraid to seek his friends and salvation. Gritting his trembling jaws, Bramble reached out to feel the cold stone of the tunnel walls. He took a deep, unsteady breath, and began to creep back the way he had come. *At least, I hope it's the way I came.* . . . With each step, the pain in his head made him feel sick and weak.

He shuddered violently, tensed his muscles, gritted his teeth. There was *no choice!* He had to keep moving. Another step in the lightless tunnel, and another. He thought perhaps the stone was rising beneath his feet and fists.

There was a shuffling noise from farther along the tunnel, and unsteady breathing. His heartbeat rising and pulsing in his throat, Bramble edged forward.

He was sure the sounds were coming closer, and he must not start to believe that was wishful thinking. He swallowed hard and blinked.

The blink . . . something was different. He frowned and blinked again, more slowly this time.

Now he was sure of it. It wasn't *light*, exactly. But there was a difference between his eyes being shut and being open. Almost . . . a lesser darkness . . .

Seemingly out of nowhere and nothingness, Bramble felt a warm hand clasp his arm. Relief and gratitude swamped him; he would recognize his sister's touch even if the light had deserted him forever.

"Bramble! Thank the Spirit I've found you. We didn't know what had happened."

Bramble squeezed Moonflower's hand, then hugged her tightly. "I hit my head, but I'm all right now," he said hoarsely. "Do you know where your mother is?"

"Just a little farther along." Moonflower cuddled him fiercely against her, then drew back. As she did so, Bramble thought he saw the gleam of her eyes against the blackness. "We've found a way out!"

"Really?" It came out in a gasping sob.

"Truly! You must have run right past it yourself!" There was giddy laughter in Moonflower's voice. "We all panicked back there, and things could have ended badly. But the Great Spirit brought us straight to another of its vents!"

Moonflower dropped to all fours, and the two young gorillas bounded along the narrowing passageway, Bramble staying so close to his sister, he trod a few times on her heels. When he actually began to make out her haunches in front of him, he could barely believe it; but it was no illusion. A faint glow outlined Moonflower in silver. Around one more corner, he saw a ragged triangle of light, so unexpected it almost dazzled him.

Against the light stood Dayflower, beckoning to them both. She gave them a huge smile. "Here's our way out!"

"This is amazing!" gabbled Bramble. "Wonderful!"

"Amazing, wonderful, and too small right now." Dayflower

laughed. "But with a bit of effort, we can make our way out in no time."

"Then let's start digging," suggested Dayflower. "I for one can't wait to see the sun again!"

They set to moving the tumble of rocks and boulders and scraping away at compacted earth and tangled roots. It was hard going. Bramble's muscles ached and he was out of breath, but nothing now could stop him digging feverishly with the others. His nails were chipped and cracked, his hands bruised, but the scent of the fresh mountain air was a constant goad to dig faster. And with every moment, with every grunt of effort, the crack of the vent was visibly widening: light flooded in to meet them, like a long golden thorn piercing the blackness.

"Moonflower, do you think you could make it through now?" asked Dayflower. The old gorilla sounded exhausted, but hopeful. "There's not much more we can do from this side. . . ."

"I think I can." Moonflower turned to hug her mother. "If Bramble and I can squeeze through, maybe we can clear that big root from the other side and shift that rock." She slapped the edge of the awkward boulder.

"If you can move those, I'm sure the gap will be big enough for me." Dayflower sounded breathless with hope.

"I'm certain we can," said Moonflower firmly. "I promise we won't be long, Mother!"

Hugging Dayflower fiercely, she drew away with a smile, ducked, and began to haul herself awkwardly through the uneven gap.

"Nearly there," came her muffled cry. "Give me a shove, Bramble!"

Together, Bramble and Dayflower pushed hard on Moonflower's haunches. With a last vigorous wriggle, the young gorilla slithered and tumbled out into the mountain air.

Stumbling upright, Moonflower turned, stretching happily. "You next, Bramble!"

He turned to Dayflower, suddenly reluctant to leave her, but she smiled.

"Go on, Bramble. The sooner you and Moonflower widen the vent, the sooner I can get out!"

Bramble nodded and grinned. "See you soon, Dayflower Mistback!"

He gripped the edges of the hole with his fingers and wriggled through. Moonflower's exit had widened the hole a little, but it was still an effort to drag himself through. No way, though, was he going to stop and go back. His sides scraped painfully against thick roots, and he grazed his knuckles on the edge of that stubborn boulder, but he clenched his jaws in determination. His head and arms were in the open air; as soon as one shoulder was free, Moonflower grabbed it and tugged him the rest of the way.

Kicking and flailing in a shower of loose earth, Bramble felt himself pop free of the mountain. He staggered upright. It felt wonderful to stand on the cool hillside; sunlight dappled the small glade where he and Moonflower stood, and his head was light with the clearness of the air. This place was not unlike their own Spirit Mouth, though as far as Bramble could tell from the sun's position, this vent was on the eastern flank of the mountain. Trees rose cool and green overhead, insects buzzed around them, and the canopy was filled with trills and cries and birdsong. Instead of that foul smoke, the scents of leaf and flower filled Bramble's nostrils.

"Come on, Moonflower." He grinned. "It's time your mother enjoyed this, too!"

The two young gorillas set to work with renewed energy, yanking at roots and stones and digging so fast and eagerly into the earth, they showered themselves with dirt. Dayflower poked her head through the opening and inhaled the air with a blissful sigh. "I can't wait to be out there."

"It gets better!" Moonflower laughed.

"And you were right about the boulder, Dayflower." Bramble gripped its top edge with both forepaws and propped his feet against the packed soil that surrounded it. He swung out once, twice, and struck the boulder with his feet. "From this side, it won't be a problem. It's loosening already."

Moonflower joined him, gripping the boulder and pulling with him.

"One-two-three-*shove*," grunted Bramble. "One-two-three—"

Moonflower gave a cry of triumph as the huge stone cracked loose from the earth and roots that held it. It sagged out; swiftly Bramble and Moonflower dodged out of its way, and Bramble clambered up the slope to push it from above. With a roaring crash, the slab came suddenly loose, tumbling down the slope toward the edge of the glade.

"Well done!" exclaimed Dayflower. "I can get through now, I'm sure of it!"

Shifting the boulder had made a big difference to the gap. Moonflower's eyes shone as her mother began to wriggle through, dislodging pebbles and earth.

It was still a tight squeeze for a fully grown gorilla, thought Bramble, but Dayflower was close to freedom . . . *so close* . . . Her shoulders were clear of the gap, and now her arms. . . . Bramble clenched his fists in excitement.

The old gorilla's eyes met his, and she smiled.

In the time it took Bramble to return her grin, Dayflower's expression changed. Delight turned to an awful terror. Her jaws opened in a gasp of horror, and her eyes widened till the whites showed around her pale brown eyes.

"Moonflower!" she shrieked. *"Help me!"*

As Bramble gaped in confusion, Dayflower's body jerked backward. He lunged toward her, grabbing one flailing arm, and Moonflower seized the other one.

"What is it?" cried Moonflower. "What's happening?"

Another great jolt pulled Dayflower back again. She screamed.

"It's got me. *Help!*"

"I don't understand!" cried Bramble. "What's got you?"

But even as his mind reeled in bewilderment, he stood up, propping his feet against the rocks and hauling with all his might. Moonflower was pulling desperately at her mother's arm, yet the old gorilla, wriggling and struggling and sobbing with fear, slipped inexorably backward into the cavern.

"Don't let me go!" screamed Dayflower. "Please, by the Spirit, hold on!"

Whatever had her was stronger than both of them. Moonflower lost her grip, falling back; Bramble was yanked in after Dayflower. Only his scrabbling feet against a boulder saved him. He fought to hold on, but as his head and shoulders were dragged into the darkness again, he caught sight of something behind the Mistback in the darkness, something huge and coiled and sinuous. The feeble light of the vent flickered and gleamed on colossal scales.

"What is it?" cried Dayflower, her eyes even more broadly white-rimmed now and bright with utter terror. "What can you see?"

Bramble's heart thundered with fear and horror as he gazed into her eyes. "It's . . . I don't . . ."

And then, with a powerful jerk, the old gorilla's arm slipped through his fingers. Dayflower gave one last, despairing scream. And then the darkness swallowed her.

Bramble kicked violently back, bringing clods of earth down on himself as he squirmed backward out of the hole. Something huge smashed against the interior of the vent, as if it was coming after him, and Bramble gave a hoarse scream.

Rocks cascaded down both inside and outside the vent, and he barely managed to scrabble away before they hit him. But Moonflower sprang forward, and it was all Bramble could do to stop her leaping through the tumbling rockfall in pursuit of Dayflower.

The roar and crash of the rocks seemed to go on for an

eternity. When the hillside settled once more and the last stone rumbled to a halt against a tree, a grim silence fell.

"Mother!" Moonflower's shriek shattered the stillness and sent flocks of birds fluttering from the canopy. "Bramble, get her back! We have to go in again!"

"You *can't!*" Bramble wrestled his sister back, dragging her to the ground as she kicked and yelled. "The rockfall has blocked the vent."

"We'll move the rocks!"

"Moonflower, no!" Bramble yelled desperately. "Even if we managed that—it'll take us too!"

"It? What was *it*? Let me get her back!"

"You can't!" Bramble flung himself on top of her, holding her down as she snarled in grief-stricken fury. "Moonflower. You've got to believe me. We couldn't fight that thing. Please."

"You still haven't said!" Her eyes blazed, but Bramble felt her body go limp as exhaustion caught up with her. Panting, she glared up at him, her eyes red. "What was it?"

"I . . . I'm not sure myself." Bramble too was gasping for breath. Hesitantly, he staggered up; Moonflower made no attempt to bolt back toward the vent. "It was bad, Moonflower. Scales, like a snake, but *so big . . .*" Another great shudder went through his bones.

Rolling over, she pounded the earth with her fists. "Why, Great Spirit? She was nearly free!"

She collapsed to the ground again. Bramble bounded to her side. If he couldn't explain what had happened—if he was barely capable of describing the thing he'd seen—the least he could do was cradle his sister as she wept for her mother.

After a time, he pulled away and went back to the blocked vent. The rock was packed tightly, and some pieces were clearly too large to move. Whatever that thing had been—whatever took Moonflower's mother—it had no chance of escaping this way.

The two young gorillas sat without speaking for a while, surrounded by birdsong and the scents of the forest. It didn't feel half so beautiful as it had when they first escaped the mountain.

But we are alive, thought Bramble. *That has to matter. The Great Spirit spared us.*

His head twisted as he heard a voice calling out, distantly through the trees.

"That's Woodnettle," he murmured. "Burbark's thugs must be checking all the neighboring valleys, and they're coming this way."

Moonflower nodded, wiping her face, clearing her throat. Her face was set in a grim scowl. "We can't let them win. Not now."

Dropping to all fours, the two gorillas bounded through the trees. At every turn, Bramble heard the rough deep voices of the Blackbacks, and he began to despair. *Where can we go? They can't help but find us.*

He and Moonflower scrabbled to a halt on a ridge. Below them, an escarpment stretched down toward a series of stone ledges. There was no clear path down.

"That looks dangerous," said Moonflower.

"We can't turn back," Bramble replied. He glanced over his shoulder. "They're getting closer!"

Moonflower took a deep breath. She seized his hand.

"I won't let Woodnettle seal me up in that place again," she growled. "Are you ready, brother?"

"I'm ready."

Together, they began to pick their way down onto the precipitous slope.

There was no chance of keeping their footing. Bramble's went from under him straightaway, and he slid on his rump, tumbling down the hillside, hitting stones and snatching at trees and branches in a desperate attempt to slow himself. Off to his right he caught glimpses of Moonflower, who fared no better; she was slithering backward, clutching uselessly at the ground, panic in her eyes.

The slide seemed to go on forever, but at last Bramble jolted to a painful halt on level ground. He lay immobile with shock for a moment, then tentatively began testing hands and feet to make sure they still worked. *Nothing broken.*

Moonflower stumbled over to him. Her fur was dusty and bedraggled, but she too had escaped without serious harm. Bramble shut his eyes and breathed out in relief.

She squatted beside him. "So where now?" Her voice sounded very small and frightened.

Bramble opened his eyes again and struggled up to a sitting position. They had landed on a broad ledge of sandstone that jutted out over . . . well, he could not describe it as a valley. It was a vast, sweeping plain that stretched to a misty horizon he could barely make out. Gullies and rivers made ragged green and silver lines, and flat-topped acacias dotted the near distance; beyond that, the land was blurred by a shimmer of distance. He could make out birds soaring over the plains, but they were no more than tiny dots. And farther out on the great sea of yellow grass, those might be vast herds of wildebeests and gazelles. . . . It all looked so open, so impossibly wide and long, so *exposed*.

"There," he said, pointing down. "The Spirit told us to go to the plains." Moonflower was silent, staring down at the expanse. Bramble reached for her arm. "It was Dayflower's wish." He almost said *final wish*, for he had no doubt that Moonflower's mother was dead.

"You're right," said Moonflower, nodding slowly and sadly. "There's nothing for us on the mountain now, Bramble. Only death."

But what awaits us down there? thought Bramble. *Blood pools on the plains. . . .*

"It's what Cassava wanted too," he said, almost to himself. "It's what he died for."

"I'm afraid," said Moonflower.

"As am I," he replied, "but at least we're together."

He took her hand, and side by side they set off down the shallow slope, toward the grass plains of Bravelands and the ancient fears that would rise to meet them.

CHAPTER TWENTY-FIVE

Fleeing was not an option. And, Prance reminded herself, she did not *want* to run. For better or for worse, the Great Spirit had brought her here, to a point where she would have the answers she sought. Perhaps that would mean her death, but it wasn't as if she hadn't prepared herself.

The lion who had hunted her down led the way; the rest of his pride escorted Prance in two close ranks. They had walked through the night, the lions' eyes glowing beside her. She was exhausted and limping from the wound she had taken in her fall.

Why hadn't the pride killed her? Perhaps, she thought, this was some twisted game that lions liked to play. She'd heard stories of how cats big and small liked to toy with their prey. Prance's hide bristled. At any moment she half expected to feel claws and teeth in her rump, dragging her down to have the life choked out of her.

As if he heard her thoughts, the big lion ahead of her turned as he walked.

"Don't be afraid, Prance Herdless. We're not going to kill you."

She cleared her throat, trying to sound as brave as she could. "Then where are you taking me? Who *are* you?" A sudden thought struck her, and she gasped. "Are you real lions—or spirits?"

The lion grunted a laugh. "We're real live lions," he assured her. "I am Gallant Gallantpride, and we have already eaten today."

"That's good," said Prance faintly.

"Besides, I am under strict orders," he added.

Taken aback, Prance almost missed her footing. Who could give a great pride leader orders? she wondered.

A watering hole loomed through the shimmering haze of the morning. It seemed barely any time until they reached its banks, but the lions did not pause to drink; they paced around its edges toward a clump of trees on the western side. Prance felt her weariness more sharply now, and the pain of her wound was worse. Yet she didn't dare halt while the lions walked on.

This bank of the watering hole was thronged with animals. Tired as she was, Prance couldn't help staring. There were zebras, wildebeests, gazelles; a group of elephants stood in the shallows, dousing one another with trunks full of water. Hippos wallowed nearby, shooting filthy looks at the crocodiles farther out. Birds perched on every branch: starlings, hawks, bee-eaters, egrets, weaver birds, and buzzards. As Prance passed, every creature stopped what they were doing to stare at her with curiosity.

Still the lions walked on. They veered away from the water and now padded through the cluster of trees Prance had noticed from a distance. In a few strides, she found herself in a broad, dappled clearing, shaded by young branches and studded with ancient white stumps. Here, the noise was overwhelming; baboons lined the trees and the sandy earth between them, hooting and hollering and whooping. Prance's ears flickered anxiously; her heartbeat was racing now.

The lions stopped. Just ahead, Prance saw a huge pale boulder, standing solitary in the clearing, its top almost flat. On it perched a vulture, and though she couldn't be sure, she was struck by the instinct that this was the one that had been stalking her. It blinked its heavy-lidded eyes as she approached and flexed its wings.

Gradually, the baboons began to quiet, and other animals approached the clearing, waiting just beyond the trees. The lions turned away from Prance and began to pace away.

"What?" she stammered to Gallant Gallantpride as he passed her. The lions had been terrifying company, but she found suddenly that she didn't want them to abandon her.

"We lions have other work to do," Gallant rumbled. He walked on, but paused to glance back and say again, "There's nothing to fear now."

Easy for a lion to say! thought Prance. Silence fell in the clearing.

There was movement behind the boulder, and Prance peered harder. A small creature was hobbling out from behind the stone.

It was a wizened, gray old baboon, and he held a mango in his paws, chewing on it as he walked. He muttered to himself and slapped a fly from his shoulder.

The baboon was almost blind, she realized as he lifted his filmy eyes. But he kept walking toward her, stopping only when she was sure he was going to bump into her. He peered up at her, spitting out a tough piece of mango skin and wiping juice from his chin. Then he moved around her, prodding and poking at her flanks and limbs, and muttering under his breath. At last he came to a halt before her and offered her the half-eaten mango. "Hungry?"

She backed away. "No, thank you." Around the clearing, the other animals were watching.

Prance waited, overcome by sudden shyness. At last the baboon turned his head to stare back at the huge boulder. He shook his grizzled head.

"Once," he said, "I could have leaped onto that boulder in a single spring. Now I can barely climb at all. That bird sits there and mocks me. Don't you, old friend?"

The vulture blinked its eyes and tilted its head. Far from a mocking gesture, it seemed quite affectionate. The old baboon grinned, revealing a few missing teeth, and turned back to Prance.

"What's your name?" His voice was surprisingly clear, if a little soft.

"I'm Prance Herdless."

He smiled into her eyes, blinking his own pale and watery ones. "Prance *Herdless*, you say. How very strange! And what brings you here?"

"The lions brought me," said Prance.

"Ah, yes," replied the baboon, "but *what* brought you here? How is it that you are a gazelle with no herd?"

"I . . . I don't know." She cast a nervous glance around. It was pure instinct. Despite what the lion had said, there could be predators lurking.

"You are safe," said the baboon. "None will harm you."

Slowly, she felt her heart calm and steady. His face was so kind and so wise, and suddenly Prance knew she had to tell this old baboon everything.

"Thank you. Thank you, because I haven't felt safe in a long time. My story . . ."

The words spilled out of her in a great rush, aching and heartfelt. The lion hunt, the death of Leap, her incredible escape, and the frightened hostility of Runningherd. Her time with the zebras, and her time alone. Her loss of the Us, and her fears for the Friendships that bound other herds. The old baboon listened to the whole tale in silence, his head slightly cocked, sucking occasionally at the mango. ". . . So you see," she said, "the Great Spirit has abandoned me. And now I'm alone."

For the first time, the baboon reacted. Bristling, he threw down his mango and rose onto his hind legs. He wagged a scolding finger in front of her muzzle, and she flinched.

"The Great Spirit abandons no creature, Prance Herdless! Indeed, from your story it sounds as if the Spirit has a special purpose for you."

Recovering her nerve, Prance couldn't help but laugh. "I doubt that! I don't mean any disrespect, but what could make you think the Spirit is interested in me?"

He stared at her, very intently. "I do not think it. I *know* it."

And suddenly, then, Prance understood. She realized who it was in front of her.

"Oh my! You're—"

"Yes." The old baboon nodded and dusted his paws free of mango scraps. "I am."

"I'm sorry," she blurted. "I didn't realize—"

The old baboon grinned. "Who do you think sent Gallantpride to find you?"

"Great Father!"

"Please, you must call me Thorn."

Prance still couldn't quite fathom it. Her mother had often told her stories about the Great Father baboon and his adventures—how he had taken on evil and kept Bravelands safe. But times had been peaceful for so long, and she knew the stories were much exaggerated over the seasons. It was hard to believe this frail old creature could be the same baboon who fought alongside the elephants and lions against Titan the Devourer of Souls.

"You are not impressed, I think?" he said.

"No . . . it's not that," lied Prance. "I just never expected to meet the Great Parent."

"Nor he you," said Thorn. He narrowed his eyes. "I've heard many stories of the gazelle who keeps cheating death. It's a strange phenomenon, but not half as odd and wrong as some of the things that have happened in Bravelands these last moons."

Prance drew herself up. It was funny, but her legs had stopped shaking, and she was suddenly unashamed. This was the Great Father talking to her—and he had summoned her himself. She dipped her head in respect, then lifted it again.

"If I can help, I will," she told him softly.

"Good, good." Great Father Thorn laughed cheerfully. "Because I have a feeling we will need all the help we can get to fix what is wrong in Bravelands."

EPILOGUE

The young snake had climbed for days, his contracting belly muscles hauling him up the mountainside, over dry rocks, under
thorny bushes, between the roots of trees. He was sore and
weary; the days had been burning hot, and the nights cold
enough to render him motionless.

His tongue flickered out: he could taste the high thin air.
Close now . . .

At least he had not made his journey alone. He had been
aware of the others all the way from his forest home, jour-
neying not with him but alongside him. Grass lizards and
worm lizards, agamas, geckos and chameleons, forest turtles,
and of course snakes of every size and nature: venomous and
constricting, vicious and timid, large and tiny. It was strange
to be among so many; his kind were usually solitary, and the
Sandtongue-speakers did not mingle. But it gave him a cold

thrill, too. They were as one. They had a common purpose, a goal and an end they all shared. Each one of them had been summoned by the same powerful voice.

The mouth of the cavern in the hillside was almost obscured, there were so many creatures crawling and slithering into it. A mass of bodies writhed and skittered; the snake joined them gladly, feeling the coils of his body slither over and under creatures like himself. It was a great brotherhood and sisterhood of cool flesh, strong in its unity. He did not truly know what had brought him to this place; all he knew was that he *must* be here.

Because he knew who had called him. All of them did.

Within the blessed, cool darkness of the cavern, the noise at last faded; the hissing and croaking and the slithering were replaced by silence as the last stragglers joined the vast Sandtongue throng.

Something moved in the shadows beyond this great cave. It was huge, gliding powerfully from a tunnel, its coils folding and slithering in what seemed an endless process. The snake gazed, awestruck and reverent like all his sisters and brothers, at his Empress. She of a Thousand Skins. The one who would swallow the world.

At last, Her vast coils settled into place, She went still. Shadows folded around her colossal body, but her yellow eyes were glaringly bright. Her voice, when She spoke at last, was beautiful: soft and chilled and menacing as deep water.

"Thank you for answering my summons, Children of the Coldblood. You have traveled far, from all over Bravelands, and your road has been hard. You have come from the plains, from the ravines and the rivers; you have come from grass and rock and forest. And you have come to hear me tell you what our kind should always have known, but what we have forgotten.

"For too long, the Coldblood have been ground down, trodden into the dirt, despised and distrusted. Hoof and claw and talon strike at us in contempt.

"But that time is coming to an end, my children. The Age of Sandtongue is upon us; the Age of the Coldblood. I, your beloved Grandmother, will lead you into that beautiful time. I will show you the way."

The hissing cries of the reptiles rose again, in a great crescendo that echoed from the cavern walls until they seemed to tremble. The young snake joined his voice to theirs, his excitement spilling over; around him, his brothers and sisters writhed and twined.

"Yes, Grandmother," they screeched and hissed and croaked. "Grandmother, we are yours!"

The sound was a torrent. It was rising, unstoppable; the young snake knew it. With Grandmother at their head, with Her cold heart uniting theirs, that flood would at last wash away all in its path.

BRAVELANDS

Baboon Forest

Watering Hole

Great Parent Clearing